Smoky Mountain Stalker

Foggy Mountain Intrigue

Book Three

Ashley A Quinn

TCA Publishing LLC

ISBN: 979-8-9853441-9-6
Library of Congress Control Number: 2022916353

ONE

The twang of a steel guitar echoed through the bar over the din of dozens of voices. Laughter rang out in pockets around the room. Jake Maxwell let the heavy wooden door swing shut behind him as he walked deeper into the building on his way to the long mahogany bar at the back. Nodding to several people he knew as he crossed the room, he didn't stop to chat. He needed a beer.

Today had been brutal. Most of the time, he welcomed the variety and challenge of being a detective. But today was a case he wanted to forget. A robbery gone wrong that left an eleven-year-old boy in the hospital with a life-threatening stab wound after he tried to defend his mother from a jacked-up teenager, looking for some quick cash to score his next hit.

That mother's pain wasn't something he'd soon forget. If she'd been able to, she would have traded places with her son in an instant.

Sidling up to the bar, Jake motioned to the bartender. The man tipped his head in acknowledgment, then turned back to the beer he was pouring. After delivering it to a customer at the other end of the bar, he walked down to Jake.

"What can I get you?"

"Guinness. Draft, please."

The man nodded and reached for a pint glass, filling it from the dispenser. Jake passed him some cash, waving off the change. Spying an open table against the wall in the corner, he took his drink and sat down. He hoped no one would venture back here to talk. He just wanted to be alone to process his day.

Normally, the cases he worked didn't get to him. But when they involved kids—well, he'd need a heart made of steel not to be affected. It didn't help that he'd worked this one alone. His partner, Tristan Mabley, was out on paternity leave. Without him, Jake didn't have anyone to talk to as things progressed. He knew he could stop by Tristan's house to talk about the case, but it wouldn't be the same. Tris hadn't been there. He didn't see the blood on the woman's hands and clothes, or the pain and disbelief in her watery brown eyes.

He lifted his glass and took a long swallow. More laughter erupted from across the room, and he grimaced. Buying a case of beer at the store and drinking at home might have been the better option. But he didn't want to be alone yet. Or to drink more than one beer. Especially on an empty stomach. His plan was to walk to a local diner and get some food after this to help absorb the alcohol, then come back and get his car and head home.

Another couple came in, holding hands. Jake watched as they headed his direction. He sank lower into his seat and prayed it wasn't anyone he knew. They sat down at a table ten feet away, engrossed in each other.

His phone dinged, and he fished it out of his pocket. Turning on the screen, he saw a text from Tristan. *Ben said you caught a bad one today. You okay?*

Jake sighed. How was he supposed to put the case out of his head if he kept being reminded it of it? Biting back a growl,

he replied. *I'm fine. Having a beer and some dinner, then heading home to bed. How's the baby? And Laurel?*

Three dots appeared on his screen, then the message. *They're fine. Stop redirecting. I'm here if you need to talk.*

He shifted in his seat, feeling a little ashamed that he'd gotten angry at Tristan; the man was just trying to look out for him. *I know, and I appreciate it,* he typed. *But don't worry about me. I'm a big boy.*

A laughing emoji appeared. *Fine. Let me know if there's anything I can do.*

Jake smiled and replied. *Will do. Tell Laurel I said hi.*

The dots appeared again, then one word. *Yep.*

Jake turned off the screen and put his phone away. He glanced up, taking a drink, and noticed a waitress had appeared at the couple's table. This girl was new. He'd remember a figure like that. Lean and willowy, but with just the right size curves so a man could get a nice handful. And her hair. Halfway down her back even in a ponytail, it shone a deep, rich, dark chocolate in the low light. He loved it.

She stepped away and turned, looking his way. Something about her face reminded him of someone.

Her eyes widened slightly when she saw him, but she schooled her features and walked over.

"Hello, can I get you anything?"

It hit him as soon as she spoke how he knew her. That husky, velvety tone wasn't a voice a man forgot. "Shay?" He'd interviewed her during the stolen babies case he and Tristan worked earlier in the year.

She blushed. "Hi, detective."

"When did you start working here?" He wasn't exactly a regular, but he came in several times a month. This was the first he'd seen her. "What happened to the motel?"

"I still work at the motel." She paused, her mouth twisting slightly. "Well, a different one, I guess, than the one you met me at. It's here in Foggy Mountain. But I needed some extra income, so I started waitressing a few nights a week. I've been here just a couple weeks." She tucked a flyaway strand of her dark hair behind her ear.

He wasn't sure he liked that she was working in such a rough place. Barney's wasn't a dive, precisely, but the police department got its share of call-outs to this place. "Everything going okay so far?"

She nodded. "Yeah. I haven't had any problems." Her gaze flitted away.

Jake narrowed his eyes. She was lying. He let it slide, though. They didn't know each other well enough—hell, hardly at all—for him to call her out on it. Instead, he nodded. "Good."

"So, can I get you anything?"

"No, I'm good for now." He lifted his glass a couple inches off the table, then set it down again.

"Okay. Well, if you need anything, just yell."

"I will. Thanks."

She offered him a polite, shy smile, then turned and left.

Jake watched her walk away. The woman had a figure to die for. Though he had a feeling, she didn't see it that way. Her tight jeans showed off the curve of her hips, but the oversize t-shirt hid everything else. And he'd noticed she was makeup-free.

Thoroughly distracted from his earlier depressing thoughts, Jake kept an eye on the pretty waitress as she made the rounds of the room. When she reached the raucous party of mostly men across the bar, Jake tensed. One of the men reached out and ran a hand up the back of her thigh.

Red filled his vision. His ass left the seat, but before he could leave the table, she stepped out of his reach and glared at the drunk. The man gave her a lopsided grin and reached for her again. This time, he snagged her wrist and dragged her down onto his lap, slapping a hand over one of her breasts. His friends laughed and egged him on as Shay squirmed in his lap.

Beer sloshed as Jake pushed away from his table and wove his way through the bar.

"Hey!" His voice boomed, silencing the group. Shay looked up, tears streaming down her face. He grabbed her arm and pulled her to her feet.

The drunk peered up at him, an unperturbed smile on his face. "Dude. You ruined my vibe. She was really doing something for me with all that squirmin'."

Disgust twisted Jake's gut. He pushed Shay back, shielding her, as he faced the man. "She's here to serve you beer, not your baser urges. I think it's time for you guys to leave."

That wiped the smirk from the man's face. He stood up, swaying a bit on his feet. "Yeah? You gonna make me?"

Jake took his badge from his pocket. "Do you want me to?"

The belligerent look on the man's face faded. He held up his hands. "You win." He glanced at his friends. "Come on. Let's go find us a place without the law."

"Make sure you settle your bill. And don't drive," Jake called as the group filed out of the booth. One of the women —a meek blonde in skintight leather pants and a cutoff white t-shirt—gave him a wary look, then walked over to the bar to settle the tab. The rest stumbled toward the door.

Once they were gone, Jake turned to Shay. "Are you all right?"

She sniffed and swiped at her face, nodding. "I'm fine." Stooping, she picked up the order pad she dropped in the fray, then spun toward the bar.

Jake frowned and followed her. "Does this sort of thing happen often?" he asked, leaning against the bar as she retreated behind it to get her next order.

"No."

The bartender who served him his beer snorted. "Liar."

She glared at him.

Jake frowned harder, his gaze bouncing between them. Finally, it settled on the bartender. "Where's your bouncer?"

"We don't have one. He quit a month ago, and our manager hasn't found a replacement."

"In a month?" Jake's eyebrows shot up.

The man nodded.

"It's not a big deal, detective." Shay plunked two pints of Budweiser onto her tray, then grabbed the cocktails the bartender slid toward her. "I can handle myself." She picked up the tray.

"Sure you can." He blocked her path. "That's why you were squirming, trying to get off that guy's lap, but only succeeding in getting his rocks off."

Her face colored. "Can you move, please?"

He ignored her and looked past her at the bartender. "Why didn't you do something?"

"I didn't see it until you came barreling across the bar."

Jake looked at Shay again. She stared at the hollow of his neck, unblinking, her jaw tight.

"Is that the worst that's happened since you've been working here?"

A single tear slid down her cheek. "Please move." Her voice came out as a shaky whisper. "I can't lose this job."

"Answer me first. Has anything worse happened?"

She looked up at him, then. A spark of anger flashed in her rich, dark eyes. "No. I just get groped on a nightly basis and called all sorts of inappropriate names. Happy?"

"Hell, no." He took a breath through his nose, then blew it out, reining in his temper. "Are you sure this is where you want to be?"

She snorted. "If I had a choice, I wouldn't be here. But I don't. Now, can you please move?"

What the hell did she mean by that? He wanted to ask more questions, but the look on her face told him she wouldn't answer any. Instead, he stepped back and let her pass. She darted around him without a backward glance.

Jake turned to the bartender. "I want your manager's number." They were going to have a chat about his staff's security.

Two

It took all of Shay Britton's willpower to hold back the new round of tears wanting to fall. Damn that detective for making her think of things she'd rather forget. Of course she didn't want to be here. What woman enjoyed being groped and hit on all the time? Not her. But she didn't have a choice. Not if she wanted to make the extra cash she needed quickly. The tips here were great.

Sniffing, then taking a deep, controlled breath, she pasted a smile on her face and walked up to her customers to deliver their drinks. She saw the pity on their faces, but ignored it. Shay had learned things went back to normal sooner if she didn't give attention to the other patrons' shenanigans.

She wandered the room, checking on the customers and taking drink orders. Through it all, that detective sat at the bar and watched her. Shay wished he'd leave. Too much scrutiny was dangerous for her. She didn't need the man digging into her life.

Finally, after an hour, he got up and left. The disappointment that punched her in the gut surprised her. She'd wanted

him to leave. She should be dancing through the bar, happy that he was gone.

Shay blamed it on hormones. With coal black hair and icy blue eyes, the man was gorgeous. And he seemed nice. Any sane, straight woman would sit up and take notice of him and wish she could be the one he came home to at night.

That was a ship that could never sail, though. Relationships weren't in the cards for her. Especially not now. She doubted they would be in the future, either. Men were trouble. She had enough of that in spades.

A hand smacked her ass as she wove through the tables. Shay's step faltered, and she glanced back to see a young man barely old enough to drink flush beet red. A shy but cocky smile lifted one corner of his mouth. She glared at him, and his smile died. Mumbling a sorry, he looked away.

Shay sighed. She might not want the detective around, but a bouncer sure would be nice. Sidling up to the bar, she gave the bartender, Joe, her order.

The rest of her night passed smoothly. No more raucous men pulling her into their laps. Just a few more slaps to the rear and several leering glances. After Joe locked the doors, Shay swept the floor and mopped it, then counted her tips and filled out her time card. With her can of mace in her hand, she exited the building, scanning the parking lot as she went. This was another instance in which she wished they had a bouncer. It would be nice to have someone to walk her to her car. She knew Joe would, but he'd high-tailed it out of here shortly after locking the doors. Said he had a hot date.

Shaking off her unease, Shay hurried to her little car. She thrust the key in the lock and turned it, then yanked on the handle, falling inside. With a quick tug, she closed the door, then slapped the lock button. Her hands shook as she put the key in the ignition.

Get a grip. She grasped the steering wheel and closed her

eyes, blowing out a breath to steady her nerves. She could hear her heartbeat in her ears. Walking to her car alone didn't usually get her so worked up. It had to be those jerks from earlier that set her on edge.

Knuckles rapped against her window. Shay shrieked and recoiled, her eyes flying open. Icy blue eyes met her gaze, and some of her fear faded.

She found the window control and rolled down the pane. "What are you doing here? You scared the life out of me." She met the detective's gaze—she wished she could remember his name. It started with an *m*. Or maybe it was an *n*.

"Why are you walking to your car alone?" His dark brows knitted in a deep frown.

"Because I'm the only one left." She held up her mace can, shaking it in his face. "I'm not an idiot."

"I didn't say you were. I'm glad you have that, but what good will it do you if some guy comes up behind you and pins your arms to your sides?"

Her lips pursed. Did he have to be so logical? "Well, then, I guess I'm screwed." She rolled her eyes. "I'm fine. Can you move, so I can go home?" She was exhausted and had to be up in four hours to go to her job at the motel.

He held her gaze a moment longer, then tapped his hand against the doorframe, straightening. "Fine." He glanced away for a second, then dug into his pocket. "Just promise me you'll walk out with someone next time. What if it had been that guy from earlier waiting for you?"

She fought the hysterical laugh that wanted to break free. That man was the least of her worries about what might be waiting for her every time she left this place. Or the motel, or her apartment.

"If you ever need someone to walk you out, you can call me." He held out a small white rectangle.

Shay frowned, but took the business card. "I'm sure I'll be

fine. But thanks." She tossed the card into her open purse and hit the button to roll up the window. He stepped back, and she shifted the car into reverse. As she drove away, she saw him standing in the parking lot, watching her leave.

She shifted in her seat and tore her gaze away from the rearview mirror. Why did he care? He shouldn't. She was a nobody. And she didn't want him to care. Never asked for it. Why couldn't he just leave her in peace?

Confused and angry, she drove home. Parking in her space outside her apartment, she climbed from her car, scanning the area around her as she walked to her front door and unlocked it. Inside, she reset her alarm and flipped all her locks. Secure as she could be, she set her purse down. It gaped, showing off the white rectangle with the police department logo in the corner. She picked it up, telling herself she just wanted to know his name. In bold black letters, it read, "Det. Jake Maxwell."

A sharp snort broke the silence in the room. "Jake." She shook her head. "That fits him. Cocky, popular. Sexy." Shay rolled her eyes and tossed the card back in her purse. "Not sexy. Don't think of him like that, Shay." Huffing, she turned and headed down the hallway. She just needed to go to sleep. To put the entire night behind her.

She just hoped the hunky detective didn't invade her dreams.

THREE

Arms loaded, Jake wiggled a finger free and pushed the doorbell at Tristan's. He heard it ring through the house. A few moments later the door swung open.

Jake's smile died as he took in his partner's appearance. Chestnut hair stuck out in several directions—like he'd run his hands through it several times and hadn't washed it in a few days—deep purple bags hung under his blue eyes, and twin furrows bracketed the sides of his mouth.

"Dude. You look terrible. Is everything okay?"

Tristan nodded, stepping back so he could enter. "Yeah. Newborns don't like to sleep. Did you know that? Logically, I did. But living it is a whole different thing." He closed the door and frowned at the stack of gifts in Jake's arms. "What's all this?"

"Gifts from the people at work. Since the baby was a little early, no one got to give you their gifts. I volunteered to bring everything over."

"Oh. Well, that was nice of them. And you. Come on into the living room." Tristan led him down the hall. "You can put everything over by the couch. Let me go get Laurel."

"You don't need to disturb her." Jake crouched and set the boxes and bags down, trying not to dump anything.

"She was just folding some laundry. I'll be right back." Spinning around, Tristan left before Jake could protest further.

It wasn't that he didn't want to see Laurel, but he didn't intend to stay long. He wanted to get to the bar to check on Shay. It had been a week since he'd seen her. She hadn't called —not that he'd expected her to—and he hadn't had a chance to stop by to check on her.

Well, that wasn't entirely true. There had been a couple of evenings he could have gone over, but he'd stopped himself for fear he'd look like a stalker. He wasn't. But for some reason, he had a need to make sure she was okay.

"Hi, Jake."

He glanced up, rising from arranging the gifts on the floor, and smiled at Tristan's wife. "Hi, Laurel. How're you doing?" She honestly didn't look much better than her husband. Her hair was a little neater, but she looked just as tired. A bright smile lit her face, though.

"I'm good. Tired. Tristan told me I should take a nap while Wyatt's asleep, but the mountain of laundry on our bedroom floor, waiting to be put away, called my name."

"Why didn't you make him fold it?" Jake pointed at his partner. "Seems you've done all the hard work lately."

She laughed. "He was helping, actually."

"Good. You both can take a break, though. I come bearing gifts." He motioned to the pile of bags and boxes at his feet.

Laurel stepped forward to look at the stack, then glanced at Tristan. "These are all from the people you work with?"

He nodded.

Tears formed in her eyes, and she fanned her face. "Sorry. Hormones. That was so nice of them." She sank onto the couch.

A baby's wail cut through the house. Laurel sighed.

"Stay." Jake put a hand on her shoulder. "You two take a load off for a few minutes. Start opening your gifts. I'll get him."

Tristan shot him an amused smile. "What do you know about taking care of a newborn?"

Jake shot him a grin. "Probably not a whole lot more than you did a week ago."

Laurel laughed and tugged on the hem of Tristan's shirt. "He'll be fine. Sit down."

"Listen to your wife." Jake pointed at the couch, still grinning as he walked toward the door.

Rolling his eyes, Tristan sat down. Jake chuckled and headed down the hall to the source of the cries. He poked his head into the nursery, and the sound increased. Wyatt lay in his crib, red-faced and screaming.

"Hey, little man. None of that, now. You need to calm down and give your parents a break." He reached into the crib and lifted the tiny infant into his arms, surprised by how small he was. Jake didn't remember his sister's baby being this small. But Ava had been full term. Wyatt was a couple of weeks early

Jiggling the baby, he walked over to the changing table to unwrap him. He loosened the swaddle and unsnapped his onesie to check his diaper. The line on the front had changed colors, so he found a new one and changed it. Wyatt's cries calmed as Jake redressed him and snuggled him into his arms. "Okay, bud. Clean and dry. Let's go find your mama."

With the baby nestled in his arms, he wandered back to the living room. He smiled as he came in, seeing Laurel holding up a tiny sleeper with a hedgehog on it, a bright smile on her face as she looked at Tristan. They glanced up as he entered.

"You look like you've done that before," Laurel said.

He smiled. "I have a one-year-old niece. She was never

quite this tiny, though." He sat down in the chair across from them.

"Do you want me to take him?" Laurel gestured to her son.

Jake shook his head. "No, I'm good. Open your gifts." He readjusted the baby, letting the boy grab his finger.

The couple dug into more presents, unearthing a stack of diapers and a dresser's worth of clothes. Little Wyatt was stocked for his first year of life.

"So, which one of these gifts is yours?" Tristan asked.

Jake smiled. "None of them." He lifted a hip and pulled an envelope from his back pocket, then handed it to Tristan.

"What's this?" Tristan turned it over.

"Open it."

Lifting the flap, Tristan pulled out a thin card and opened it. His eyebrows shot up, and he glanced at Jake. "A gift card to a baby store and another for a restaurant?"

Jake nodded once. "Yep. You can get whatever you still need for the little guy. And then I figured, as new parents, you could use a break one evening. I'll babysit." He looked down at the baby in his arms, then back at his partner. "Look. We're already bonding."

Tristan laughed. He raised the cards. "Thank you, Jake. This was really thoughtful."

"You're welcome." He shifted Wyatt again and rested his left hand on the arm of the chair, tapping his fingers against the fabric. Jake wanted to glance at the clock but stopped himself. Shay had gone a week without him playing bouncer. Another day wouldn't hurt. He hoped.

"You okay, Jake?" Laurel's soft voice drew his attention.

"I'm fine. Why do you ask?"

She shrugged. "You just seem a little preoccupied."

He waved his hand. "Nope, I'm good."

Tristan narrowed his eyes. "I call bullshit." He stood and

took the baby from Jake, handing him to Laurel, then turned to Jake. "Come on."

Biting back a groan, Jake stood. He didn't really want to talk, but Tristan was like a bulldog. He wouldn't give up until he had answers. So, he followed his partner through the house to the kitchen.

"Talk." Tristan opened the fridge and grabbed a bottle of water, offering it to him.

Jake waved it off. "I'm fine."

Tristan cracked the lid and took a drink, leaning against the counter.

"You're not going to let me leave until I tell you what's bothering me, are you?"

"Nope." He took another drink.

Jake sighed and ran a hand through his hair. "That's kinda hard to do when I'm not even sure what that is."

"How about you start at the beginning?"

He stuffed his hands in his pockets and looked at the floor. Brow furrowing, he tried to put into words the emotions—the worry—running through him. "So, do you remember the housekeeper at the motel where we went looking for Veronica Chapman during the stolen babies case?"

Tristan straightened, his features going hard. "The house-keeper?" Jake could see the wheels turning in his brain as he thought. "Dark-haired, quiet woman?"

Jake nodded. "Yeah. So, she's working as a waitress at Barney's."

"Okay?" Tristan frowned. "Lots of people change jobs."

"It's in addition to the motel. A new motel." Jake waved a hand. "But that's not the point. I went in there last week after that robbery case where the kid got stabbed, and she was working. A group of her customers got a little rowdy, and one of them pulled her down onto his lap and wouldn't let her up. I stepped in. Once she was safe, I asked where their bouncer was. Turns out they don't have one. Old one quit, and the manager hasn't hired a new one." He shook his head.

"So, you want to go check on her?" A sly smile quirked one side of Tristan's mouth. "I knew you were sweet on her when we were at the motel."

A corner of Jake's mouth lifted to match Tristan's. She'd intrigued him back then with her quiet demeanor and pretty face; that had only grown. He thought he'd hid his interest, though, with the way he tossed off Tristan's comment about his charm. Apparently not. "It's not that. I got the feeling she didn't want me there. That she was trying to hide something."

Tristan's smile died. "You think she's into something illicit?"

Jake shook his head. "No. I think she's scared. Of what—or who—I don't know." He crossed one arm and rested his other elbow on top of it, pressing the backs of his fingers against his mouth as he glanced out the window over the sink. "She blustered at me like a fierce kitten, but she was terrified. I could see it in her eyes."

"We never ran a background check on her, did we?"

"No. And I can't now. I have no reason to."

"Well, it looks like you'll have to do things the old-fashioned way." Tristan walked forward.

"What way is that?"

"Charm her." He slapped Jake's shoulder. "Women fall at your feet. Should be a piece of cake."

Jake groaned and rubbed his temples. "She's resistant to my charms."

Tristan laughed. "Be persistent. If you're really concerned about her, don't give up."

"No, I won't. Something's wrong." Jake's gut always steered him in the right direction. If it said something wasn't right, something wasn't right.

"So, why are you still standing in my kitchen?"

Four

Shay knew the moment Detective Maxwell stepped into the bar. The hair on the back of her neck stood up, and a tingle raced down her spine. She glanced toward the door and saw him standing there, scanning the room.

It had been almost an entire week since she saw him. She thought maybe he had lost interest in her, but apparently, she was wrong.

A small thrill raced through her; one she quickly squashed. There would be none of that. She wasn't interested in Jake Maxwell—or any man.

He took a seat near where he sat the last time. Shay kept to the other side of the room, thankful none of her tables were near him. He still hadn't seen her. Maybe she could keep it that way and he would leave, thinking she wasn't working tonight.

"Yo, Shay!"

She bit back a groan as the bartender, Matty, called her name, raising the two pints she hadn't had room for on her tray on her last run. So much for Detective Maxwell not knowing she was here. She walked over and took them, offering him a polite smile. "Thanks." Keeping her eyes away from the detective's table, she delivered the drinks.

As the night wore on, and the crowd thinned out, the other waitress working went home, leaving Shay to cover the entire bar. It normally wasn't an issue—Shay was used to closing on her own. But being alone meant she now had to speak to Detective Maxwell.

She checked on every other table, some of them twice, before she wandered over to him. "Hello, detective. Are you doing all right?" She gestured to the soda glass in front of him.

"I could use a refill." He picked up the glass and drained the rest of the dark liquid.

"Okay. Coke?"

He nodded.

She returned to the bar to get his drink, then brought it back. "There you go." She reached for the empty glass. "Let me know if you need anything else." Shay started to turn away, but curiosity stopped her, and she glanced back. "Detective? Why are you still here?"

"I like the soda." He lifted his new cup and took a drink. Those white-blue eyes sparkled over the rim.

Shay huffed. "Sure you do." She spun away, angry. But whether it was just at him for hanging around or at herself, too, for feeling—something, she didn't know. He unsettled her, and she wished he'd just go away.

For the rest of the evening, she did her best to avoid him, only stopping by when she noticed his drink was low. After the third refill, she started to wonder if he intended to sleep tonight. If she drank that much caffeine so late, she'd never fall asleep. Maybe it was a cop thing. Didn't they live on strong coffee and donuts?

Though, if the man ate donuts, it didn't show. Muscles flexed in his tanned forearm every time he lifted the cup to take a drink. His biceps bulged as his elbow bent, telling her any sweets he ate got worked off in the gym.

Shay shivered as the image of him shirtless and sweaty entered her mind. She rolled her eyes at herself and pushed it away. Entertaining those kinds of thoughts wouldn't help her peace of mind.

At last call, Detective Maxwell got up, leaving money on the table. She breathed a sigh of relief as he finally exited the bar. When she went to his table, shock rendered her immobile for several moments. He'd left a hundred-dollar bill. A handful of sodas came to less than twenty bucks.

She scooped the money up and stuffed it in her apron, then wiped down the table with quick, angry strokes. Did he think he could buy her affection? Or was this his way of setting up another meeting between them? Was he betting she'd be unwilling to accept the excessive tip and try to return it?

Gritting her teeth, she cleaned the rest of the tables that needed it. He had another think coming. She'd keep his damn money and only thank him if he came in again. Shay rolled her eyes, knowing that's exactly what would happen. He'd be back. She was sure of it.

Once she finished with the tables, she swept the floors and counted her tips before filling out her time card. Matty stuck around, restocking the bar, and finished just as she did. Shay was thankful. She really didn't like walking out alone.

"Have a good night, Matty." Shay smiled at him over her shoulder as she took her keys from her purse.

He raised a hand and got into his beat-up silver pickup.

Finding the right key, Shay unlocked her door and got in. As she put the key in the ignition, she glanced up. A black SUV sat in the corner of the lot. Its lights turned on and it rolled forward.

Unease skated up her spine, and she hit the door locks.

The other car's window rolled down, and the air left Shay's lungs on a relieved whoosh as Detective Maxwell's face appeared and he waved at her.

With a frown and her lips pursed, she glared. That same annoyance and anger from earlier crept in. She thrust her car into gear and sped out of the lot. Let him pull her over and give her a ticket. He'd get an earful about leaving her alone.

But as she drove away, a small thrill coiled in the pit of her stomach, secretly glad he cared. It had been a long time since *anyone* cared what happened to her.

FIVE

The digital clock on Jake's dash turned over another minute. He pressed harder on the accelerator, hoping he could still catch Shay. With Tristan still out on paternity leave—which ended tomorrow, thank God—he was pulling long days to stay ahead of the workload. The sheriff gave him a couple of uniforms to help some, but it wasn't the same as having a seasoned investigator working with him.

He made the turn onto the road Barney's was on. As he drove into the lot, he let out a curse. Her car was gone. He knew she was supposed to work tonight because he saw her car earlier when he drove past. Banging a hand against his steering wheel, he turned around. He'd drive past her apartment. Make sure she made it home okay, at least.

His SUV's engine hummed as he accelerated away from the bar. Trees whizzed by in the dark, and he tapped his fingers on the wheel as he drove. What was he doing? He barely knew this woman. Why did he care so much? She certainly didn't seem to want him to. But he'd be damned if he could get her out of his head. It had to be the fear he saw in her eyes. Something was wrong. He just wanted to help.

Jake rounded a bend, and his headlights illuminated a white sedan on the side of the road. He hit his brakes and pulled up behind the car, recognizing it as Shay's. A thin stream of smoke rose from one corner of the hood.

Heart in his throat, he got out of his SUV, one hand on the butt of the gun at his hip. A rustle in the trees to his right drew his attention. He removed his weapon from its holster and the flashlight from his pocket, sweeping the light over the car. Seeing no one inside, he changed direction and headed into the forest. His heartbeat hammered in his ears as his adrenaline spiked. He forced himself to go slow and to pay attention. Even without the leaves on the trees, the low cloud cover tonight meant he saw nothing past the beam of his flashlight. He strained his hearing, hoping for a clue to what he heard—to Shay—but nothing except the sound of the wind met him.

A shadow of movement on his left was his only warning before a cold liquid hit his face. Seconds later, searing pain engulfed his eyeballs. He'd been pepper-sprayed. "Oh, fuck! Goddamn, son-of-a-bitch!" He blinked furiously, turning toward the source. He'd be lucky to hit anything like this. Tears flooded his eyes, and he struggled to keep them open. "Freeze, police!"

He heard a soft gasp.

"Oh, no! Detective Maxwell?"

Jake dipped the tip of his gun toward the ground. "Shay?"

"Oh, geez. Oh, I'm so sorry. I just saw a man coming into the woods with a gun, and I reacted. Are you all right?"

"No, I'm not all right. You fucking pepper-sprayed me. My eyes are on fire." He holstered his gun and took off his sweater to get to the t-shirt underneath. He needed to wipe his face. "Do you have any water in your car?" He whipped his t-shirt off. The cool air barely registered. He was too focused on the burning in his eyes. Pressing the shirt to his face, he moaned.

"A little, yes." She laid a hand on his arm, nudging him to turn around. "It's back this way. Come on, I'll guide you. I'm so sorry."

"You know, I was a little leery of that stuff being your only means of protection, but you've got some damn fine aim. What are you doing in the woods, anyway? Why aren't you with your car? And what happened?"

"I hit a deer. It didn't die in the accident, just ran off into the trees. I was trying to find it. I didn't want it to suffer. Then I saw you and—" She heaved a sigh. "I'm sorry."

"You keep saying that." His foot hit a root, and he stumbled. Her hands clutched his bicep, keeping him upright. "Thanks," he mumbled.

"You're welcome. Be careful. There are a couple more roots here." She helped him over them.

"Where's the little ditch?" He'd crossed a small depression on the side of the road before he entered the woods.

"We're almost to it." She tucked her hand around his elbow. "Okay, step down."

Jake stumbled through the ditch and up the other side, banging into her car. He pressed his shirt harder to his eyes, squeezing them shut. His temples throbbed now as a headache blossomed to go along with the fire in his eyes. "Where's that water?"

"I'm getting it." He heard the car door open and close, then she pressed a plastic bottle into his hand.

"Thanks." He dropped his shirt and tipped his head back, pouring the water in his eyes until it was gone. It helped, but he needed a lot more. "Christ, what kind of pepper spray did you use? Bear spray?"

"It's just regular pepper spray. But I got you right in the face. I'm sorry."

"Stop apologizing."

"Sorry." She groaned, then chuckled at herself. "I'll stop talking now and call for help."

Jake shot a hand out in her general direction and snagged her shirtsleeve. "Just drive me back to town in my car. It'll be faster than waiting on an ambulance. I can call your accident in on the way."

"What? Do you have to? I mean, I only hit a deer. It's just my car that's damaged."

Something in her voice made him pause. That fear was back. But this was something he couldn't compromise on. "I have to. Another unit could come up on the scene after we leave. If they don't know where you are, they'll initiate a search. It'll waste resources, not to mention you could get in a heap of trouble for leaving the scene of an accident."

"Fine." Her voice was soft.

Jake turned toward his vehicle. "Help me into my car."

She took his elbow again and guided him to the passenger seat. He climbed inside and buckled up. Shay got into the driver's seat.

"Are you okay to drive?" He hoped she was. He really didn't want to wait for an ambulance.

"Yes. I wasn't hurt. Just shaken up." She started the car. "Where am I going?"

"You can just take me to my house. All I need is to flush out my eyes. I can do that in the shower." He gave her some quick directions, and she pulled off the shoulder.

Six

The tires on Detective Maxwell's car hummed over the road as she followed his directions to his house. She couldn't believe her luck. Of all the people to stop—after more than one car drove by—it was him.

Shay cast a glance at him. She was thankful it was dark so she couldn't see the rippling muscles she'd caught a glimpse of in the light from his flashlight. He still had his t-shirt pressed to his eyes. She didn't know what happened to his sweater; it was probably still in the woods. He'd stripped pretty quick, trying to wipe away the spray.

She felt terrible. She'd seen the gun and just reacted.

"Is it getting any better?" she asked.

"No. Drive faster. I'll make any speeding tickets go away."

She edged the speedometer needle a couple miles per hour higher, not willing to go any faster. Despite his promise, she had no desire to get pulled over. That meant questions. Ones she didn't want to answer. She'd likely still have to answer some after hitting that deer. A deep frown split her face when he reached for the radio clipped to the dash and called in the accident. Hopefully, she could just get by with signing a statement, and the police department wouldn't want any more personal information than her name.

Ten minutes after they left her car, she turned into the driveway of his small, gray-sided house with its neat flowerbeds. She hurried around the front of the vehicle to help him navigate to the door.

"Which one of these is the house key?" She held up the key ring with its eight different keys.

"I can't see it to tell you. Just start trying them. It's silver."

Shay found a silver key and thrust it into the knob. It wouldn't turn. After three tries, she found the correct key and let them inside. He pushed his way through the door and into the foyer. She followed him inside.

"Do you need help getting to the bathroom?"

"Just keep me from knocking anything over." He walked forward, a hand outstretched. The other held his shirt against his face.

Shay kept her eyes glued to his surroundings and off his powerful torso. They made it down the hall to his bedroom and the en suite bathroom without incident.

"Leave the door cracked," she said as he crossed the threshold. "Just in case. I'll wait out here."

He didn't respond, but the door didn't close all the way.

She stared after him another moment, then turned around and surveyed the room. It looked like any bachelor's bedroom. Heavy wooden furniture filled the space. A navy bedspread covered the mattress. On the walls, black and white art prints of mountains brought a small element of nature into the space. Shay could tell this was a man's bedroom.

The shower turned on, and she heard the rattle of the shower curtain sliding back, then into place again. It was quickly followed by a yelp and a curse. She hurried forward, edging the door open a crack. "Are you okay?"

"Yeah. Water was cold."

Satisfied he hadn't hurt himself, she backed away. The adrenaline from the past half hour was wearing off, and her knees shook. She wanted to sit down, but the only place in the room to do so was the bed. Somehow, sitting on the detective's bed felt too intimate.

But it was that or the floor. Sitting on the floor would only make him ask questions, so she perched on the very edge of the navy comforter. While she waited for him to emerge, she tried not to think about him in the shower. About what the rest of him looked like without his clothes. If it was anything like his torso, she'd probably melt into a puddle at his feet.

He probably had sexy toes too.

Groaning at herself and her wayward thoughts, Shay forced her mind onto other things. Like how she was going to pay to fix her car. She didn't want to dip into her emergency funds, but she needed a working vehicle. Hopefully, it was fixable. Buying a new car was not in her plans. That would wipe out everything she'd saved. She probably should have opted for something more substantial to begin with, but her little compact was easy on gas, which meant more money in her savings.

The water shut off, and she heard the rattle of the shower curtain again. Moments later, the bathroom door swung open and Shay forgot how to breathe. Water droplets clung to his skin and the dusting of dark hair on his torso. They cascaded down ripples of muscle, getting caught in the happy trail that disappeared beneath the towel he clutched around his waist. Her gaze followed the water, only snapping back to his face when he chuckled.

Face flaming, she shot off the bed. "I'll just wait out"—she gestured to the door—"there." She fled before he could say anything.

In the hallway, she paused, scrubbing her hands over her face. "Oh my God," she whispered. Tonight was turning into a nightmare of epic proportions. She needed to get out of here before it got any worse and she embarrassed herself further.

Dropping her hands, she wandered deeper into the house in search of a phonebook. She needed to call a wrecker to go get her car and take it to her mechanic. And she needed to get a taxi to take her home.

The living room was devoid of phonebooks, so she wandered into the kitchen. If he was like her, he kept it in a drawer. When she opened the long one beside the fridge, she hit paydirt. Lifting the large yellow tome free, she thumbed through the thin pages until she found the section for towing companies.

"Allen Towing is a good company."

Shay yelped, dropping the book. It hit the floor with a loud thwack. She cast a quick glare his way, then stooped to pick it up. "Thanks. How did you know that's what I was looking for?"

He shrugged. "Why else would you need the yellow pages?"

"For food?" In truth, she was starving. She'd forgotten her lunch bag, so she'd had to rely on the snack food they kept at the bar to hold her hunger at bay. She could only eat so many peanuts and pretzels.

"At this time of night?"

He crossed to the fridge, which was much too close for Shay's liking. She edged away. "Waffle House is open twenty-four hours."

He glanced back, a half-smile on his face and a twinkle in his icy eyes despite the redness in them. "True. But they don't deliver." He straightened, holding two Chinese takeout cartons. "Here. Fried rice and sweet and sour chicken."

"What? No. I'm fine."

He straightened, all traces of his smile vanishing. "I can

hear your stomach growling." He set the containers on the counter and opened a cupboard, removing a plate.

"Detective, really, I'm fine. I'll eat when I get home."

"I think you've earned the right to call me Jake after blasting me with pepper spray. And it'll be awhile before you get home. My vision is still blurry." He opened another drawer, taking out a spoon to put food on the plate.

Guilt churned her stomach again. "I'm sorry."

"I told you to stop apologizing. I understand why you did it. I should have announced myself." He picked up the plate and put it in the microwave, then turned to look at her. "Call your tow truck, but I think it's best if you just bunk here tonight. I'll take you home in the morning."

Her eyes grew wide. Sleep here? Under the same roof as him? Where she would wake up to him tousled and ten times sexier from sleep? That was a hard no. "I'll just call a cab, but thanks."

"At this hour, you're better off just staying here. One will have to come from Asheville. There's only one Uber guy here in town, and he goes to bed after running the drunks home. We're well past that point." The microwave beeped, and he turned to get the food out.

Shay glared at the back of his head. Why did he have to be so logical about it? So what if she wanted to wait on a cab from Asheville and pay its exorbitant fee?

But she didn't. Not when she had a car to fix—or perhaps buy. Her shoulders slumped as defeat set in. It looked like she was sleeping here.

Jake opened the drawer again and removed a fork, then held the plate up to her. "Eat. I'll call the tow truck."

"I can—"

"I know you can." His voice was soft as he cut her off. He arched an eyebrow, a hint of that smile coming back as he gestured for her to take the plate.

Shay rolled her eyes. "Fine." She took the dish and retreated to a stool at the island. Her stomach grumbled louder, and her mouth watered. It took all she had not to shove a giant forkful into her mouth, but instead take small bites.

While she ate, he called a wrecker for her and had her car towed to her mechanic, using his credit card as a reserve for a cash payment tomorrow when she could get to the tow truck company's office to pay for the tow. It bothered her that she was beholden to him, but she didn't use credit cards. Not anymore.

Once her car was taken care of and her belly full, fatigue hit her hard. A yawn cracked her jaw as she took her plate to the sink.

"Come on. I'll show you to the guest room."

She followed him wordlessly down the hall, where he stopped at the door next to his room.

"Sheets are clean. There's extra blankets in the closet." He snapped his fingers. "You need something to sleep in."

Before she could tell him she'd just sleep in her clothes, he spun away, entering his bedroom. He returned a moment later with a folded t-shirt. Deciding it would be best not to argue— she just wanted to go to sleep now—she took the shirt.

"Thank you. You've been very kind, even though I probably don't deserve it." She suppressed a wince as she took in his red, swollen eyes. The poor man looked like he'd been attacked by some angry bees.

"Nonsense. I'm glad it was me who stopped to help you. But next time, don't go wandering off into the woods after a deer. Call for help instead."

Shay rolled her lips in and nodded. "Yeah." She would have saved herself from the rollercoaster of emotions she'd been on since she pepper-sprayed him. Plus the ones that would no doubt hit in the morning.

"Well." She offered him a smile. "I guess I'll see you in the morning."

He nodded. "Do you have to work at the motel?"

"Yes." She'd nearly forgotten about her other job. "I'm supposed to be there at eight tomorrow. Though with everything that happened, I'll call my boss in the morning and tell him I'll be a little late. I need to pay the tow truck driver and find a rental car first."

"I have a car you can borrow, actually."

"What? Oh. No, I'll be fine. You've done plenty for me already."

"Don't be stubborn, Shay. It's just sitting in my garage. I don't drive it much. It's too conspicuous for me to take to work."

Curiosity got the better of her and she had to ask. "What kind of car is it?"

A smile twitched his full lips. He tipped his head toward the kitchen, then walked that way. "Come look."

She stared at him for a long moment. Unbidden, her feet carried her toward him. He opened the garage door and flipped on the light. Shay's eyes widened as she took in the vehicle asleep in the bay. "That's a vintage Porsche 911." She glanced at him. He stared at her, shock in his puffy, red eyes.

"You know cars?"

She shrugged and walked past him, wanting to get a closer look at the gorgeous white car. "My grandpa liked cars. Especially European ones. Some of my earliest memories are of sitting in his garage, eating those tube popsicles while I watched him tinker with the old Mini he owned." Her throat closed as she thought of her family. Shay turned back to the house.

"Hey." His hand on her arm stopped her. "Are you okay?"

"I'm fine." She refused to meet his gaze. "Just ready for bed." Shay dashed past him, not stopping until she reached

the guest room. She shut the door and leaned against it, closing her eyes. Tears pressed against her eyelids. She drew in a shaky breath and stepped away, dashing at the moisture on her face. Crying wouldn't help. Besides, she'd shed all the tears she had to shed over her family a long time ago.

It only took her a few minutes to change and get ready for bed. She slid between the sheets of the full-size bed and closed her eyes. Shay figured she'd have trouble dropping off to sleep, but to her surprise, she drifted off within minutes.

When she woke hours later, it was to the smell of coffee and running water. She sat up, pushing the covers back, and rubbed her face, yawning. As her brain connected to her surroundings, some of the apprehension and dismay from yesterday crept back in.

She sucked in a breath and swung her legs over the side of the bed. It wouldn't do her any good to dwell on those emotions. Finding her discarded clothes, she changed. After running her finger over her teeth with some water and using the restroom, she ventured out into the living area.

Her nose drew her to the kitchen, where a full pot of coffee sat waiting. It took her a couple of tries to find the right cupboard, but eventually, she found a coffee mug and poured herself a cup of the steaming brew. She took a sip and closed her eyes, savoring the flavor. Apparently, not all cops drank swill.

"It's good stuff, isn't it?"

Shay jumped, sloshing hot coffee over the rim. She cursed and spun around, setting the cup on the counter so she could run her hand under cold water. "Do you have to sneak up on me?" She turned on the water and thrust her hand beneath the spray.

"Wasn't trying to."

She huffed and shut the water off, steeling herself to turn around and look at him again. The first sight she'd gotten was enough to scramble her already foggy brain. She wasn't awake enough to deal with him in all his sexy glory.

A paper towel appeared in front of her. "Thanks." She took it and dried her hands, then turned to face him.

Desire punched her in the face. Fresh from the shower, water still clung to the dark waves of his hair. Clean-shaven, he was close enough she could smell his aftershave. It mingled with a scent that was all Jake. Still half-asleep, Shay had little defense against the man and the effect he had on her. She picked up her coffee and took another sip. It scalded her tongue, but she didn't care. It helped distract her from the man smiling at her.

"So, how did you sleep? My mom picked out that mattress. It's a little firm for my taste, but she loves it."

"Oh, um, it was fine. I was pretty tired." She took another sip of her coffee, then changed the subject. "How soon will you be ready to drop me off at the mechanic's shop? I want to call my boss at the motel and tell him I'll be late, but I'd like to give him an estimate of when I'll be there."

Jake paused, pouring himself a cup of coffee, frowning at her. "I told you last night you can borrow my car. That hasn't changed, so you can leave whenever you want."

Her eyes widened, and she cast a quick look at the garage door. "What? No. I can't drive your Porsche." She knew the value of a car like that. And what it would cost to repair it if she dinged it up. No thanks.

He tipped the coffee carafe and filled his mug. "Then take my SUV." He put the carafe on the warming plate, then looked at her. "There's no point in you renting a vehicle when I have two."

Shay studied him for a moment. He stared right back at her. "You don't even know me, Jake."

He lifted one shoulder. "I know enough. And you look like you could use a friend. Let me help. Please?"

It was the soft please that did her in. He wasn't demanding or trying to take over. He just wanted to help. Truly and sincerely help. And she sensed no malice or ulterior motive in his offer. "Fine." She sighed. "I'll take the SUV."

A bright, sexy smile erupted over his face, stealing her breath. Shay lifted her cup and took another drink, letting the scalding heat unscramble her brain.

"Great. The spare key is hanging by the door there." He tipped his head toward the garage. "Keep it as long as you need."

"You're sure?"

"Yes."

She sighed again. "Okay. Well, thank you."

"You're welcome." Jake lifted his cup, but paused just before he took a drink. "You know—and I'm not prying here or asking you to share anything you're not willing to—but I just want you to know if you ever need anything, just ask. I meant what I said about being a friend. If you need one, I'm here."

To Shay's horror, she felt tears press in on her eyes again. "Thank you," she pushed through her tight vocal chords. Lifting her cup, she took another drink and turned away. The tears pressed harder, and she decided lingering would just make her embarrass herself, so she crossed to the sink and dumped her mug. "I'm going to head out. Thank you for letting me crash here and for the use of the car. I'll get it back to you soon, I promise."

He frowned at her, that crystalline gaze telling her he saw past her ruse, but he said nothing. Instead, he nodded. "Take as long as you need."

She offered him a watery smile, then snagged the spare keys off the hook and hurried out the door, escaping as the first tears fell.

Seven

Jake tossed his sunglasses onto the passenger seat of his Porsche and rubbed his scratchy eyes, glad he was done for the day. The puffiness was gone; it had mostly disappeared by the time he woke up. But the redness and irritation had remained. Once he rolled into work, Tristan took one look at him, and, after getting the full story, burst out laughing. Jake couldn't blame him. If the situation were reversed, he'd be laughing too.

He cranked the engine and put the little sports car into gear. As much as he didn't like driving the flashy car for work, he was glad he convinced Shay to borrow his SUV. The woman was stubborn. She was determined to go it alone, and he didn't know why she was so against accepting help. Her attitude—and the tears he caught a glimpse of—made him want to discover more about her. Find out what made her tick, and why she was so secretive and alone.

Jake ran a hand over the back of his neck as he drove. That was the start of his very long day. Even having Tristan back hadn't helped. Between the paperwork, the new cases they'd drawn, and his scratchy eyes, Jake had a fierce headache. All he wanted was to go home and sleep. But he knew once he climbed into bed, he'd only wonder how things went for Shay today.

So, he made the turn away from his house and toward Barney's to check on her. She probably wouldn't be happy to see him, but that was tough shit. He was more determined than ever to unravel the mystery of Shay Britton. That feeling he had that something wasn't right with her was still there, and it was louder than ever.

When he pulled into the bar parking lot, he was surprised to see it so full. Then he remembered what day it was. Friday. People were out celebrating the end of the work week. He squeezed his car between two trucks near the rear of the lot and got out. Gravel crunched under the soles of his boots as he walked to the front door.

Music blasted him as he stepped inside. Three waitresses wove through the tables tonight, and two bartenders took orders behind the long mahogany bar. He frowned when he still didn't see a bouncer. The manager assured him after his phone call that he was looking. Jake didn't understand why it was so hard to find someone. Any beefy dude who could look mean would do.

He scoped out the tables, looking for an empty one. There weren't any, so he headed for the bar. Taking a seat near the end, he turned his back to the wall so he could see the room. Shay's dark ponytail swayed as she set a pint glass down in front of a customer. The man reached up and caressed her hip. Before he could rise from his stool, she deftly plucked it off and stepped away. One thing he'd learned watching her was that she could normally take care of herself. He didn't like it, but that's the way it was. Not for the first time, he wondered why she didn't look for a job that paid what her two jobs did combined. Working for one of the local factories would pay better, and they were always hiring.

"What can I get you?"

Jake glanced up at the bartender. "Something on tap." He handed the man his credit card to start a tab, then turned his attention back to Shay. She flitted about the room, taking orders and delivering the last few drinks on her tray. He knew the moment she spotted him. Her shoulders stiffened and a frown knit her eyebrows. Jake still didn't completely understand why he made her uneasy, though he suspected it had to do more with his job and with the fact that she didn't trust anyone, than him personally.

A glass of dark beer landed in front of him. He picked it up and took a sip without taking his eyes off of her. She walked toward him, holding his gaze.

"Your eyes look better." She slid in next to him, then motioned to the bartender, giving him her next order.

"Yeah. They feel better too. Still scratchy, but not like earlier. How'd things go with your car?"

The frown on her face deepened. "Not as I'd hoped. The deer busted my radiator and fan assembly. Not to mention the headlight as well as the crumpled bumper and hood. It's all fixable, though."

"That's good. Do you know when you'll get it back?"

"It'll be next week sometime. You can have your car back. I'll get a rental."

Jake waved a hand. "I'm not worried about it. Keep it as long as you need."

She twisted a cocktail napkin in her hands, then looked at him. "Why are you being so nice to me? At times, I haven't even been polite to you."

He took another sip of his beer as he formulated an answer. Finally, he decided to go with the truth. "Because something about you screams that you're scared. Of what, I don't know. I'd be lying if I said I don't care what. But for now, I'm leaving it alone. I just want you to know that I'm here to help. Even if that means you just borrow my car for a few days."

A muscle in her jaw ticked as she stared at her hands and the napkin she now shredded. Jake wrapped a hand over hers, stilling her movements. Startled at the touch, she jumped and looked at him.

"If you want to talk, I'm a good listener."

She pulled her hands away. "Thanks." She looked at the bartender. "You about done with my order, Matty?"

The man gave her a pointed look and put an empty glass under the beer tap, filling it.

Deciding he'd pushed her far enough, Jake sat back and nursed his beer. She cleaned up her napkin shreds, then loaded her tray, offering him a tight smile as she walked away. He sighed, shaking his head. He'd find out what had her so scared. And he'd fix it.

For two hours, Jake sat on the same barstool, watching Shay work. With a crowd like this, he wasn't about to leave. When a scuffle broke out at the pool table, he wandered over and flashed his badge. It was enough to break up the two parties and stop the argument in its tracks. Then he went back to his barstool.

"Wouldn't it be easier if you just asked her on a date?"

Jake turned his attention to the bartender, Matty. The man stood a few feet away, drying glasses.

"If I thought she'd say yes. But that's not why I'm hanging around, anyway."

Matty arched an eyebrow. "Sure." His tone said he thought Jake was trying to sell him a load of crap.

A scowl darkened Jake's face. He'd be lying if he said he

didn't find Shay attractive. She was beautiful. But he was here to protect her. Not to score a date. "What do you know about her?"

The man shrugged. "Not much. She's been here about a couple months now. Keeps to herself. Mentioned that her family is dead once, but that's about it."

That explained why she ran out of the garage last night after she mentioned her grandpa. "She say where she's from?"

Matty shook his head.

Jake drummed his fingers on the bar top. He had a lot of work to do to get to the bottom of what put that fear in her eyes.

Commotion on the far side of the room pulled him from his thoughts. He looked over to see the man who'd pulled Shay onto his lap the other night take the tray from her hands, setting it on a nearby table. She squawked as he hauled her into his body, then twirled to the music.

In an instant, Jake was off his stool and on his way to her side. Two men stepped into his path when he was a few feet away. They folded their arms, the bigger of the two arching an eyebrow at him.

Jake glared at them. "Did you guys learn nothing the other night?" He raised his badge.

They just shifted their weight, though a bit of uncertainty entered the eyes of the smaller man.

"Move. Or I'll make you move." His voice dropped to a lower tenor.

The men looked at each other. Jake growled and pushed past them. He was at the couple in two strides. Reaching out, he snagged Shay's arm and spun her out of her captor's arms.

With a glare, the man rounded on him. "You again?"

"Yeah. Me. You're real dense, aren't you? The lady's not interested."

The man thumbed the corner of his mouth. "I don't know. She danced real nice."

Jake bit back another growl, relying on his police training to keep his cool. What he really wanted to do was to plant his fist into this guy's face. "How about you leave? Keep the lady from pressing assault charges."

"Jake—"

He cast a glance at her, willing her to be silent. Pressing charges would be a last resort. It hadn't slipped past him that she was skittish around law enforcement.

"So," he turned back to the man, "what do you say? Time to leave?"

Anger glittered in the man's eyes. Jake had a feeling the only thing saving him from a punch to the face was the badge on his belt. The guy knew better than to slug a cop.

With one last glare at Jake and a hard look at Shay, the man stomped away. His friends followed, and they all left.

Jake turned to Shay, who was already walking away. "Shay."

She kept going.

"Shay."

"What?"

"Are you okay?"

"I'm fine." She slapped her tray on the bar and barked her order at the other bartender, Joe. When he started working on it, she spun to face Jake. Fire flashed in her eyes, making him pause.

"Save your speech about how this job isn't safe. I'm not leaving."

He held up his hands. "I wasn't going to ask you to."

"Good." She held his gaze for a moment, then huffed. "But, um, I think maybe you're right, and I need more than mace for protection." She bit her lip as she tapped a foot on the sticky floor. "Do you think you could teach me some self-defense?"

Jake rocked back on his heels, surprised. "Sure."

"Thanks." She picked up the beers and loaded them onto her tray, leaving him there wondering what flipped the switch and allowed her to ask for help.

EIGHT

S hay avoided Jake as much as possible for the rest of the night. She still didn't know what made her ask him to teach her self-defense. What it was about him that begged her to trust him. She didn't. Not yet. But he'd come closer than anyone else in the last three years. And she was truly tired of being manhandled. It would be nice to extricate herself from men like that obnoxious drunk without having to rely on someone to come save her. Jake wouldn't always be around to step in.

At last call, Jake settled his tab, but didn't leave. He stayed at the bar, watching as she and Matty closed down. He even grabbed a rag and helped dry the stack of glasses that came out of the dishwasher. When they had everything closed up and ready for opening tomorrow, he followed her and Matty into the back so they could get their things. The three of them exited through the back door together.

"Why did you park all the way back there?" She nodded to the white Porsche.

"It was one of the few spots left when I got here."

"That's your car?" Matty stared at it, wide-eyed. "What's a cop doing with a car like that?"

Jake chuckled. "It was a project car I bought when I graduated high school. If I hadn't become a cop, I'd be a mechanic."

An engine revved. Shay turned in time to see a truck come out of the shadows near the side of the building, heading straight for them. It bumped over the uneven parking lot, the headlights coming on to blind them.

Shay's heart thudded in her ears, and she froze. Suddenly, she understood how the deer she hit felt when she came around that bend.

Jake knocked her sideways, hitting her like a battering ram. The breath left her lungs as she hit the ground with him on top of her. He rolled them out of the path of the truck. Just as suddenly as he grabbed her, he released her. She rolled to sit up and saw him pop to his feet, gun raised.

The truck fishtailed in the gravel as the driver swung around. It didn't stop. Shay's heart leaped into her throat as the pickup bore down on Jake. He stood his ground, legs spread and weapon aimed at the truck's windshield. But, still, it didn't stop. Jake fired.

Shay jumped as the retorts echoed through the night. The windshield splintered, and the vehicle veered to the side. It crashed into the building and came to a shuddering halt.

Jake advanced, gun aimed at the driver's side of the truck. He reached for the door handle and yanked it open. Shay covered her mouth with a gasp as a hand flopped out. She could see the driver slumped forward in the seat.

"Damn." Jake stepped onto the running board and reached in, pressing his fingers to the man's neck. Swearing again, he hauled the man out of the vehicle and laid him out on the ground. He glanced back at her. "Call for help." His gaze moved past her and he frowned. "Where's Matty?"

Her stomach plummeted to her toes, and she spun around. "Matty?"

She heard a groan and ran toward the shadows behind her. She found him clutching his leg. Her stomach rolled as she took in the gruesome sight. It was twisted at the knee, his foot facing backward. "Oh, geez." She sank to her knees next to him and put a hand on his shoulder. "Just hang on. I'm calling for help." She dug into her purse, looking for her cell. Once she found it, she dialed 911 with shaky fingers. When the dispatcher came on the line, she started to tell the woman what happened, but Jake yelled for her to bring him the phone.

Shay scrambled to her feet and ran as fast as she dared over the dark, uneven ground. "Here."

He took the phone, putting it on speaker, then identified himself. Shay only caught part of what he said. Her eyes were on the man covered in blood. It was the same man who grabbed her earlier. Twin holes marred his shirtfront, oozing blood every time Jake pressed down as he performed CPR. Another hole in his face showed Shay an angle on his molars she didn't want to see.

She didn't know how long she sat there staring. Long enough for the ambulance to respond. Sirens split the night, closely followed by the red and blue flash of emergency lights.

"Shay."

Her name registered, and he looked at Jake. Blood covered his hands. He frowned at her.

"Sugar, are you okay?"

She looked at the man, then glanced around at the myriad of first responders now on the scene. It surprised her to see more than just an ambulance crew.

"Shay?"

"I'm okay." She turned her gaze on him again. "I'm fine."

She sucked in a breath, battling back some of the brain fog. "Is he—?" She gestured to the man.

Jake nodded. "Yeah."

"What about Matty?" She rose to her feet, intending to search for the bartender.

"I pointed a crew toward him." He tipped his head to the scene behind her.

Shay spun around to see several emergency personnel kneeling around her co-worker.

"Come on. I need to clean up my hands and talk to Ben." He motioned for her to follow him toward an ambulance.

"Ben?"

"My boss. The sheriff, Ben Davidson."

"Oh." Still a bit dazed from shock, she followed him, then watched as he poured water over his hands to clean the blood off. As he dried them, someone called his name. Shay glanced over to see an older man walking toward them. His salt-and-pepper hair caught the swirling lights and reflected it back.

"Hey, Ben."

"What happened?" He cast a quick frown at her, but directed his question at Jake.

"The truck came at us, tried to run us over. I grabbed Shay and dove out of the way. It came back around to try again, and I fired three shots. He lost control and hit the building. I don't know how the bartender hurt his leg. Probably diving out of the way as well."

"Do we know why the guy wanted to run you over?" His question was again directed at Jake, but his gaze took in her too.

"He's been bothering Shay at the bar." He tipped his head toward her.

Inwardly, Shay groaned. She didn't want to get involved with the police, but it didn't seem she had a choice tonight.

"He grabbed her earlier tonight and forced her to dance.

Last week, he pulled her down onto his lap and wouldn't let her up."

Ben looked at her, tilting his head as he studied her. "That what happened?"

Shay nodded. "Jake stopped him both times. The guy wasn't very happy. But he never indicated he'd try something like this." She flapped a hand at the carnage.

"Okay. I'll need you both to fill out statements. Jake, I need your gun."

Jake lifted the weapon free of its holster.

"Why do you need his gun? He was defending us."

Ben took the weapon. "It's standard procedure. The gun is evidence. I'll log it, and later, our crime scene investigators will process it." He looked at Jake. "You're also on administrative leave, effective immediately."

Jake scrubbed a hand over his jaw and nodded. "Tristan's going to love this."

The sheriff flashed a grin. "He just had two weeks off."

"Because his wife had a baby."

Ben shrugged, still smiling. "Turnabout's fair play. He'll get over it."

"Not without whining a lot first." His gaze traveled past Ben. "Speak of the devil."

Shay looked behind the sheriff to see a gray truck pull up on the scene. A tall man got out, his long legs eating up the ground as he walked toward them. Her eyes widened as she took in the look on his face. Pissed off warrior fit him well. She didn't remember him looking like this when she met him at the motel a few months ago.

His steely gaze raked over her, then Jake. "You two all right? All dispatch said when they called was that you'd been involved in a shooting."

Jake nodded. "We're fine." He quickly rehashed the night's events.

Shay didn't think it was possible, but his expression got darker the longer Jake talked. She shrank back when he turned those eyes on her.

"And you did nothing to encourage the guy?" He arched an eyebrow over those steely eyes.

Anger pushed away any fear she felt at the accusation in his gaze. Her spine stiffened. She didn't get a chance to say anything, though. Jake stepped in front of her.

"Back off, Tristan. This isn't her fault."

"I'm not accusing her of anything. Just trying to get all the facts."

"The *fact* is that this isn't her fault," Jake growled.

Ben stepped between them and held up his hands. "Let's take a step back, okay? Jake, Tristan's just doing his job. Tris, maybe pull back on the bad cop routine a bit, yeah?"

Tristan blinked and his face softened. He glanced at Shay. "Sorry. I truly didn't mean to accuse you of anything. I just want to make sure I get the full picture of what happened."

A little of her anger faded. "I understand. And to answer your question, no, I did not do anything to encourage that man."

His head bobbed once. Shay cast a look at Jake. He'd relaxed some as well.

"Okay. Jake, Shay, why don't the two of you come with me, and I'll take your statements." Ben motioned them to follow him. "Tristan, start processing the scene."

Shay's eyes roved over the area once more before she followed the sheriff. *What a mess.*

At his cruiser, the sheriff removed two clipboards and attached witness statement forms to them. Shay took it from him with a tight smile. She uncapped the pen, then glanced over the sheet, fighting to keep her expression neutral as she processed all the information it wanted. Curses flew through her mind. She couldn't give them that.

But what choice did she have? If she provided false information, it would only take a quick inquiry for them to find out she lied. Correct information would jeopardize her safety.

Shay felt the press of emotions again and clutched her pen so hard her knuckles turned white. She wasn't ready to run. To change her name again.

She glanced at Jake through her lashes. His head was bent as he filled out the form. Her heart lurched. Swallowing hard, she turned her eyes back to her clipboard. This is what she got for letting a sliver of hope shine. For thinking maybe she could have a friend—or more.

Angry at herself and at her situation, Shay put the pen to paper and started to write, making the only choice she could. Herself.

NINE

Pounding echoed through the house, loud enough Jake could hear it over the music pulsing in his ears as he ran on the treadmill. Stopping the machine, he hopped off, pausing his music as he walked out of his home gym to answer the door.

Whoever was on the other side banged again. Jake quickened his stride and threw it open. Tristan stood there, a glower on his face.

"What crawled up your ass?" Tristan wasn't typically quick to anger. Not like this. It was enough to make Jake frown.

"We need to talk."

Curious what this was all about and what had him upset, Jake stepped back so he could come in.

"What do you know about Shay?"

Jake stilled, concern replacing the curiosity. He closed the door. "Shay? Why?"

"Just answer the question."

Anger flared to life in Jake's eyes and heated his veins.

"How about you tone down the assholery and talk to me like my partner instead of a cop? What's gotten into you?"

"Your girlfriend. She's not who you think she is. There's something shady about her, and she's got you bamboozled."

Jake snorted and headed for the kitchen to get some water. "What the hell are you talking about? I'll give you that she's hiding something, but it's because she's scared, not because she's into anything criminal." He opened the cabinet and removed a glass, ignoring the girlfriend comment. It wasn't worth the air to argue.

"You sure about that? I ran her info from the witness statement. Shay Britton doesn't exist. Her social security number came back to a man named Floyd Meister. He died in 1992."

Surprise made Jake pause, hand on the faucet.

"You knew, didn't you?" The accusation in Tristan's voice rankled.

"No." Jake glanced at him, his eyes hard, then turned on the water, filling his glass. "I suspected something was wrong; I told you that. She just seemed really scared and distrustful. But I didn't know she was using an alias. That probably explains why she was working at the motel and at Barney's. I bet neither place verified her ID. Do you know who she really is?"

Some of the heat left Tristan's eyes. "No. I came here hoping you knew before I submitted a warrant for her."

Alarm bells went off in Jake's head. "You can't."

Tristan frowned. "What? Why not? She's a material witness, and she lied on an official document for an attempted homicide and police-involved shooting investigation. The only legit information on her statement was her address. And maybe her phone number. It came back as a prepaid cell."

"She lied for a good reason. I'm telling you, Tris, she's running from something—someone."

"So, what am I supposed to do? Ignore it?"

"Yes. For now, at least. Let me talk to her and find out

what's going on. I'll get you the correct information, and maybe we can fix whatever has her scared."

Tristan scrubbed his hands over his face and groaned. "I don't like this." He sighed. "But I trust you and your judgement. I'll sit on it as long as I can."

"Thanks, Tristan. I appreciate it." He leaned back against the counter, thinking about the best way to find her quickly. "Do you happen to have her number with you?"

One of Tristan's eyebrows shot up. "You loaned her your car, and you don't even know her phone number?"

Jake lifted a shoulder. "It's not like she's hard to track down. She's either working one of her two jobs or at home."

Tristan rolled his eyes, then opened the junk drawer and found a pad of paper and a pen. "I hope she answers for you. She wouldn't for me." He wrote down the number and address, then tossed the pen on the counter, glancing up. "I'm leaving now before I get in deeper. Don't tell Ben I gave you all that info." Grumbling about how he hoped he could keep his ass out of trouble, Tristan walked out of the kitchen. The door slammed as he let himself out.

Drinking his water, Jake pulled the notepad closer to read what Tristan wrote. He tore the paper off and stuffed it in his shorts' pocket, then set his glass in the sink. Calling her would be his last resort. She never gave him her number, so she'd wonder how he got it. That alone might keep her from returning any message he left.

He'd start the old-fashioned way. A glance at the clock told him she was done with her motel job for the day. Which meant she was either at home or at the bar. He was betting Tristan had already checked both and only came here when he couldn't find her. Jake was hoping the bartender would give him information he wouldn't give Tristan.

After changing clothes, Jake hopped in his Porsche and made the short drive to Barney's. His SUV wasn't in the lot, which didn't surprise him. He parked near the door and went inside. The few people there at this time of day glanced at him, then went back to their drinks. Jake let his eyes adjust to the dim interior, then headed for the bar.

"She's not here." The bartender gave him a frosty look as he dried a pint glass. It was the same guy from last night who worked with Matty.

"I know. I'm hoping you can tell me where she might be. I need to talk to her."

The man shrugged. "No idea. She came in before we opened and told the manager she was quitting, then asked for the money she was owed. He gave it to her and she left."

Dammit, she was running. "She didn't say anything about why she was quitting or where she was going?"

"Just that the atmosphere here was too rough for her. She didn't say anything about where she planned to go. I figured she was just going to find another job in town." He set the glass down and picked up another.

Jake tapped his palm on the bar top. "Okay. Thanks for the info. If you hear from her, tell her to call me?"

The man paused and eyed him for a moment. "She's in trouble, isn't she?"

"Maybe. But not with the law." He backed away. "Tell her to contact me if you see her." The bartender nodded, and Jake left.

Outside, he climbed back into his car and started the engine. Tapping his finger on the steering wheel, he debated where to go next. If she was clearing out, that left the motel and her apartment. And her car. But if she was scared, she'd leave in his SUV. She wouldn't wait on her car to be fixed.

He picked up his phone and called the repair shop where she had her car towed as he drove out of the parking lot toward the motel. The mechanic quickly confirmed she hadn't been in since yesterday morning. At the motel, his conversation with her boss was similar to the one he had with the bartender, which left him with just her apartment to check. But something told him he wouldn't find her there, either. She was already gone.

A tense ten-minute drive confirmed his suspicion. The parking lot at her apartment complex was devoid of his SUV. He parked outside her door and got out. He'd knock, just in case she left his car somewhere else and took a cab home.

Rapping his knuckles on her door, he waited. The place looked empty. She had the curtains drawn on the front window and the lights were off inside. He knocked again, but still didn't get an answer.

With a groan, he turned around, taking his phone from his pocket. "You better call me back if you don't answer, sugar." He dialed the number on the paper, but as he was about to hit send, the door next to hers opened and an older woman stepped out.

"You here looking for Shay?"

Jake lowered the phone. "I am, yes. Do you know where I can find her?"

The woman glanced around and stepped closer. "That depends. What do you want with her?"

"I'm just a friend trying to help."

She narrowed her eyes, searching his gaze. Something in his eyes must have deemed him trustworthy, because she continued.

"I saw her earlier as she was leaving. She had a couple of suitcases and loaded them into some black SUV. I asked what happened to her car, and she said she hit a deer. That the SUV was a rental. When I asked if she was going on a trip, she told me it was just a little vacation."

"Did she say where?"

The woman shook her head. "No. Just that she was looking forward to the warmer weather. I figured she meant

Florida. I know that's where I'd go if I wanted warm this time of year."

"Me too. Okay. Thank you. If you see her, will you tell her to call Jake?"

"I sure will." She smiled at him.

Jake waved as he climbed into his car. Warmer weather. At least he had a place to start looking.

TEN

Jake stared at his phone, willing it to ring. He'd left several messages on Shay's voicemail in the last twenty-four hours, but she still hadn't called him back. She'd also ignored all his texts. Frustration clawed at him. Against his better judgement, he'd told Tristan to put a BOLO out on his car. He didn't want to spook her. But if she was in enough danger to run because she felt like she had to falsify a police report, then he wanted to find her and make sure she was safe.

He picked up the device and woke the screen. His thumb hovered over the phone icon, debating whether to call her again. She needed to answer his calls. Before he had no choice but to make the BOLO for more than his car.

Growling, he tapped the icon, then touched her name in his recent calls list. He drummed his fingers on the arm of his chair, waiting for her voicemail to pick up so he could leave another message.

"Please stop calling me, Jake."

It took him a moment to realize she'd answered. When he did, he sat forward and his heart did a little flip into his throat. "Shay, where are you?"

"Not in Foggy Mountain." She sighed. "Please stop calling. I'm sorry I took your car. Once I get a new one, I'll leave it somewhere, then call you to let you know where it is."

"I don't care about the car, Shay. I care about you. Where are you? Please let me help."

"I can't. It's too dangerous. Just forget about me. I'm sorry."

"Shay—" A beep in his ear told him she'd hung up. He cursed and stood, immediately calling her back. It rang several times, then rolled to voicemail. Jake cursed again, then called Tristan, pacing while he waited on his partner to answer.

"Mabley."

"She answered. I called, and she answered."

"I know."

Jake stopped pacing, a frown forming. "What do you mean, you know?"

"I got a warrant for her phone when I put a BOLO on your car. And before you start, it was just so we could get a location on her. She's in Myrtle Beach, South Carolina, by the way."

"I don't know whether to punch you or kiss you."

Tristan laughed. "I vote neither. Now go find her before I have to alert Myrtle Beach PD to pick her up. She's at a motel near the water. The Silver Dolphin." He rattled off the address. Jake repeated it to himself, committing it to memory as Tristan continued. "Ben's giving us leeway, but it's only going to last so long."

Jake blew out a breath. "Thanks, man. I owe you."

"No, you don't. Just find her." He hung up.

Relief hit Jake hard, but it only lasted a moment. He still had to get there and locate her before she moved on.

Stuffing his phone into his pocket, he ran to his bedroom to pack. After dragging a small suitcase out of his closet, he threw several changes of clothes and his toiletries into it, along with his reserve weapon and some ammunition. He hoped he wouldn't need it, but he'd be damned if he'd leave without it.

On his way out the door, he grabbed the other set of keys to his SUV. The door slammed behind him as he yanked it shut, then hurried to his car parked in the garage. Tossing the suitcase in the backseat, he got in and hit the button to open the overhead door, then started the engine. It roared to life, and Jake smiled. He needed to rethink which car was his everyday vehicle when this was all over.

Backing out, he hit the gas and headed for the highway. Myrtle Beach was a five-hour drive. He prayed she'd still be there when he arrived.

The miles passed in a blur. Darkness settled around him as he neared the city, which he appreciated. She'd be less likely to spot him coming. He pulled off the road long enough to enter the motel address in his GPS, then resumed his drive. The minutes ticked by like hours, making Jake edgier the closer he got.

Finally, the sign came into view. He drove past, looking for his car, but didn't see it. That didn't mean much, though. There was a rear lot. Turning around, he pulled into the motel's parking lot and drove around.

Bingo. His car sat on the end near the stairs, close to the lot's rear exit. He kept going and left the motel, heading down the street to park at a shopping center. Hurrying back, he went beneath the stairs and leaned against the wall to wait.

He needed a plan. At this hour, she wasn't likely to come out until morning. Someone would call the cops on him if he lingered under the stairs all night.

His fingers fiddled with the spare key in his pocket, and an idea formed. He found the bottom button on the remote and pressed it. The horn blared to life on the SUV and the lights flashed as he activated the panic alarm. Curtains twitched down the row as people glanced outside. After several moments, the car stopped its fit. Jake waited, hoping she'd come out to make sure all was well.

Two minutes after the alarm stopped, the door above him opened. He shrank back against the wall, hiding in the shadows. The last thing he wanted was for her to see him and dart back inside, barricading herself.

The soft shuffle of her feet on the concrete stairs sounded, then she appeared at the base, her focus on the car. Jake crept out from his spot until he was in the open. As she rounded the car, checking it for problems, she saw him.

Her eyes went wide, and she froze. "How did you find me?"

"Tristan got a warrant for your cellular data. We got your location when you took my call. And no, I didn't know he did it."

She narrowed her eyes and crossed her arms. "But you took the information anyway."

He walked closer. "Damn straight. I don't know what you're running from, but that ends now. It's time to fight, Shay."

Her dark eyes took on a hard, but hollow, look. "You have no idea what I'm up against. This isn't some simple stalking case."

An anger started on a slow burn in his belly. "You're being stalked, but it's not really stalking? Is that what you're saying? Then what is it?"

Her lips twisted, and she tapped her toe on the pavement. "None of your business."

Tired of the run around, he moved forward. Unlocking the car, he opened the back passenger door and pushed her inside.

"What—Jake! What are you doing?"

"Getting answers." He followed her in and shut the door.

She reached for the opposite door handle, but he grabbed her arm. "Don't. You need to talk to me, Shay."

"No. I don't want to put anyone else in danger. This is my problem."

"Yeah? How's that working out for you? How long have you been running?"

She stilled and tears swam in her eyes. "Three years," she whispered. A tear tracked down her cheek.

Jake cursed, gentling his hold. He slid his hands down her arm to hold her hand. "Please let me help."

ELEVEN

The air inside the SUV threatened to stifle Shay. So many emotions attacked her from every angle, she didn't know which way was up. They clogged her throat and held her breath trapped in her lungs.

It was the soft, "Please let me help," that did her in. The dam broke, and she collapsed, sobbing against his shoulder. She let three years of fear and worry loose on his shirt, soaking it with her tears.

All the while, he held her, stroking her hair and murmuring nonsense. The tenderness set her off all over again. It was something she hadn't seen much of in her adult life. Not since—

Shay slammed the door on that line of thought. She couldn't go there. Not if she wanted a chance at halting her tears.

Sobering, she sat up and looked at Jake with watery eyes. "I'm sorry."

He brushed the hair away from her face and smoothed the streaks of tears on her cheeks. "You keep saying that. I don't want apologies. Tell me what's wrong."

She searched his eyes, but again, saw no ulterior motive for helping her. But could she trust him? And if she did, what would that mean for his safety? Sure, he was a cop, but that didn't mean much in her situation. Did she have a choice, though? She couldn't go on living like this. The crushing despair and lack of hope were slowly killing her.

And the entire reason she ran was because she wanted a life. What she had wasn't living. It was surviving.

That thought galvanized her decision. She wanted more than survival. Jake was offering her a chance to live again.

"Okay," she whispered, then cleared her throat. "Okay. But not here. Can we go upstairs?"

He studied her eyes for a moment before nodding. "Lead the way."

They slid out of the car, and he followed her up the stairs to her room. She unlocked the door, then closed it behind them, locking it. Her fingers lingered on the security chain as nerves assailed her. She wanted to tell him everything, but wasn't sure she could.

"Shay."

His soft voice, full of understanding and patience, broke through her fear, and she turned around. Taking a shaky breath, she crossed to the small dinette set in the corner, sitting in one of the two wooden chairs. Jake sat down across from her.

She folded her hands on top of the table, staring at them. "I'm not sure where to start." She raised one hand to her mouth and bit the edge of her thumbnail, staring at the painting on the far wall.

Jake covered her other hand with one of his, startling her. She looked at him.

"What made you run?"

"Ultimately?"

He nodded.

"I wanted a life."

One dark eyebrow winged toward his hairline. "This is living?"

"Compared to before, yes." At least she could be relatively sure he wasn't watching. Wasn't waiting for her to come home. "But no, not really."

"Okay, let's start at the beginning. What's your real name? The one you put on the witness statement, the one you told me, is fake."

"Not entirely. My full name is Mackenzie Shaylene Brighton. I thought about doing something completely different, but I knew I'd have a hard time answering to something I wasn't used to. Mack and Kenz or Kenzie were all nicknames people used for me, but no one ever called me by my middle name. So, I became Shay."

"Mackenzie." He tested the name. "That's nice."

She thought so too. And she liked the way it sounded coming from his lips. It had been so long since she'd heard anyone call her that. She pressed the back of her hand to her mouth, holding back more tears.

He squeezed her hand. "What started all this?"

Swallowing hard, she lowered her hand. "A few years ago, I met a guy. At the grocery store, of all places. I wanted a box of granola bars, but there was only one left of the brand I liked, and it was way at the back, on the top shelf. Even standing on the bottom shelf, I could just get my fingers on it. He came along and plucked it down, handing it to me. I thanked him, and he went on his way, but we saw each other again in the parking lot." She disengaged her hand from his, smoothing it over her hair.

"He asked if I had any more trouble. I said no, but it would be nice if he was around the next time I shopped, since those bars were usually hard to reach. He laughed and said maybe that could be arranged. Then he asked if I wanted to go for a drink. He seemed so normal, you know? So, I said yes."

She blew out a breath and let her hands fall to the table, crossing her arms on it. "Things went great for a few months, but he slowly started eroding away my freedom. He didn't like this friend or that one. Didn't want me going over to my parents' house for lunch on Sundays or helping my grandpa with his car." Her voice caught on the last word and tears spilled over her eyelids before she could stop them. Taking a shaky breath, she wiped them away and continued.

"It took me a while to realize what he was doing, but once I did, I broke things off. We hadn't moved in together—that was one of the things he was pressing for, but something kept stopping me—so all I had to do was tell him it was over."

"Except he didn't want it to be over," Jake cut in.

Shay nodded. "Yeah. I would come home from work and he'd be waiting in my apartment. Like nothing happened. I threatened to call the police, but he just laughed and asked who would believe me over him?" She took an unsteady breath. "He's a cop. And a decorated one at that."

Jake jolted in surprise and sat forward. "What? A cop?"

She nodded.

"So, what did you do?"

"What could I do? He never hit me. It was all psychological abuse. He made me feel like I was nothing. That no one would believe me, not even my family. So, I let him stay. I wish I hadn't." More tears welled in her eyes, and she sniffed.

"Finally, my mom noticed I seemed depressed. She showed up at my apartment one day while Brett was at work and laid out everything she thought was going on. I couldn't argue with her. It was all true. I was just astonished she didn't hate me. He'd verbally beaten me down into a shell of my former self. Into a woman whose sole job in life was to make him happy. Mom's the one who packed my suitcase and drove me to her house. She sent my grandpa over to my apartment to change the locks and put in a rudimentary alarm system; something that made a lot of noise and would hopefully scare him off if he tried to break in."

"Did it work?"

"Not really. He disabled it all and made a mold of the lock to forge his own key. But I still insisted on staying by myself. Deep down, I knew Brett would stop at nothing to keep me. I didn't want my family in the middle of it." She looked at the scarred tabletop, picking at a scratch. "It didn't matter, though." She looked up, eyes bleak. "He killed them, then made me feel like it was my fault."

Jake's shocked inhalation matched the widening of his eyes. "Explain."

"He and I had an argument. After my mom's intervention, I had a little more backbone because I knew I had my family in my corner. I came home from work and he was inside my apartment again, watching TV like he belonged there. I started throwing things at him—pillows, small knick-knacks—and told him to get out. He just walked up to me and wrapped me in his arms and told me I needed to stop being unreasonable. That we belonged together and all he wanted was to keep me happy." She let out a shaky breath. "By that point, I was crying. I was so angry and frustrated. But he mistook it for capitulation and let me go. Said he was going to make me a cup of tea and then we'd talk about which pieces of furniture I wanted to keep when I moved in with him." That same frustration she felt then reared its head now. She picked at the scarred tabletop again, chipping off flecks of varnish.

"As soon as he entered the kitchen, I ran. Just grabbed my purse and keys and left. I needed some space and some time to think. To come up with a plan. I couldn't move in with him, I knew that. I might have lost my self-esteem, but some part of me recognized our relationship was toxic." She paused, looking up. "I drove around for hours, trying to figure out how to regain my independence. While I was gone, he called my family and told them I was missing. They went out looking for me and had an 'accident'." She air-quoted as the first tears fell. "The official report says the car went off the road and flipped, then caught fire. But I know he had something to do with it."

"Oh, man. I'm sorry, Shay."

She swiped at the moisture on her face. "He twisted it all around. Made me feel like it was my fault they were dead, because they were out looking for me. I spent months wallowing in grief and guilt. I kept thinking how they'd still be alive if I hadn't gotten so angry and left. It got to a point that I didn't want to live." She sniffed and shifted.

"Then I ran into my best friend while I was out running. She took one look at my gaunt face and all the weight I'd lost and hauled me into a coffee shop and forced me to talk. The next thing I knew, I had enough cash to get me a hotel room for about a week and a cheap car—because he'd convinced me to sell mine shortly after my family's accident."

She shook her head, wishing she could see Piper again to thank her. When she left, she'd been so overwhelmed she hadn't been able to force more than a quick, "I don't know what to say," past her tight throat. Piper had told her that her surviving and starting a new life was thanks enough.

And she'd tried. But he'd found her. "I spent a few months living in Pittsburgh. It seemed far enough away, but not too far for comfort."

"Where are you from?"

"Amandale, New York. It's near Buffalo." She leaned back and hugged herself. "Anyway, I thought just starting over would be enough. But it wasn't. He tracked me down, showed up at my apartment and outside my job. But by then, I had a new perspective. I wasn't going back."

"You said you ran because you wanted a life. What happened?"

Shay brought her hand up and chewed on her thumbnail again, staring off into space as she fought to stay out of the emotions of the past. "He started contacting people I worked with, meeting them accidentally on purpose at grocery stores and coffee shops, spreading lies. I was a pharmacy technician. He would tell them he recognized them from when he picked me up or dropped me off at work. Said he was my boyfriend. Then he'd ask how I was doing at work. That he was concerned about how I was handling things. He kept hinting that I had a problem with painkillers without actually saying it. It finally got back to my boss, and he pulled me in, questioning me about it. I denied everything, of course, but I was forced to go through a drug-screening and they put me on probationary status."

Dropping her hand, she met Jake's gaze. "He did the same thing he did to me back home—isolated me from everyone. But this time, he couldn't make me doubt myself. I knew if I wanted a real life, I needed to start clean. Mackenzie Brighton needed to cease to exist."

"So you reinvented yourself?"

"Yeah. One of the other techs, she believed me when I said it was all lies. She used to run with the wrong crowd when she was young and pointed me toward someone who could get me a new identity. I wiped out my savings and gave the guy my car to sell to cover the cost. As soon as my papers were done, I dropped it off, took my documents and hopped on the first bus I could get."

"And it led you to Foggy Mountain?"

"Actually, it led me to Charlotte. I worked at a bar for tips for a few weeks, staying at a seedy motel to keep costs down. I saved up for a car, then moved again. I did that every few months until I was sure he wasn't on my trail. I've stayed in Foggy Mountain longer than anywhere."

Jake took a deep breath and scrubbed his hands over his face as he let it out. "Until one drunk threatened everything by exposing you."

"Yes. If I'd put my real name on that form, I'm sure he'd have found out. Brett's smart and charming. Someone would be watching for my name to pop up somewhere."

"Okay." Jake leaned on his forearms on the table. "What if we let him know?"

"What?" Her heart thudded in her chest at the thought. She didn't want to end up back under Brett's thumb.

He held up a hand. "We have an advantage. He doesn't know that I know the truth. That my partner and my boss are going to know the truth. This time, he can't isolate you. You won't fall for it like you did the first time, and we won't fall for it like the people in Pittsburgh."

She thrust her hands into her hair and stood. "God, I don't know, Jake." She walked to the window, flicking back the edge of the curtain to look out. It had started to rain. The soft drizzle left puddles on the ground. Water beaded on the cars below. The dark, bleak sky fit her mood.

"It'll be okay, Shay."

Spinning around, she pinned him with her stare. "You don't know that. He killed my parents and my grandpa. Because of me. Because he wants me all to himself. He won't hesitate to kill you or Tristan or Ben or anyone else who gets in his way. I can't be the reason someone else dies. Not again."

Jake stood, his expression hard as he walked toward her. He took her shoulders in his hands and gave her a little shake. "Listen to me, Shay. You are not the reason your family died. He is. He killed them because of his obsession. You did nothing to cause their deaths."

Tears flowed down her face. "Yes, I did. I—"

"No. No. You did nothing. He manipulated you and mentally and emotionally abused you. *All* of this is because of *him*."

She wanted to believe him. Wanted it to be true. But she'd spent so long thinking this was her fault, that she did something to make him act this way, that her brain refused to accept the alternative. But, oh, how she wanted to.

A sob broke free from her chest. Jake pulled her into his arms and held her tight.

"Not your fault, sugar." He kissed the top of her head. "We're going to stop him. I promise."

Shay clung to him and his words, praying he could keep his promise. Whether she believed it wasn't her fault or not, she was tired of running. She wanted to live.

TWELVE

A rumble of thunder woke Jake. He'd checked into the room beside Shay's after garnering a promise from her that she wouldn't run again.

Lightning flashed, and another clap of thunder followed. Jake sat up, glancing at the clock. It was nearly five. There wasn't much point in attempting to go back to sleep. They needed to head back to Foggy Mountain so they could meet with Ben and Tristan and make a plan.

He showered and dressed, then went to the coffee shop he remembered passing on his way here last night to get them coffee and breakfast. He hoped sleep gave Shay a chance to process everything that happened and what was going to happen. She needed to recognize that she had hope.

His mouth twisted as he pulled into a space at the motel and stared up at her door. She'd been without hope for so long, he feared she wouldn't be able to climb out of the well of despair she was in. Even though she'd agreed to his plan, he felt like she still didn't quite believe it was possible to escape her ex and climb out of the hole.

Jake opened his door and got out. No matter. He'd do

enough believing for the both of them until they stopped the guy and she could see it for herself.

He dashed up the steps through the rain and knocked on her door. When she didn't answer, he glanced around, noting both his cars were still in the lot. Unless she called a cab and left, she was in there.

A frown darkened his face as he prayed that wasn't the case. Last night, it seemed like while she wasn't ready to believe it was possible to get out from under her ex, she was ready to try. He knocked again, louder. "Shay? It's me."

When she still didn't answer, he let out a soft curse and went to his room. He'd asked her to leave her connecting door unlocked in case of an emergency. Hopefully, she listened.

Setting their food down on the little table, he opened his door to her room, then tried the knob on hers. It turned in his hand and he said a quick prayer of thanks.

"Shay?" Pushing it in, he looked around. Her suitcase was on the bed, open.

The bathroom door opened and she walked out in a towel. She saw him and shrieked, her hand flying to the knot between her breasts.

"Jake! What are you doing in here?"

"Sorry." He backed into his room, keeping his eyes on her face. One glance lower was enough for him to know he wanted to see her without the towel. "I knocked. When you didn't answer, I got concerned. I got us some breakfast. Knock when you're decent." He pointed at the inner door, then closed it.

"Son-of-a-bitch," he whispered, leaning his head against the door. He'd done a damn good job of ignoring his attraction to her. She was in no position to start a relationship. He wasn't interested in complicating her life any more.

Backing away from the door, Jake picked up his coffee and took a gulp. The searing liquid left a fiery trail down his throat, but it cleared his head, gaining him some perspective.

Lusting after her wouldn't help anything. He needed to bury all that until she was free to decide if she wanted to pursue a relationship. Harboring feelings for her now would only make his life harder. Nothing could come of it.

When she knocked on the inner door five minutes later, he'd gotten a better grasp on his emotions.

"Hi," he said, opening the door. "I got you a muffin and a black coffee." He gestured to the sack on the table. "I hope that's okay."

"It's fine. Thank you." Her gaze flicked to his, then she skirted past him and sat down, pulling the bag toward her.

Jake took the seat across from her and sipped his coffee.

"You're not going to eat?" She peeled back the wrapper on her muffin.

Wordlessly, he took the second muffin from the bag and bit into it.

"So, what exactly is the plan?" Shay glanced up at him through her lashes.

"Talk to Ben and Tristan. Other than that, I don't really have much of an idea yet. We need to find proof he orchestrated your family's deaths. It's the only way to ensure he stays away from you." That wasn't necessarily true, but Jake didn't want to think about what would have to happen to keep Brett away otherwise. They were better off proving old crimes than inducing new ones.

"You're sure this will work?"

"If we can prove he planned their deaths, yes."

She fiddled with her coffee cup, turning it in her fingers. "And if we can't?"

"We'll find a way." He covered one of her hands with his for a moment and squeezed. "Are you about finished? We have a long drive ahead."

Shay nodded, but kept picking at her muffin. Jake frowned. "Are you okay?"

She tore off another small piece of her muffin and put it in her mouth, glancing out the window. "No," she finally answered. "But I'll be okay." She pushed the muffin away, picked up her coffee, and stood. "I'm not very hungry. Let's just go."

Jake frowned, but said nothing. There was nothing to say that would make it better. Empty words wouldn't help, so he stayed silent.

They disposed of their trash and gathered their bags, then Jake checked them out. He followed her out of the parking lot, then through town to the interstate.

Buildings and trees whizzed by and the terrain gradually changed as they entered the mountains. A half an hour from home, he called Tristan.

"Hey, Jake. How's the hunt going?"

"I found her. We're on our way home now. Can you grab Ben and meet us at my house in about thirty minutes?"

"What? Oh, I don't like the sound of your voice. Why do I get the feeling I won't like this?"

"Probably because you won't. I know I don't. Just meet us there."

Tristan sighed. "Yep."

Thirteen

Jake pulled into his driveway behind Shay. He was glad to see Tristan and Ben had already arrived. It meant less time for Shay to think about what they were doing.

Although she'd had five hours alone in the car to think.

Heaving a sigh, he got out and met her in the drive. She glanced at him before looking at the porch. Ben and Tristan rose from the swing, their imposing forms and intense expressions making her shrink in on herself.

"Come on." His voice was quiet as he put a hand on her back. "They're here to help."

She gave a short nod and let him lead her up the steps.

"Ms. Britton, I'm glad to see you're safe," Ben said, his expression softening some.

"Thank you." She took a deep breath and glanced at Jake.

He offered her a nod, encouraging her to say what he could see in her eyes.

She looked at Ben again and held out a hand. "It's Brighton, actually. Mackenzie Brighton. You can still call me Shay."

After a brief widening of his eyes, Ben smiled and shook

her hand. "It's nice to meet you, Mackenzie Brighton." He looked at Jake. "Let's go inside and talk, shall we?"

Jake nodded and stepped forward, unlocking the door. The four of them filed inside. He led them to the living room. Shay sat on the couch, so he sat next to her, offering her moral support. Ben and Tristan perched on the remaining chairs.

"So, Ms. Brighton, why don't you fill us in on what's going on and why you ran?"

Shay twisted her hands together in her lap and stared at them. Jake put his hand over hers and squeezed. She turned her face to his.

"It's okay." He squeezed again.

She studied him for a moment, then sucked in a breath and looked at the other men. "My ex-boyfriend psychologically and emotionally abused me and killed my family to isolate me. I ran so he couldn't keep me under his thumb any longer."

Tristan cursed and stood, walking to the window. Jake eyed him, worrying about how he'd take this turn of events. His wife had been in an abusive household throughout her childhood.

Ben cleared his throat. "What do you mean by he killed your family?"

Shay launched into a recap of what she told Jake at the motel. By the time she finished, a vein pulsed in Tristan's forehead, and Ben's eyebrows practically touched.

"I understand now why you thought you couldn't trust the police," Ben said. "But I'm glad you did. Tell us more about him." He took a notebook and a pen from his pocket.

"His name is Brett Jorgensen. He's a sergeant with the Amandale Police Department just outside of Buffalo, New York."

"How old?" Ben asked, head bent as he wrote.

"Thirty-two."

"Do you know his birthdate?"

She rattled it off, and he wrote it down.

"What about his family?"

"He doesn't have any that I know of. He told me he's an only child and that both his parents passed away. His dad in a car accident when he was in high school, and his mom from an aneurysm about five years ago."

"Do you know their names?"

"Rick and Tricia."

Ben nodded. "What about his friends? Did you ever meet any of them?"

She lifted one shoulder. "A few. He liked to keep me to himself. But we went to a couple of parties. There was one guy he talked about and hung around with more than anyone. His name is Eric Steiner."

"He ever talk about previous girlfriends?" Tristan asked.

She looked over at him where he still stood near the window, listening. "Not really. He mentioned a woman named Mary a few times. I never learned her last name."

"Ever see any pictures?"

"No."

"Okay," Ben cut in. "What about his habits? Routines? What can you tell us about those?"

Shay frowned and looked at Jake for a moment before looking back at Ben. "I'm not sure what that has to do with what he did to my parents."

Jake squeezed her hands again. "We're looking for sources of information. Places he might go to hide evidence or people he might confide in or enlist for help."

"Oh." She shifted and blew out a breath. "Um, well, he was a creature of habit. On the days he had to work, he'd get up, workout, go to work, then come home. On Fridays, he went to a local bar with Eric and maybe a few other friends. I never went." She glanced down at her hands laced with Jake's, then up at him.

He smiled softly, silently encouraging her to continue.

"I used those nights for myself. Read a book or watched a movie. Took a walk. Just something that I could do alone. I didn't get much time to myself." She gave him a tremulous smile, then looked at Ben. "On the weekends, if neither of us had to work, we'd do something together or just spend time at either his place or my apartment."

"What kinds of things did the two of you do together?"

"Mostly hiking and camping. It was one of the things I liked most about him in the beginning. He liked the outdoors as much as I did. Otherwise, we did the normal date things. Dinner, a movie, that sort of thing."

"Okay." Ben tapped his pen against the notepad. "Are there any other people you can think of he might confide in?"

She bit her lip, then shook her head a moment later. "No. Eric would probably be the only one."

"What about places he liked to go? You mentioned the bar. What's the name of it?"

"O'Toole's. They'd go bowling too. He was even in a league for a while."

"This was in Amandale?"

She nodded.

"What about where you went hiking?" Jake asked. "Did you frequent certain places?"

"Actually, yes. He liked a state park that wasn't too far away. Darien Lake."

Ben scribbled in his notebook again. "All right. I think that's a good place for us to start." He looked up. "I'll get in touch with some old colleagues from the FBI."

"The FBI?" Shay cut in. Jake could feel her tense.

Ben nodded. "He crossed state lines when he sought you out in Pittsburgh. Plus, I can't contact his local department without tipping him off. Same with the sheriff's department up there. He could have friends in it. I'll probably involve the New York state crime bureau, though."

"Once you talk to Eric, Brett will know. He'll start looking for me even harder."

The tension in her shoulders grew. Jake tightened his hold, turning to put a hand on her knee. "Hey. Don't worry, okay? Ben's good at what he does. We'll dig up what information we can from here. I think the feds and the state police are just more for surveillance. We can't tail him from here."

"Jake's right," Ben said. "We need to track his movements. I won't tip him off that you've gone to the police with your story. You're still safe here."

"I'm confused." She looked from Ben to Jake, then Tristan and back to Ben. "I thought the plan was to draw him out?"

"Only if we need to, I think. Why don't we start by seeing what we can dig up first? If nothing comes of our investigation, we'll talk about bringing him out of the woodwork."

Jake's mouth flattened. While he didn't like the idea of using Shay as bait, it might be the only way she could be free of her ex.

She let out a soft snort. "Okay. But I can about guarantee we'll be talking about how to make him show his face around here. He wouldn't leave a trail connecting him to my family's accident. Brett's controlling, not stupid."

"I understand, but it's still worth the time to investigate. I don't want to put you in danger if we don't have to. None of us do." His gaze took in Tristan and Jake.

Jake nodded. "Ben's right. Let us tear his life apart—quietly. We might end up surprised. He sounds like he's arrogant enough to think he won't get caught, and that could make him careless."

Her shoulders slumped. She turned her hands over in his

and squeezed. "Okay." She sighed. "You got my hopes up. Now, I just want this over with."

He squeezed back. "I know. And we'll do our best to make it quick."

Shay nodded. "Thank you." She looked at Ben and Tristan. "All of you." Her eyes watered. "I'm thankful I landed here. I'm so tired of running. Of hiding. I want my life back."

"And you're going to get it." Jake lifted a hand to push a lock of hair out of her eyes. Determination to give this woman everything her heart desired hit him hard. She deserved so much more than the life she'd led the last few years. "Don't worry, please? We won't fail."

With a shaky breath, she nodded. He palmed the back of her head and leaned forward, pressing a soft kiss to her forehead. All while praying he wasn't lying.

Fourteen

Shay stood in front of the bathroom mirror at Jake's and frowned at her reflection. She looked tired. And haggard. The stress of the last couple of days was showing. Maybe tonight she'd be able to get a good night's sleep. Though where that would be, she didn't know. She'd given up her modest, furnished apartment when she ran, forfeiting her security deposit when she broke her lease. Tomorrow, she'd have to stop by the manager's office and see if he'd let her have her apartment back. If not, she would need to dip into her savings for a security deposit and first month's rent for another place. Assuming she could find another furnished apartment in the area. They were few and far between.

Sighing, she leaned on her hands on the counter. That still didn't solve her dilemma of where she would sleep tonight. She could probably get a room at the motel she cleaned. She needed to talk to the manager about getting her job back, anyway.

She pushed off the counter and left the bathroom to head back to the living room. When she entered, she paused and glanced around. Jake still sat on the couch, his phone in his hand, but Ben and Tristan were gone. "Where did the others go?"

Jake glanced up. "Tristan went home, and Ben went back to the station to make some calls." He laid his phone on the coffee table and stood, walking toward her.

The hair on the back of Shay's neck rose as he neared. It nudged her closer to him, but she planted her feet. Giving in would be a disastrous idea. She didn't need more complications in her life.

Instead, she cleared her throat. "Oh, well, okay. Can you take me to the motel? I want to talk to the manager about getting my job back. I'll just rent a room there for now. I broke the lease on my apartment when I left."

"No."

She frowned. "What do you mean, no?"

"No." He shrugged. "You're not going back there. You can stay here."

"What? Why not? Ben said I was safe in Foggy Mountain."

"You are. But on the off-chance Brett catches wind of our investigation or of the one into the bar incident—because Ben can only withhold your real name so long—I want you somewhere I can keep an eye on you."

She searched his wintery eyes. "And that's here?"

He nodded. Shay bristled. She'd had enough of domineering men. "No."

It was Jake's turn to frown. "No?"

Shay shook her head. "No. I'll be fine on my own. I don't need a keeper."

Understanding widened his eyes, and he held up his hands. "I'm not trying to dictate anything, Shay, I swear. I just want you safe. Staying with me—or hell, even Tristan or Ben —would be the best option to do that. If you don't want to stay with me, that's fine, but let me call one of them. You shouldn't be alone. Not while things are heating up."

Shay pressed her lips together, rolling them inward as she thought. She didn't want to admit that he was right, but she knew she'd feel a lot better being close to someone if Brett managed to track her down. "Fine, I'll stay here."

His smile lit up his face and set off the butterflies in her stomach again. Maybe she should stay with Ben instead.

She quickly dashed that thought. The sheriff was nice, and she had no doubt he'd keep her safe, but she wouldn't feel comfortable with anyone but Jake. He'd come after her, cared about her, when no one else did. He might throw her lady parts into a state of ardent rapture, but she trusted him to keep her safe and to have her best interests in mind.

"Great. Since I'm on leave, and your case isn't an official investigation, Ben told me to start digging into Brett's online presence. Do you want to help, or would you rather do something else? You can do anything you'd like. You don't even have to stay here if you don't want to. Just make sure you're around people and keep your phone close."

"Oh, um, I guess I could go talk to my boss at the motel. See if I can get my job back."

Jake frowned. "You're not doing the same at the bar, are you?"

She shook her head. "No. I think my waitressing days are done."

"Good." He touched her cheek with one finger, leaving a trail of tingles in his wake. "You're too classy for a place like that."

Heat suffused her cheeks. She licked her lips, transfixed by his eyes and the tenderness in them. Desire flared to life in her belly. She saw an answering passion leap to life in his eyes, turning his icy blue irises to blue-brushed steel. The hand on her face cupped the side of her head. His fingers delved into her hair, sending the tingles over her scalp.

His jaw flexed as he looked down into her eyes. She

watched as the desire in his eyes banked, and he stepped back. "I'm going to go get started on that internet search. Be careful when you go out. If anything seems weird, call me."

Shay gave him a shaky nod, incapable of speaking. The tingles had paralyzed her vocal chords. He swept his eyes over her face one last time, then he turned and walked away.

Her breath left on a whoosh. She covered her heated face with her hands and let out a soft groan. Staying here was such a bad idea.

Fifteen

Jake rubbed his temples, a headache pounding behind his eyes. He'd been staring at his computer screen for hours, looking for dirt on Brett Jorgensen. The man didn't have much of an online presence. A few snapshots of him doing outdoorsy things with friends—including Eric Steiner—and a couple of dinner photos with the same friends were about all Jake found. He'd run the man's name through a background check and discovered he was what he said he was. There was nothing to indicate the man was a cold-blooded killer or an emotionally manipulative bastard.

He still didn't like the guy. The smile on his face in all the pictures rang false. Like he was trying too hard. It was a smarmy, politician's smile. The one Jake's local congressman always plastered on his face during his meet-and-greets and during interviews.

But he could be biased. Shay's story had clouded his objectivity when it came to the man.

Deciding he needed a distraction, he clicked off of Jorgensen's background check to search news reports for the car accident that killed Shay's family. He found several from local news outlets. They stated her grandpa was driving, and the car went off the road, going over a berm and flipping several times before coming to a stop in a field. The car caught on fire before rescue could arrive and all three occupants died.

Jake grimaced as he read the details. What a horrific way to die. He wished he could get his hands on the official report, including their autopsies. But that would tip off Jorgensen. They needed another way to get the information.

He made a note on a legal pad, then went back to the background check database. He'd run Jorgensen's parents and check the details of his story. Typing their names in and approximate death dates, he tapped a finger on the mouse as he waited for the database to collate.

His eyes grew wide as the message, "No record matches your entry," appeared on the screen.

"What?" He clicked back to his web browser and typed in Jorgensen's mother's name, looking for her obituary. He scrolled through a number of Tricia Jorgensens, but none matched the woman he was looking for. Trying Patricia Jorgensen, he got similar results.

"What the hell is going on here?" Jake frowned and tried the dad. More of the same appeared. There were no deaths of a Rick or Richard Jorgensen that happened from a car accident at the time Brett would have been in high school.

"Why would he lie about his parents being dead?" Muttering to himself, Jake pulled up Brett's background check, reading it again. It seemed on the up-and-up. His gaze stopped on the section about his family. He squinted and leaned closer, as if that would change what he read. It had both parents marked as deceased. "So, they are dead?"

Growling, he wrote down the information about the parents and ran a separate search on each one. Both came back as entry not found, even after he removed the death information.

"What in the actual hell is going on here?" Jake picked up the phone and called Ben. Maybe the sheriff would have some insight Jake couldn't see.

"Davidson."

"Ben, it's Jake. I ran the background on Jorgensen. His parents don't exist."

"What do you mean, they don't exist?"

"I looked up both names, couldn't find obituaries for either. Checked Brett's record again, and ran background on both parents with the birth and death dates from it. No names came up."

"None?"

"Nope."

"What the hell? There should be something."

"Yep."

Ben sighed. Jake could picture him running a hand over his short-cropped hair. "I don't see us getting more information without talking to the local authorities up there. I know we promised to keep Shay's location a secret, but we're not going to get answers without actually speaking to people who know him. Assuming they'll even talk to us. I don't exactly have a legal leg to stand on."

Jake sighed. "Yeah, I was thinking the same thing. So how do we go about protecting her while we inquire about him? She's already balked at having to stay with me."

"You could take her somewhere. Don't tell anyone where you're going except me and Tristan. Actually, scratch that. Don't even tell us. Then Jorgensen can't say we lied about where she is."

Wheels started to spin in Jake's head. That had merit. But whether she'd go for it, he didn't know. "I can ask her and see what she says."

"Do your best to convince her. This could get ugly."

"Agreed. Okay. As soon as she gets back, I'll talk to her.

She went to get her job back at the motel. They put her right to work." And she'd have to quit again if they left. Jake scrubbed his jaw and bit back another sigh.

Ben chuckled. "Oh, you've got your work cut out for you. If it helps, tell her that Mara Roth at the equestrian center would probably give her a job in the stables, no questions asked, once y'all come back and this is over."

"That's good to know. I'll tell her. Thanks, Ben."

"No problem. Let me know what you decide."

"I will." They bid each other goodbye and hung up.

Jake bowed his head, tapping his phone against his forehead. "Damn." Blowing out a breath, he sat back. Things just got much more complicated.

He woke up his computer screen. This time, he logged into the federal fingerprint database. Jorgensen would have prints on file because of his job. Jake wanted to see if any of the information they had differed from what they knew.

Typing in Jorgensen's name and date of birth, he found the record. It brought up his image, address, full name, and occupation. The man had no criminal history and everything else matched.

Jake's mouth twisted, and he stared at the screen. They were missing something. He just didn't know what.

Clicking off the fingerprint database, he went back to their standard background check site and put in the name of Jorgensen's friend Eric Steiner. He was reading through the man's details when the front door opened.

"Hey." Jake glanced up from his desk in the corner of the living room at Shay as she came inside.

She smiled at him. "Hi."

The weary satisfaction on her face pulled him away from the computer. "You look like you had a good day."

Shay shrugged and set her purse down, then kicked off her shoes before coming further into the room and dropping onto the couch. She curled her feet up under her. "It was okay, I guess. I got my job back, and I put in several hours of work. It'll be nice to have an almost full paycheck this week."

A slight frown drew Jake's brows together, knowing he was about to kill her good mood. He took a steadying breath and got up to sit beside her on the couch. "About that—"

Her relaxed expression turned sour, and her feet hit the floor. She aimed a finger at his face. "No. I just got my job back. I'm not quitting."

Jake rubbed his forehead. "I don't want you to quit, but we've found some—inconsistencies in Jorgensen's background." He dropped his hand. "We can't resolve them without talking to his superiors and friends."

She frowned. "What kind of inconsistencies?"

"His parents. The names on his background check don't match to anyone that age with those birth and death dates. I can't get to his actual birth certificate without filing a records request form, because he was born in Massachusetts. They don't have an online database. Everything has to be printed and mailed. The moment I make that request, if he has someone keeping tabs on his records, he'll know someone's checking into him."

Shay brought her hand up, chewing on her thumbnail again. She glanced away, thinking. "Why would he lie about his parents?"

"I don't know. But it makes me wonder what else he lied about. And how he managed to get a job as a police officer. Those background checks are much more extensive than the basic one I ran today. They actually talk to family and friends."

"In person?"

Jake paused, frowning. "No, not always."

"Maybe he hired actors for them to talk to."

It was possible, but they'd have to be very well-versed in his life. "But how did he falsify the records? The department would need a copy of his birth certificate. They'd verify it. How long has he worked there?"

"He said he started not long after his mom died. I met him about two years after that."

"Okay. I need you to think. What did he tell you about them? All the details, Shay."

She chewed that thumbnail again, her brows furrowing. "There really weren't many. He told me they were dead and didn't seem to want to talk about them. I got the feeling he didn't have the best relationship with either of them."

"Did he ever casually mention anything about them? Perhaps when something reminded him of them?"

The furrow deepened. "Not really. Once, my mom asked him about them. He told her the same thing he told me, that they were dead. She asked what they used to do, and he said his dad was a mechanic and his mom worked in retail. That he came from a real working-class background."

"And this was in Massachusetts?"

"I think so. He told me that was where he was born, and that he'd moved to Amandale after his mom's death. I just assumed he came from there."

"Did he have an accent?"

She blinked twice. "Actually, no."

Jake bit back a curse.

"What does that mean?"

"That he either worked hard to lose it, or he's not who he says he is." He was betting on the latter.

"Why would he lie?"

"Because maybe he's done what he did to you to some other woman, and it caught up with him." Jake stood, needing to move. "I still don't understand how he passed the law enforcement background check, though."

She turned to look at him. "So, what does this mean?"

"It means it's more important than ever that we leave

town. Let Ben and Tristan dig into him, into your family's accident, and find the truth."

Shay hung her head. "They need to talk to people, don't they?"

Jake pursed his lips and nodded. "I'm afraid so."

"How are they going to get that information? What reason do they have to dig into Brett's life? I mean, sure, he followed me to Pittsburgh, but he hasn't followed me here. Do they have jurisdiction?"

His frown deepened as she hit on what could be a problem for them. "No. Ben will have to convince the local police up there to open an investigation into your ex."

Shay wrinkled her nose and rolled her eyes. "That will never happen. He'll turn on the charm and the chief will tell Sheriff Davidson he's lost his marbles."

She was right, but there was another way, he realized. It went against all his protective instincts, but it might be the only way—and the quickest—to free her from Jorgensen. He hurried to her side and sat next to her. Covering her hands with his, he held her gaze. "There's another option."

"I'm not going to like this, am I?"

"No. But if you want to break free of him, it might be the only way."

Her fingers twitched beneath his, and she sucked a corner of her bottom lip in, worrying it as she glanced away. When her gaze met his again, he could see a weary acceptance in her eyes.

"You want me to out myself, don't you?"

Jake nodded. "We let him know where you are. Create something—an online post, official record, something like that—and let the chips fall. If he comes here and starts harassing you, it gives Ben the clout he needs to open an investigation."

"Like what? He's going to be suspicious of me just

popping up after two years. He knows why I ran and why I changed my identity. If I start using my real name, he'll wonder why. It'll make him cautious."

"Right." An idea formed as he listened to her misgivings. His heartbeat quickened at the thought. It was radical, but it could work. "What if we had a good reason, though? One that would make sense?"

"Like what? I can't think—"

"Marry me."

Sixteen

Shay blinked, and her mouth dropped open. She knew she looked like a fish, but she couldn't get any words out. Did he just ask her to marry him?

"E-excuse me?"

"Marry me." He shifted, twining his fingers through hers. "Think about it. It makes perfect sense. If he thinks we fell in love and want to get married, you'd have to use your real name to make it legal. Not only would it draw him here, it could upset him enough that he slips up and says something he shouldn't."

"But—" She closed her eyes and swallowed, still unable to believe what she was hearing. "Marriage?"

"We don't have to actually get married. Well, probably not, anyway. Filing for the paperwork would be enough. It would show we're serious, that it's not a hoax. The license is valid for sixty days. That might give us enough time to draw him out and conduct our investigation."

"Yeah, but you're assuming he'll find out about our license application in that timeframe. How long does it take for something like that to hit the wire? Would it?"

"No, but we can couple it with an engagement announcement. What if you contact your friend, Piper? Can we trust her to be in on our secret?"

"Of course." Piper would love to help them take down Brett. She'd been ready to castrate and quarter him before she helped Shay leave.

"Then she can spread the word. I'm betting he monitors her social media, waiting for her to post something about you. What if she goes dress shopping for your wedding and posts about being excited to come down here to see you marry the love of your life?"

Shay yanked a hand free and chewed on her nail. What he said made perfect sense—and it sounded like a good plan. But could she put herself out there like that? Saying she wanted away from Brett and taking an active role in doing so were two entirely different things. He scared the bejesus out of her. She was terrified she'd end up under his control again.

But what was life without risks? And if she wanted a life, this was a risk she *had* to take. Shay heaved a sigh and met Jake's gaze. "Fine." She groaned, pulling her other hand from his to drop her head into her palms. "What do we do now?" She sank further into the couch cushions and closed her eyes. What was she doing? This was insane.

But it had merit. It also had its pitfalls. She was now connected to a man who set her nerve-endings on fire and made her libido wake up and dance. If she didn't fall for Jake for real, it would be a miracle.

"Call your friend."

She opened her eyes, getting caught in his in the pull of his icy blue eyes. Inhaling a breath, she nodded. "Okay. Now?"

"Yes. No." He frowned. "He might be monitoring her phone."

Shay's eyes widened. "He can do that?"

"It's possible. Do you two communicate in any way?"

"I have an email address that's tied to a different name I made up. We send each other messages on that. And she checks it on a public computer at least once a week. More if we're having a conversation."

"When will she check it next?"

"Saturday."

He grimaced. "It's only Monday. What if you called her at work? Even if you just left a message telling her to check her email."

"That would work. She's a pharmacy tech at the local hospital. I doubt Brett would put a trace on that phone. They get so many calls. He wouldn't even know where to start." She took out her phone and dialed the number for the hospital by rote. It was the same place she used to work.

"Maybe." Jake held out a hand. "Let me leave the message just in case he tapped the phone. He might recognize your voice."

"Oh. Okay." She handed him the phone as it rang. It seemed far-fetched Brett would go to such lengths, but the more Jake and his colleagues uncovered about her ex, the more she realized he was capable of some crazy things.

"Hi, yes, I'm calling about a prescription for Shay Britton."

Shay leaned closer, trying to hear the other end of the conversation. She could just make out a feminine voice on the line, but it didn't sound like Piper. Jake noticed and put it on speaker.

"What's her birthday?" the woman asked.

"Birthday? January 22, 1989." He made a face at Shay that said he was just making things up as he went. She smiled at him.

They heard clacking as the woman typed. "Hmm, I don't seem to have a record of a script for her. Can you spell the last name?"

"B-R-I-T-T-O-N."

More clacking echoed over the line. "No. Still nothing."

"That's weird. I spoke with one of the techs there earlier about her prescription. I think she said her name was Piper."

"Okay. Let me transfer you. Maybe she knows what's going on with it."

"Great, thank you."

Shay held her breath.

"This is Piper."

Tears formed in Shay's eyes. It had been so long since she heard Piper's voice.

"Yes, hi. I'm calling about a prescription for my wife, Shay Britton."

Silence stretched for a beat. "Shay Britton, you say?"

"Yes. Her doctor was supposed to have emailed a script over."

Piper cleared her throat, and Shay heard her typing. "Birthdate?"

"One, twenty-two, eighty-nine," Jake said.

"I don't see anything here. You're sure he faxed it?"

"Not faxed. Emailed."

Shay prayed Piper understood.

"We don't accept emailed prescriptions. You'll have to contact her doctor's office and have them fax it."

"Oh? Okay, I'll have to do that. If I can get through. You know how their phone services are. All those automated choices, then you wait fifteen minutes to even talk to a real person. It'd probably be faster to send an email directly to them." He paused.

"Yes. Emails are a great communication tool."

Shay's heart jumped into her throat. She nodded at Jake. It sounded like Piper had gotten the message.

"Okay, well, thanks for your help. I'm sure we'll talk again soon."

"I think we will, yes. Have a good day."

"You too. Bye."

"Bye."

Jake pulled the phone away from his ear and ended the call. "Think she got the message?"

Shay grinned. "Yes. I could hear it in her voice. She'll probably check her email the first chance she gets. Can I borrow your computer?"

He pointed to the desk. "Have at it. I'll fix us some dinner while you message her."

"Sounds great." She stood and made it a few steps before she paused to look back at him. "Jake?"

"Hmm?"

"Thank you."

A smile brightened his face. "You're very welcome. Mackenzie."

Her name rolling off his tongue had the same effect on her as the last time, and she blushed. With a nod, she continued to the desk, thankful he left. She needed to regain her equilibrium.

Sitting in the desk chair, she opened the web browser and logged into her anonymous email account and started a draft email. The first one she sent was quick, in case Piper logged in soon.

Piper,

Things are happening. Too much to put into this quick message. Another will follow soon if you haven't already received it.

-Mack

Shay hit send, then opened another message box and started typing. She laid out their plan and what they wanted from her to begin with. Explained who the man was on the phone and stressed the importance that she not call on anything but a public line for now.

Rereading what she wrote, Shay fiddled with a few things, then hit send. Now they waited.

She drummed her fingers on the desktop, staring off into space, antsy. She'd been living in limbo so long, to have things moving again—to have the prospect of getting her life back and taking the steps to achieve that—it made her restless.

Getting up, she wandered to the window and looked out. Jake lived on a quiet street. There were a few families across from him—she could tell by the sidewalk chalk art and colorful toys in the driveways and yards. But there was little traffic. It wasn't a main thoroughfare, which made it great for raising kids. It made her wonder why he chose the location.

Maybe he just liked the quiet. Shay stepped away from the window and went in search of him. Smells were starting to drift toward her from the kitchen. She walked in to see him stirring something on the stove. "What are you making?"

He glanced back and offered her a smile. "Nothing fancy. Just spaghetti."

"Can I help?" She wandered closer.

"You can get the plates out and dish out some salad." He nodded toward a cabinet by the sink, then at the fridge.

"Sure." Shay found the plates, then the salad fixings in the refrigerator.

"Did you email your friend?"

"Yeah. Hopefully, she'll respond tonight through either a message or a phone call. I told her to use a public phone or someone else's." She turned on the water and ran the lettuce under it.

"Good. I know it sounds like a crazy plan, but it's our only shot."

"I know." She shut off the water and grabbed the cutting board leaning against the wall and a knife from the block. "I just want to be free. When I left the other day, the despair hit me all over again. It was awful. I just felt like there was no hope. No future for me." She slid the knife through the lettuce with a satisfying crunch. "I don't want to live like that again. Not unless this doesn't work and I don't have any other choice."

"It'll work, Shay."

She glanced at him, surprised by the vehement conviction in his voice. Her smile was a touch sad. "Who are you trying to convince? Me or yourself?"

He gave a small snort and tipped his head. "I have to believe this will work. You deserve to have a life."

Her gaze caught on his icy blue eyes, and emotion clogged her throat again. She swallowed hard and turned back to her lettuce prep. "Thank you."

"We'll get him, Shay."

She kept cutting, having nothing left to say on the subject. She could only pray it worked.

Seventeen

J ake tried not to stare at Shay over the dinner table. She ate with the same grace she did everything else. Pretending to be her fiancé for the foreseeable future would be a test of his willpower. Something about her spoke to him. He'd wanted to get to know her better before her life went topsy-turvy.

He cleared his throat and twirled more pasta onto his fork. "We should talk. About the plan."

She stopped chewing for a moment, looking at him, then swallowed. "What about it?"

"Well, for starters, do you want me to use the name you've been living under, or do I start calling you Mackenzie?"

She shrugged, staring down at her plate, twirling her fork through the noodles. "Either is fine."

"That's crap."

Her eyes met his, round with surprise.

"You've reinvented yourself, yes. But that doesn't mean you aren't still Mackenzie Brighton. That's who you were for over twenty years. Now that you're working to get your life back, you need to decide who you want to be. Shay or Mackenzie. What name do you call yourself?"

Her gaze dropped back to her dinner. She spun more noodles around before letting out a breath and setting her fork down on her plate with a clank. "Mackenzie. I call myself Shay so I don't trip up, but when I look in the mirror, I see Mackenzie."

He smiled. "Good. I'll do my best to call you that from here on out."

She rolled her lips in and nodded.

"So, now that the name thing is out of the way, where do you want to get married?"

The fork she just picked up clattered against her plate as she dropped it. "I'm sorry, what?"

"We need a story to tell people. Part of that is where we're getting married. This is something we need to let Piper know too. I was thinking maybe a local park. I know all the magistrates, so it shouldn't be a problem to get one of them to perform the ceremony. Hypothetically, of course." He wanted to hammer out as many details as possible. The better their backstory, the more believable this would be. And the easier to convince Ben this was the right move.

She hummed. "Of course."

"We should probably look into clothes and rings."

Her eyes grew wide? "What? Why would we need those things? We aren't getting married."

Jake put his fork down and propped his elbows on the table, clasping his hands together. He glanced away, twirling his thumbs. He knew she opposed such a drastic step, but if it became necessary? Would she still? He wouldn't.

He looked at her again. "If marrying you becomes necessary to keep you safe, I won't hesitate."

The whites of her eyes showed for a brief moment before a

fierce frown overtook her face. She pushed back from the table. "I don't need a husband to protect me. I've done fine by myself for three years. I'll go along with the engagement charade, but I will not marry you. You and your colleagues better come up with a good plan to catch Brett, because you only have sixty days. After that, well"—she held her arms out, then dropped them so they smacked against her thighs—"if I have to leave, I will."

Tears formed in her eyes, and she wiped them away with an angry swipe. "I don't want to become myself again, only to have to give her up. But I will."

Jake stood and rounded the table, taking her biceps in his hands. "Sh—Mackenzie, I don't want that, either. And I'm going to do everything possible to keep it from happening."

"Except marry me. I'm not marrying you."

"Except that. But if you ask, I will."

She searched his eyes. Jake held her gaze, steady.

"Why?" A small wrinkle formed between her eyes. "Why would you join your future to mine just to keep me safe? You barely know me."

Jake skated a hand up her arm to cup the side of her head. Her silky hair spilled over his hand and brushed his arm with a gentle caress. "In case you haven't figured it out, I want to. I want to get to know you. I did before I knew anything about your past. When this is all over, I'll still want to." His voice ended low and just loud enough to hear.

Her hand came up to hold his wrist. The pupils in her dark eyes grew larger, and the tip of her tongue darted out to wet her bottom lip. Jake shuffled closer, his thumb sweeping across her cheekbone and down to her mouth. He wiped away the moisture she left behind, feeling the warm puff of her breath on his hand. His body tightened.

Her phone rang from the living room, jolting them apart.

"I better go answer that. It could be Piper." She was already backing away.

"Yeah." He ran a hand through his hair and blew out a breath as she turned. Holy hell, what just happened?

EIGHTEEN

Mackenzie snagged her phone from the coffee table, recognizing the area code as Amandale's. She slid her thumb over the screen. "Piper?"

"Mack? What the hell is going on? You're faking an engagement?" Piper didn't waste time.

"First of all, it's so good to hear your voice." Emotion clogged her throat, making her voice thick.

Piper sniffed. "Same, girl."

Swallowing around the lump in her throat, Mackenzie continued. "Where are you calling from?"

"I'm on a payphone at the gas station on the edge of town. And no, I wasn't followed. I made sure. Now, explain, please. Your email outlined your plan, but didn't give many details. How did you meet this guy? Why are you doing this now? It's been three years."

"I know." Mackenzie sighed and sat down. "I met Jake earlier this year when his partner's wife was missing. They were running down a lead and ended up at the motel where I worked. Anyway, none of that matters. I hadn't seen him in months, then he walked into the bar where I was waitressing.

Then he kept coming back. I had some issues with one of the patrons, and long story short, the guy tried to run us over in the parking lot a few nights ago and Jake shot him."

"What! You're not hurt, are you?"

"No. Nothing more than a few scrapes and bruises. Jake knocked me out of the way. Again, the details of that incident aren't relevant. What is, is the fact that I had to fill out a witness statement."

"Oh, shit."

Mackenzie let out a soft snort. "Exactly. I used my assumed name, then took off. Jake tracked me down and demanded to know why I lied."

"And you told him?" Incredulity raised Piper's voice an octave.

"He already knew I was lying about who I was. They figured out that much when they ran my social security number, I suspect." She ran a hand through her hair, taking a steadying breath. "And I'm tired of running, Piper. I want my life back. I want *a* life. Jake said I wasn't living. That I was just surviving. He's right, and I don't want to do that anymore. So, will you help me?"

"You know I will. But what happens if this doesn't work? If you out yourself to Brett, then they can't pin anything on him?"

"Then I reinvent myself a second time and go on the run again." But she prayed it wouldn't come to that.

"Okay." Mackenzie heard Piper sigh. "So, you want me to make some social media posts about your upcoming nuptials?"

"Yes. Let people know you're excited to be my maid-of-honor. Take some pictures of yourself dress shopping."

"Do I need to buy anything?"

"You can. I'll reimburse you if you do. Or you can tell the

shop owner you saw a dress at another shop and need time to think about which one you like best."

"I like that idea. All the fun of dress shopping, but without the pain in my wallet."

Mackenzie chuckled.

"When do I get to come there and meet this guy? He sounds... intriguing."

"I don't know if that's a good idea. If Brett shows up here, it could put you in danger."

"Pfft. Whatever. He could just as easily get to me here. So, when's the wedding?" Piper giggled.

A smile spread over Mackenzie's face, and she rolled her eyes. "There isn't one, remember? But how about this? If we get close to the end of our sixty-day license period, you can come down. It'll lend some authenticity to the charade."

"Deal. Just promise me you'll be careful. Not just with Brett, but with this new guy too. I don't want to see you end up with a broken heart."

Mackenzie's gaze flicked to the kitchen doorway. She could hear Jake cleaning up their dinner mess. She hoped her heart stayed intact too. "I'll be fine. Don't worry about me."

"I'll always worry about you, Mack. You're my friend."

Oh, there went the waterworks again. Mackenzie fanned a hand in front of her face and sniffed. "I love you, Piper. Thank you for always being there." She didn't deserve it. Not after cutting Piper from her life when she was dating Brett.

It took a moment before Piper responded. Mackenzie heard a sniff. "Anytime, girl. Look, I better go before someone wonders why I'm standing her blubbering." She sniffed again. "Keep me posted, please."

"I will."

"Daily updates, Mack. I mean it."

"Scout's honor."

Piper snorted. "You were never a scout. But I believe you anyway."

Mackenzie giggled. "I'll talk to you soon."

"You better."

They said their goodbyes. Mackenzie pulled the phone away from her ear and stared at it for a long moment before turning off the screen and setting it on the coffee table. She leaned forward, elbows on her knees, and rubbed her forehead.

"Headache?"

She jumped and let out a little squeak. Narrowing her eyes, she looked at Jake. "Geez. Are you part ghost or something? Didn't I ask you to stop sneaking up on me?"

He held up his hands. "Sorry. I'll make sure to stomp my feet next time."

Unbidden, a corner of her mouth lifted. She waved a hand at him. "Sorry, you're fine. I'm just a little edgy."

Tilting his head, he eyed her for a moment, then walked forward, hand outstretched. "Come on."

She frowned. "What? Where are we going?"

He tipped his head. "Out. Do you have a heavy jacket and some gloves?"

Her frown deepened. "Why? It's not that chilly yet."

Jake dropped his hand. "Humor me, please?"

Mackenzie huffed and stood. "Fine. They're in my suitcase." Jake brought it in for her earlier, but she hadn't unpacked anything yet. She'd tried, but her brain had yet to process she wasn't running anymore.

"Go get them and meet me in the garage." A coy smile toyed with his lips.

Intrigued, Mackenzie hurried down the hall to her room and dug her winter coat and gloves out of her suitcase. She snagged her purse and made her way back through the house to the garage. When she stepped through the door, she paused on the top step as she took in the sight before her.

Heart rate kicking up a few notches and her breath quickening, she couldn't take her eyes off of Jake. He'd donned a leather jacket and gloves and now straddled a Harley.

"You going to stand there and stare, or are you going to join me?" He held out a black helmet.

"Um." She swallowed. "You want to take me on a motorcycle ride?"

He nodded, lowering the helmet when she didn't move. "The open road always helps me think, and it burns off some energy. I thought it might do the same for you." He lifted the helmet again and looked at her expectantly.

Mackenzie had never been on a motorcycle. She'd been in some fast cars—driven them—but she'd never been on a bike.

A quick thrill went up her spine at what it might be like to be plastered to Jake's back as he wound them through the mountain roads. At what the icy wind might feel like flowing around her.

Her feet moved forward of their own volition. Halfway across the garage, she found her voice. "Okay."

He grinned. "Put this on. You can leave your purse here." He nodded toward the workbench to her right at the rear of the garage.

Mackenzie detoured and set her bag down, then took the helmet, pulling it over her head and buckling it under her chin.

"Climb on." He motioned to the seat behind him, pulling a second helmet over his head.

She threw a leg over the bike and settled onto the leather seat. Tentatively, she gripped the sides of his jacket, keeping as much distance between them as she could. The sight of him on the bike already had her hormones spinning. And now she could feel his body heat. This was so not a good idea. Maybe she should get off. Plead a headache and go inside.

He withdrew a garage door remote from his pocket and

opened the door. After returning it to his jacket, he inserted a key and turned it, then pulled in a lever on the left handlebar. "You ready?" He glanced back.

"I think so." Her brows dipped as her tongue overruled her brain. What happened to getting off?

Jake pushed a button, and the bike roared to life, loud in the enclosed space of the garage. Mackenzie yelped and jumped. She felt more than heard him chuckle.

"You might want to hold on tight," he yelled, then yanked her hands around his middle.

She yelped again as the move pressed her flat against his back. The bike lurched forward, and she clutched fistfuls of his coat in her gloved fingers.

With a brief pause at the end of the driveway to check for traffic, he turned right, and they roared down the road.

Wind whistled through her helmet, loud in her ears. She relaxed a fraction as the miles ticked by, sitting up enough that she could see the landscape whizzing by. There was just enough light left to see the trees.

They rode for nearly thirty minutes before Jake slowed and turned down a single-track forestry road. He wove up the mountain until the trees opened, revealing more stars than Mackenzie could ever remember seeing.

The bike rolled to a stop, and Jake cut the engine. Mackenzie removed her helmet and climbed off.

"Wow! This is incredible." Face turned to the sky, she spun in a circle as she stared at the stars and the long, brilliant arm of the Milky Way.

"Yeah. I come here a lot when I need to think. Even in the daytime." He tucked his helmet under his arm and stood beside her.

"How did you find this place?"

He shrugged. "I've lived here my whole life. I grew up exploring the Smokies."

"Well, it's beautiful. Thank you for sharing it with me."

"You're welcome."

Mackenzie closed her eyes and inhaled a deep breath of the brisk, pine-scented air. It filled her lungs, sending a zing through her. This was living. Her alter ego, Shay, didn't take motorcycle rides with men she found attractive. Didn't stop to savor the forest and the crisp, fall air. She worked and worried about saving enough money to start over again when she needed to.

Opening her eyes, the shadow of boulders to her left called her name. She walked over and perched on them, leaning back. "Can we just sleep here?"

Jake chuckled and sat beside her. "Might get a bit chilly by morning. But maybe we can come back one day soon with tents and sleeping bags."

A soft smile played on her lips. "I'd like that." Shifting, she looked at him, just able to make out his features in the moonlight. "So, tell me about yourself, Jake Maxwell."

He turned to her, his light eyes reflecting the moon. "What do you want to know?"

Mackenzie lifted one shoulder. "Whatever you want to tell me. You know my life story, but I don't know anything about you, really."

"Okay, let's see. The basics—I'm thirty-one, and I was born here. My dad died in a mining accident when I was eleven. I have a sister, Leanne, who's younger than me. She's married and has a one-year-old daughter named Ava. My mom's name is Belinda, and she raised us alone after dad died."

"She never remarried?"

Jake shook his head. "I don't think she wanted to. She always said dad was the love of her life and there would never be another."

"That's both sweet and sad."

"I agree. But I'm not going to push her into something she doesn't want. She says she's happy the way she is." He shrugged.

"What made you want to be a cop?"

"His accident, actually. I remember the police officer coming to the door to tell us about the accident. He was very kind and sat with us for a while. He came to the funeral, too, and answered every question we had about what happened. The guy made what was a terrible event bearable by being compassionate. I wanted to do that for others."

Mackenzie grinned. "I'd say you've succeeded."

He chuckled. "I guess, but I can honestly tell you I'm not helping you just because it's my job or because I think you deserve compassion."

Even in the low light, Mackenzie could see the fire light in his eyes. An answering one lit in her belly. She shifted, sitting on her hands so she wouldn't grab him and kiss him.

Clearing her throat, she looked up at the stars. "So, what do you do in your free time apart from helping damsels in distress and riding motorcycles?"

She heard him exhale, but kept her eyes on the sky. Her body hummed both from his words and his proximity. If she looked at him, it wouldn't matter that she sat on her hands.

"I tinker with my Porsche. Hike and fish. Do some hunting on occasion. What about you?"

She snorted. "What free time?"

He chuckled. "If you had free time, what would you do? What did you do before things went sour with Brett?"

Mackenzie searched her memory. That felt like a lifetime ago. "I liked hiking. That continued with Brett. I also liked to dance. I haven't done that in years, though. I used to go every Saturday night with Piper. Sometimes Friday too. We wouldn't even drink. Just go and let loose."

"Fast stuff?"

She nodded. "Though I liked a good slow dance too. If the guy was right. And the song."

Jake scooted forward off the rock and stood.

"Time to leave already?" Mackenzie knew she sounded dejected, but she didn't care. She wasn't ready to leave.

"No. I have a better idea." His phone screen lit up, illuminating his handsome face. Music started to play through his phone speaker. He looked up at her and smiled. "Dance with me?"

Mackenzie's spine straightened. "Dance?" Considering her reaction to his nearness, she wasn't sure that was a great idea.

He walked forward, hand outstretched. "Yeah. You know. That thing people do where they sway to music."

She rolled her eyes, a smile emerging. "Smart aleck."

His smile widened. "Maybe." He tipped his head, the look in his eyes asking her to dance again.

Mackenzie drew in a breath and stood. She'd probably regret this, but it was hard to say no to Jake. That smile of his made her want to do things she knew she shouldn't. Things that would complicate her life more than it already was.

The moment his fingers closed around hers, she knew she was right. Even through their gloves, his touch had an effect on her. A zing shot up her arm, making her shiver.

"Cold?" He laid the phone on the rock behind her, then pulled her into his body. "Dancing will warm you up."

Oh, if he only knew. She was sweating beneath her coat. But she didn't dare tell him the reason she shivered. She didn't want him to let her go.

They swayed to the music, relaxing into each other's arms as the song went on. Mackenzie forgot how entertaining feelings for Jake complicated things. Those thoughts and all her worries about Brett melted away as they danced. All that was left were her growing feelings for the man holding her.

As the song ended, she pulled back enough to look at him.

His gaze caught hers. A new song started, but Mackenzie didn't hear it. The music and the world around them faded away.

Jake brought a hand up, skimming her cheek. Her lips parted as desire quickened her breath. She stared into his eyes as he dipped his head. In the moonlight, his white-blue eyes glowed, silently asking permission to kiss her.

Mackenzie stood on her toes and sealed her mouth to his. It didn't matter that it was a bad idea. She wanted—needed—to know how it felt.

Light from a thousand suns went off behind her closed eyelids, blinding her to everything except the feel of his kiss. She clutched the back of his jacket, anchoring herself as his mouth moved over hers. His hands delved into her hair, angling her face for the best access. Mackenzie felt like she could drift up to become one of the stars as he plundered her mouth.

The more he probed and caressed, the more she floated. And the more she needed to return the favor. He tasted better than she could have imagined. Like coffee and something uniquely Jake.

She let go of his jacket to run her hands up his chest and over his shoulders, wanting to feel the silky strands of his wavy dark hair beneath her fingers. To find out if she could make him moan the way he made her moan. Gripping the strands, her nails raked his scalp. She felt his sharp intake of breath and smiled.

He drew back to look at her. "This was not my intention when I asked you to dance," he said, voice low. "I just wanted to give you back something that made you happy."

Moisture swam in Mackenzie's eyes, her heart expanding tenfold. She framed his face and reached up to place a gentle kiss on his lips. "Thank you."

He pecked her mouth once more, then released her. "We should probably get going. It's getting late."

Mackenzie nodded. He picked up his phone, shutting off the music. She followed him to the motorcycle and donned her helmet again before climbing on behind him.

The bike roared to life. She wrapped her hands around his waist and leaned into his back. She didn't see the darkened scenery as they rode back to his house. Her mind was a jumble of thoughts as she processed what happened and what it meant. Could she go back to being just friends with Jake? Did she want to?

No, her inner voice said. And it was right. She didn't want to go back to the way things were. But, still—was a relationship wise? What would happen if she had to run again? If she got involved with Jake, could she leave him if she had to?

She didn't have any answers and knew that her life was more complicated now than it was just a couple of hours ago. But for the first time in a long, long time, Mackenzie felt something other than fear and isolation. She wasn't about to let that feeling go.

Nineteen

"You ready?" Jake looked at Mackenzie over the hood of his SUV. Her face was pinched as she stared at the courthouse.

She glanced at him, some of the anxiety in her expression fading as they made eye contact. "I guess."

"We can still come up with another plan." He wasn't sure what, but he'd think of something.

"No." She rounded the front of the vehicle. "This is a good plan. And it's the fastest way to draw him out and to make him make a mistake. Let's do this."

Jake held out a hand to her, and she took it. They walked up the courthouse steps, and he held the door. Mackenzie passed into the building with a tight smile.

"Relax," he whispered into her ear. "People will think you don't like me."

A small, genuine smile graced her face.

"That's better." He took her hand again and squeezed it. "Everything will be fine. The license is just part of the plan. We'll never use it."

She looked at him, eyes full of nerves. "I know. It's not

that. Doing this—" She broke off and looked around before inhaling a shaky breath. "This sets the plan in motion. There's no going back."

Jake squeezed her hand again. "No. No going back." He stopped and faced her, taking her other hand too. "We don't have to do this."

Mackenzie shook her head. "No. I meant what I said outside. It's a good plan. It's just scary. I've been hiding from my problems for a long time."

He reached up and brushed her cheek with his fingers. "But you're not alone now."

That small smile returned. "I know. It's the only reason I'm not on the other side of the country right now." She tugged on his hands. "Come on. Let's do this."

Jake returned her smile. "Okay."

They walked through the metal detectors, then headed down the hall to the records department. The clerk, whom Jake knew well, smiled at him as he approached.

"Detective Maxwell. What can I do for you today?" She frowned. "I thought the sheriff put you on administrative leave because of what happened at Barney's."

"Hi, CeCe. He did. I'm not here for a case." He glanced at Mackenzie, smiling, then back at the clerk. "We're here for a marriage license."

The woman's hazel eyes grew wide and her mouth rounded to a perfect O. She recovered quickly and offered them a bright smile. "Well, that's just wonderful. Come around to the inner office and we'll get all the paperwork done." She got up, disappearing from view.

Jake led Mackenzie around to the door and let them inside. From an office ten feet ahead, CeCe beckoned them to enter. They filed inside, sitting around the desk.

"Okay." CeCe scooted her chair in, smiling at them, and woke the computer. "I need your birth certificates, social security cards, and driver's licenses. Have either of you been married before?"

"No," Jake said.

Mackenzie shook her head and withdrew her social security card and license, as well as both their birth certificates from her purse, passing them to the woman. Jake dug his license and social security card from his wallet and slid them across the desk. CeCe laid the items out, typing pertinent information into the computer. She cast a coy look at Jake.

"So, does this mean I have to find someone new to flirt with?" She grinned.

Jake laughed at the older woman. "I think Mackenzie will understand. Right, honey?" He turned to her and smiled.

A grin covered Mackenzie's face. "Maybe I'll share."

CeCe laughed. "Oh, I like you." The printer behind her spit out a single page. "So, when's the big day?"

"We're not sure yet," Jake said. "It's a bit sudden, so we're still working out the details." He looked at Mackenzie, giving her a tender smile to sell the charade. "We just didn't want to wait."

"Oh." CeCe put a hand over her heart as she spun around to take the paper from the tray. "That's so lovely. I just love this part of my job." She turned back, laying the document on the desk in front of them. "Okay, check that over and make sure all the information is correct."

While Jake and Mackenzie leaned forward to check the document, CeCe printed another form.

"Look good?" she asked.

They both nodded.

"Perfect. I just need your signatures on this." She laid the second document on the desk. "It's the application. Then I need the sixty-dollar license fee and you're all set."

Jake scrawled his name on the application, his hand shaky. He covered it up by quickly dropping the pen and opening his wallet to take out the sixty dollars. Even though he knew this was a ruse, it sure felt real.

He glanced at Mackenzie as he passed CeCe the money. It wasn't hard to imagine her as his wife. He could picture them coming home to each other in the evenings, discussing their days. Spending their nights cuddled together under the blankets after they slaked their hunger for each other. His body heated as the memory of their kiss last night flooded back.

"All right, that's all I need."

CeCe's voice cut through his fantasies, and he blinked. Offering her a smile, he picked up the license from the desk and stood. "Thanks, CeCe."

"Sure thing. I expect to see pictures." She raised an eyebrow at him, grinning.

He returned her smile. "I'm sure you won't let me forget."

"Nope." She laughed, then held out a hand across the desk to Mackenzie. "Congratulations. You've got yourself a good one."

Mackenzie smiled and returned CeCe's handshake. "Thank you. He's something, that's for sure."

CeCe chuckled. "I think she's got you pegged, detective."

"Very much so." He kissed Mackenzie's cheek, then took her hand. "Come on, dear. Let's go finalize some more wedding plans." He waved to CeCe and led his new fiancée from the office.

"Now what?" she asked as they left the records department.

"Now we go tell Ben and Tristan the new plan." He didn't think Ben would go for turning Mackenzie into bait, so he figured it was better to ask forgiveness than permission in this case. It's why he hadn't already called him. With the legwork they'd put in so far, he'd be more likely to acquiesce.

She sighed, nodding. He led her through the courthouse to the building down the block that housed the police station.

After signing Mackenzie in as his guest, they wandered into the bullpen.

"Tristan." Jake lifted a hand in greeting as they approached his partner.

The other man looked up from his desk, frowning. "What are you two doing here?"

"We need to talk. Is Ben in his office?"

Tristan's frown deepened. "Yeah. What's going on?"

Jake tipped his head and started walking again. "Come on."

"What—" His words cut off with a growl as Jake led Mackenzie away, heading for the sheriff's office.

"Why do you delight in making him angry?" Mackenzie asked as Jake rapped on Ben's door.

A grin slashed his face. "It's fun. I mean, look at him." He glanced at Tristan as he approached. The man's dark eyebrows slanted inward over his bright blue eyes. "His feathers are all ruffled."

She rolled her lips in, mirth sparkling in her eyes. "You're awful."

"Keeps him on his toes."

The door swung open as Tristan reached them. Ben frowned as he took in his visitors. "Sorry. I was on the phone with Gemma," he said, mentioning his wife.

Tristan's frown changed its focus. "She okay?"

Ben nodded. "She was just making sure I remembered her doctor's appointment this afternoon. Pregnancy brain made her forget to remind me before I left this morning. Why are you all here?"

"Good question," Tristan said, frowning at Jake.

"We need to talk. Mackenzie and I came up with a new plan."

"Mackenzie?" Ben glanced at her.

She shrugged. "If Brett's going down and I'm getting my life back, I want to be me."

Ben studied her for a moment, then gave a quick nod. He stepped back. "Come in and explain this new plan. Though I think I'm afraid to ask."

They filed into Ben's office, and Tristan closed the door.

"So, we were talking last night about what you wanted to do and the feasibility of that plan." Jake said. "Jurisdiction is going to tie our hands."

"Right. That's why we were going to talk to the locals in Amandale and see about convincing them to reopen the death investigation on Mackenzie's family." Ben crossed his arms, leaning against his desk. "It's the quickest way to call Brett's actions into question."

"No. The quickest way is to get him to come here." Jake held up the paper in his hands.

Ben took it, eyes widening as he read. "Are you insane? You're getting married to catch the guy?"

"What?" Tristan snatched the paper from Ben's hands.

"No. We're only making it look that way. What do you think the chances are he lets her get married without trying to stop her? We use the sixty-day license window to lure him down here and nail him on stalking charges. We can investigate her family's deaths after we have him in custody."

Ben closed his eyes, resting his fingers against his forehead for a moment before he looked at Mackenzie. "You agreed to this?"

She nodded. "I know it's a little crazy, but it's a good plan. We contacted my best friend, Piper. She's agreed to post some things to her social media, adding some legitimacy to our plan." She looked at Jake. "And I've been thinking I should post to mine. I never closed my accounts—just let them go dormant. We could get some engagement photos taken, and I could post them."

He nodded. "You need a ring too. We need to—"

"Hold on." Ben waved a hand. "I agree this idea has some merit, but do you have any more of a plan than 'lure him down here'?" He air-quoted, then flattened his hands, palms up. "What happens if he shows up and just kidnaps her?"

"He won't." Mackenzie's voice was firm.

"What makes you so sure?" Tristan asked.

"Because I know Brett." Her gaze took in them all. "He'll want to make my life miserable. Make me doubt everything, including my feelings for Jake and Jake's feelings for me. He'll want me to come crawling back to him. It's all about control. If he kidnaps me, he's not in control. And he'll have a harder time getting me to behave the way he wants if he rips me out of my life here."

"This will work, Ben." Jake held his boss's gaze.

Ben crossed his arms again, pursing his lips. He studied Jake, then looked at Mackenzie. "Are you sure this is what you want? It's dangerous."

"I know. But I want to be free of him to live as myself again without fear. If we work together, we can stop him."

With a sigh, Ben scrubbed a hand over his face. "Fine. Jake, she's your responsibility. Keep her safe. And keep me apprised of everything that happens and any plans you make. Understood?"

Jake nodded, the knot in his stomach disappearing now that Ben had green-lighted their plan.

"Go." Ben motioned to the door. "Get out of my office, all of you." He walked around behind his desk.

Snatching the marriage license from Tristan's fingers, Jake gave Ben a quick two-finger salute. "Come on, Mack." He took her hand. "Let's go announce ourselves."

Tristan shook his head as they passed, then followed them out. "And I thought I had some harebrained ideas."

Jake tossed a grin over his shoulder. "You've rubbed off on me."

Rolling his eyes, Tristan stopped beside his desk. "Just be careful, okay? Don't take any unnecessary risks." His gaze took them both in.

"We'll be careful," Mackenzie said. "I have no intention of ending up in his clutches again. I might have been hesitant to confront the problem, to confront Brett, but I'm not anymore. If this is what it takes to be free, so be it."

Tristan smiled. "I like your spunk. Just don't let your desire to be free overrule your brain."

She nodded. "I'll think things through. No blind leaps, I swear."

"Good." He sat down. "If you two need anything, call."

"Thanks, Tristan." Jake met Tristan's gaze head-on. His partner stared at him hard for a moment, conveying through the understanding glint in his eyes that he understood Jake's need to keep Mackenzie safe. It was the same look Jake had given him months ago when Laurel was in danger.

Jake nodded and backed away, pulling Mackenzie with him. "We'll see you later."

Tristan lifted a hand and they left.

"Where are we going now?" Mackenzie asked as they left the police station.

"We need to talk to my mom and sister. I don't want them to hear about us and think I slighted them by not telling them about you."

She pulled him to a halt. "Are we telling them the truth?"

He glanced away, staring at the gently swaying trees lining the street. He wanted to, but he also didn't want to force them to lie. Neither woman was very good at it. But they wouldn't believe he'd asked a woman to marry him after knowing her for such a short time.

"I think we have to." He looked at her. "They know me

too well to believe I'd keep such a serious relationship a secret from them until I proposed. We just need to stress the idea that they have to treat you like our engagement is real. Everyone needs to believe we're madly in love."

She inhaled a breath, then pasted a bright smile on her face. "Then what are we waiting for?"

His expression lightened. "You're really embracing this."

With a tip of her head, she shrugged. "No point in half-assing this. Brett needs to believe our relationship is real, so we need to act like it is or he'll catch us in our lie."

He took a step closer. "Is that such a good idea after last night?" His voice dropped as the heat of remembered kisses flared between them.

Her pupils dilated. She licked her lips. "Probably not, but what I feel for you scares me less than Brett."

Jake pressed his lips together, processing what she said and what she didn't say as he held her gaze. Dipping his head, he pressed a quick, fierce kiss to her lips. "You don't need to be afraid of me. Of us. You and me may not be a wise idea right now, but I'll never hurt you, and I'll always respect you and your wishes."

She raised a hand, brushing it over his jaw. "I know," she whispered. Clearing her throat and blinking furiously, she let her hand fall and stepped back. "Let's go meet your family."

TWENTY

Nerves assaulted Mackenzie as the doorbell rang at Jake's. When they left the police station, he called his mom and his sister and asked if they could get together for dinner that night. They'd agreed, so after stopping at a pawnshop in the next county to find her an engagement ring, they bought groceries and came home to make dinner.

She swiped her hands down her thighs as Jake answered the door. It was unnerving how much she wanted his family to like her.

"Hi, guys." Jake stepped back to let them enter.

"Hi, honey." Belinda breezed inside, her eyes on her son. "So, do you want to tell us what this is all about now or are you going to make us wait until—" She broke off as she caught sight of Mackenzie. "Well, hello."

Mackenzie lifted a hand and gave a small wave, offering the dark-haired woman a smile. "Hello."

"Jake?" Belinda turned to him.

He held out an arm, ushering her and his sister, who now stood beside her, deeper into the house. "Dinner's pretty much ready. Let's talk while we eat. All you need to know right now is this is Mackenzie."

Leanne nudged her mother toward the dining room. "Go. Sit down. I want to hear this." She eyed them both with amused speculation.

Letting out a breath as the two women turned away, Mackenzie escaped to the kitchen to bring out the food. Jake hadn't been lying. He knew his family would be brimming with questions the moment they stepped in the door, and she wanted to make everyone as comfortable as possible.

So, after their trip to the pawnshop, she made him stop at the grocery to get things to make her favorite meal—homemade chicken pot pie. She also bought a king-size chocolate bar. Picking out a diamond ring for a fake engagement—with the short, balding man in the loud Hawaiian shirt that needed a few more buttons buttoned, staring at her like he wished he could trade places with Jake—left her with the need for comfort food. Chocolate was quick. The chicken pot pie would help extend her relief. She'd need it to get through this awkward dinner.

Jake had already set the table, so she ran a knife through the pot pie, then donned the gray oven mitts sitting on the counter. She picked up the dish and its trivet from the counter and headed for the dining room.

Conversation ceased as she entered. Mackenzie gave the two women what she hoped was a sunny smile and set the pan down in the center of the table.

"That smells wonderful," Belinda said. "What did you make?"

"Hey." Jake held out his hands. "How do you know I didn't make it?"

Leanne laughed. "Because you can make the basics. That" —she pointed to the pot pie—"is much more than basic." She looked at Mackenzie. "Mom's right. It smells great. Chicken pot pie?"

Mackenzie nodded. "It's my favorite meal. I hope you like it."

"I'm sure we will." Belinda offered her a kind smile. She held up her plate and looked at Jake. "The serving spoon is next to you. Dish that out so you can explain who this lovely woman is and what's going on."

Jake picked up the spoon. "You might want to eat first." He heaped a spoonful of the pot pie onto her plate.

Belinda frowned, some of the relaxed expression on her face fading. She set her plate down, staring at him as he filled Leanne's plate, then Mackenzie's and his own.

Mackenzie shifted, picking up her fork, then putting it down again while she waited for Jake to serve himself. She traced the thin decorative edging on her plate, feeling the bumps and swirls under her finger.

"Okay, we all have food. Explain what this is about, please?" Belinda lifted a forkful of pot pie to her mouth. Her expression changed as she chewed. "This is delicious, Mackenzie."

Smile tight, Mackenzie picked up her fork. "Thank you, Mrs. Maxwell."

"Call me Belinda, please." She gave a warm smile and scooped up another forkful of her dinner as she turned expectant eyes on her son.

Jake blew out a breath, glancing at Mackenzie. She fiddled with her food again and said nothing, too nervous to force more than a simple phrase past her vocal chords.

"Mackenzie is a friend. She's been on the run from an abusive ex-boyfriend for the last three years. In an effort to help her get her life back, we applied for a marriage license today."

Leanne dropped her fork. "Holy shit."

Belinda stared at him, open-mouthed.

Mackenzie pushed her fork through her dinner again while Jake launched into a more detailed explanation of what happened and why they applied for a marriage license. By the time he finished, Leanne sat wide-eyed and angry in her chair, while Belinda grew increasingly tense. It took all Mackenzie had not to get up and tell him to forget it all. That it was crazy and to just forget about her. His mom's and sister's reactions said that in spades. It was clear they both thought he was insane for helping her.

But she didn't. She stayed. Yes, it mattered to her what they thought, but she was also out of options. Jake was her only chance at seeing Mackenzie Brighton living in public again.

"You really think he killed your family?" Belinda asked, turning shrewd eyes on her.

Mackenzie swallowed and nodded. "The weather was good. I suppose the deer theory could be true, but Grandpa was a good driver. I can't see him losing control that way." She withdrew her hands from the table and folded them in her lap, staring at them. "I'm sorry to have involved your son in my problems."

"Nonsense." Belinda's voice had a snap to it.

Mackenzie looked up.

"I'm glad he convinced you to let him help."

"You are?"

Belinda nodded. "No one deserves the life it sounds like you've lived the last several years. And I made peace with Jake's profession a long time ago. He's good at what he does."

"Oh." Mackenzie studied her for a moment. "You're really okay with the plan we've concocted?"

"Yes. I hope it works."

"Me too," Leanne said. "I also kinda hope you get married

for real. This pot pie is amazing." She grinned, a teasing glint in her eyes, lightening the mood around the table.

Mackenzie smiled, some of her nerves dissipating. "I can give you the recipe."

"Good. But I still want you around to do the family dinners. I hate to cook."

"It's true," Belinda said. "Her husband does most of the cooking at their house."

"Speaking of," Jake said. "Where is Bryce? And Ava?"

"At home. I didn't want her crawling around distracting us, so he stayed home with her. I'll fill him in when I get back."

"Okay." Jake picked up his fork. "I have to stress, though, that you don't tell anyone else the truth. The world needs to think our engagement is real."

Leanne mimed locking her mouth and throwing away the key. "Congratulations."

Jake laughed. "Thanks, brat."

Mackenzie smiled again and relaxed, lifting a forkful of food to her mouth. Suddenly ravenous, she dug into her dinner while she listened to Jake banter with his family. It was nice, she realized.

Melancholy dimmed her smile a bit. She missed family dinners.

Twenty-One

Mackenzie eyed the park, swiping her hands along the tops of her thighs as Jake pulled into the parking lot. Children ran around the playground equipment while their mothers—dressed in sweaters and tall boots, sipping coffee—stood to the side, deep in conversation. Beyond them, people strolled down the paths, some alone, some with others. But it looked like she and Jake were the only ones here to take pictures.

Last night, Jake walked his mom and sister to their car alone. Mackenzie assumed he wanted to make sure they really were okay with what he was doing. Which he probably did. But he also asked his sister—who was a professional photographer—to take some engagement photos for them today.

"Leanne's already here." Jake pointed out the windshield to a car in the next row over. A dark-haired woman straightened from bending into the cargo area of her SUV, a bag in her hands.

Mackenzie nodded, still running her hands up and down her thighs. "Yep." She turned wide, apprehensive eyes on Jake.

"We're really doing this, aren't we? I mean, I know we set things in motion with the marriage license, but posting pictures—that's what brings him here."

"I know." He reached out and took her hand. "And I know I'm asking you to do a lot of trusting. But I promise I will keep you safe."

She nodded again, turning her eyes away as she did her best to corral her emotions and tamp down her nerves. "Let's go. I think she's waiting on us." She withdrew her hands and opened the car door, stepping out.

Together, they crossed to Leanne's car, greeting her.

"You guys look great. You ready?" Leanne smiled.

Mackenzie rolled her lips in and nodded while Jake said yes.

"Great. I know the perfect spot where we can start." She tipped her head toward the park. "Come on."

Still silent, Mackenzie followed her with Jake at her side. He didn't speak, either, but she had a feeling that was due more to the fact he had his head on a swivel as he assessed their surroundings. Why he felt the need, she wasn't sure. Brett wouldn't know to come here yet. They'd told no one outside their small circle, and the marriage application wasn't public record until they filed the signed license.

Regardless, though, it helped comfort her. He truly had her well-being at heart.

"Okay. You two stand in front of the water." Leanne gestured to the pond before them. "I thought we'd start with you both facing me. Jake put your arms around her waist. Mackenzie, put your hands over his."

"Like this?" Jake wrapped his arms around her waist, tugging her tight into his body.

Mackenzie's hands flew up to cover his. Wide-eyed, she looked straight ahead.

Leanne frowned. "Mack—can I call you Mack?"

"Sure. Or Kenz, or Kenzie. Or Shay. It doesn't matter." She swallowed and clamped her lips together to stop the babbling. Why was she so nervous? They'd talked about this, about the plan, *ad nauseum*. She shouldn't be nervous.

"You need to relax. If you look like you were dragged here kicking and screaming, no one will believe you two are madly in love."

Mackenzie nodded and drew in a deep breath. Leanne was right. She needed to get her act together.

"Can we try a different pose first?" Jake asked.

"I suppose," Leanne said. "What did you have in mind?"

Instead of answering, he spun Mackenzie in his arms. She let out a little yelp, landing against his chest.

"What are you doing?"

"Helping you relax."

"By spinning me like a top?"

He grinned. "Had to get your attention somehow." His expression sobered. His hands came up to frame her face. "We're going to start like this. I want you to focus on me. Don't think about what we're doing or why we're doing it. It's just you and me. This is about us."

"There is no us," she muttered.

His hand slid beneath her hair at the base of her skull, his fingers cradling the back of her head. With his thumb, he exerted enough pressure to tilt her face up to his. Goosebumps erupted over her skin at his touch, and a flutter kicked off in her belly.

"Says who?" He leaned down and feathered a light touch of his mouth over hers.

Mackenzie's eyes slid closed as she swayed into him. He lifted his head, and she opened her eyes to see him smiling at her.

"That's better."

An answering smile bloomed over her face. "Just us, huh?"

He nodded. "Pretend you love me."

That wouldn't be hard. She feared she was rapidly sliding down that slope. But he was right. She needed to play her part.

For the next thirty minutes, she smiled and acted as though she hadn't a care in the world. Once she broke through her nerves and did what Jake suggested, making the shoot about them and not Brett, she was able to relax and enjoy herself. They played in the leaves, stole a few kisses, and acted like a young couple in love.

Leanne let out a whistle, drawing their attention. Laughing, Mackenzie pushed Jake away as he threw another handful of leaves at her and turned to his sister.

"I think I have plenty." She grinned. "Though you two can go on playing if you want."

Chuckling, Mackenzie walked toward her. "I'm good. I'm ready for some hot cider or some coffee." There was a bite to the air, and her nose was cold.

"That sounds wonderful. Jake, you're buying." Leanne looked at her brother with a wicked smile.

He shrugged. "Works for me." He looped an arm around Mackenzie's shoulders while Leanne stowed her camera gear. "So, how soon can you have the images to us?" Jake asked as they headed for the parking lot.

"I'll edit a few of the best ones tonight and get them to you before I go to bed. I know you're on a time crunch. I'll post a full album later in the week. You can bill the first ones as a preview."

Mackenzie stiffened slightly at the reminder of what they were doing.

"Sounds good." Jake squeezed her shoulders, his hand wandering lower to curve over her hip.

Any apprehension that had managed to creep back in fled at the feel of his hand caressing her body. Maybe she should just stay within touching distance of him through this whole ordeal. She'd be too caught up in the need racing through her body to think about the havoc going on in her life.

"We'll see you at the coffee shop."

Jake's voice snapped Mackenzie out of her thoughts. She waved at Leanne and followed Jake to his car. He unlocked the doors, but before she could open it and get inside, he backed her into the door and leaned close.

Fireworks went off in her head, spreading their hot tendrils down her neck and into her limbs. She looked up at him. Heat blazed in his icy eyes.

"You know how you said there is no us?"

She nodded.

"I want there to be an us. Maybe not now. But when this is over? I think we need to talk about there being an us."

His words only made the fire in her blood burn hotter. She didn't want to wait for later. Unwise or not, she wanted to be with him now. Life was too short. Rising on her toes, she pressed her mouth to his. He grunted and folded her into his arms, deepening the kiss. His tongue skated along hers, and a floating sensation came over her. It took her a moment to realize he'd lifted her feet off the ground and pushed her up the car door to gain better access. She clutched handfuls of his hair and kissed him back.

The honk of a car horn drew them apart. From the corner of her eye, she saw his sister drive past. Undoubtedly, she was cackling as she drove away.

Taking a shaky breath, Mackenzie let go of Jake's hair and slid her hands down to his shoulders. He stepped back, lowering her feet to the ground.

"I don't think we need to talk about that us thing anymore." She brushed his hair back into place.

He studied her. "Are you sure?"

Mackenzie nodded. "Yeah. I'm done running. From everything."

A slow, sexy smile spread over his face. He dipped his head. "Okay, then." His mouth descended on hers again.

She hoped his sister didn't mind waiting.

TWENTY-TWO

Beyond tired, Mackenzie towed the vacuum cleaner and her cart into room 204. After not sleeping much last night and cleaning all morning and afternoon, she was ready to go home and nap.

Leanne had given them the photos she took last week, and Mackenzie had posted several shots to her social media. Piper had done the same. Since then, she'd been waiting for the other shoe to drop. Every little noise made her jump as she imagined Brett waiting outside, staring through the windows, trying to find a vulnerability to get to her. They'd kept the curtains tightly closed since she posted the pictures, but it didn't help her nerves. It almost made it worse, because she couldn't see outside.

She just wished he'd show up. Then she could relax.

Gathering the bedding, she dumped it into the linen basket on her cart, then grabbed clean sheets and made the bed. After dumping the trash and changing the bag, she wiped down all the surfaces, then swept the floor. Once the main room was clean, she moved to the bathroom. Spraying the shower, she hummed to herself, trying to bolster her energy reserves. This was her last room. She planned to go home, take a little nap, then make dinner before Jake got home. The sheriff had him on administrative duty while they completed the investigation into the incident at the bar.

They'd settled into a routine over the last few days. He'd get up, make coffee, then head to work just as she emerged from her room. Then she'd spend several hours cleaning at the motel before coming back and making dinner. After dinner, they'd sit outside if the weather was nice enough and just talk. When it wasn't, they'd watch TV and chat. She'd learned a lot about Jake Maxwell in the last week.

Like he preferred sausage to bacon and iced tea to soda. He was also much more intelligent than she thought a lot of people gave him credit for. Though maybe she was wrong; he was a detective at thirty-one, after all. But she'd had time to peruse his books—an interesting mix of thrillers and non-fiction—and had read a couple.

Their conversations stemming from her questions about his reading habits, led to discussions lasting late into the evening. He made her think. And laugh. For the first time in a long, long time, she felt normal.

He hadn't tried to kiss her again since the night they went stargazing. Even when things got interesting the couple of times he taught her some self-defense, he'd walked away before anything could happen. She wished he wouldn't have. Maybe she'd sleep better. It would give her mind something else to dwell on besides all her worries while she tried to fall asleep in the quiet of her room.

Humming louder to drown out her thoughts, she finished the bathroom and left the room. After stowing the cleaning supplies in the upstairs janitor's closet, she wandered down to the office to get her purse and clock out.

"All done, Shay?"

Mackenzie startled as the manager called her by her alias. She turned and smiled at him. "Yes. It was an easy day. None of the guests made a mess."

"Good to hear. Before you go, you should know, we have a new long-term renter. Room 113. Says he's here on extended business. He said he'd like if you could make his bed each morning and give him fresh towels, then full service once a week unless things look particularly dirty to you."

Suspicion made the hair on the back of her neck stand up. "Oh, okay. Did he say what time would be best? I don't want to disturb him if he's still sleeping."

"I told him that. He said he'd put the 'Do not disturb' door hanger out at night and take it off in the morning once he was up and about."

She nodded. "Sounds good." She started for the door, but paused with her hand on the bar. "This guy—was he early thirties, about six feet tall? Dark hair and hazel eyes?"

Her manager frowned, but nodded. "Actually, yes. How did you know?"

Mackenzie waved a hand and thought fast. "Oh, well, I saw him earlier. Coming from that way. That's why I wondered."

"Oh, yep, that's him."

"Okay, great. I'll see you tomorrow, then."

"Have a good night." He lifted a hand in farewell, and she pushed through the door.

She made it to Jake's SUV, which she was still driving thanks to deeper issues with her car, before her breath stalled in her lungs. *He was here.* Her gaze darted around the motel, landing on room 113. No car was out front and the curtains didn't twitch. But she could feel his eyes on her.

Unlocking the car, she climbed in and hit the lock button. She jabbed the start button and backed out of her space, eyes searching all her mirrors as she drove back to Jake's. No one appeared to be following her, but that didn't mean much. Brett seemed to always know where she was when he was around.

To be safe, she made a few nonsensical turns, then drove home, parking in the garage, a space normally reserved for Jake's Porsche. Once she told him her suspicions, he'd understand. His SUV was common enough, but it was better not to broadcast that she lived here if Brett did somehow manage to follow her from the motel.

Inside the house, she dug into her purse for her phone so she could call Jake. "Where the hell is it?" She pulled it open further, tilting it into the light, but still didn't see it. Frustrated, she dumped the contents over the granite counter. Papers scattered and tubes rolled. Her lipstick fell to the floor, clattering on the tile. Her phone landed on top of the pile. She scooped it up and unlocked the screen, quickly calling Jake.

The call rolled to voicemail, so she hung up and scrolled through her contacts until she found the number for his desk phone. He'd had her add it and the number for the station. Tapping the screen, she lifted the phone to her ear and listened to it ring. It, too, rolled to voicemail.

Mackenzie growled. "He tells me to call if I need something, then doesn't answer. You're on desk duty. Answer the phone!" She stabbed the phone screen to call the station.

"Sheriff's office. How may I direct your call?"

"Hi, this is Mackenzie Brighton. I'm trying to reach my fiancé, Jake Maxwell. He's not answering his cell or his desk phone."

"I think he's in a meeting with the sheriff. Give me one second."

Mackenzie heard a click as the woman on the other end put her on hold. She drummed her nails on the countertop, then decided to make the best of her wait and started sorting through the items she dumped out of her purse. She didn't need most of the papers that fell out.

"Ms. Brighton?"

She stopped sorting. "Yes?"

"He said to give him a few minutes and he'll call you right back. Unless it's an emergency? Do you need help, ma'am?"

She let out a sigh. "No. I'll wait for him to call back. Thank you." She hung up, growling again.

Heaving another sigh, she went back to sorting. Maybe it was a good thing he wasn't available yet. She should probably calm herself and get her thoughts in order so she didn't sound like a lunatic.

After she finished putting her purse back to rights, she opened the freezer and got out the meat for dinner. They were having tacos.

Her gaze landed on the canisters. *And cookies. We're having cookies.* She pulled them forward and lifted the lids to make sure there was enough flour and sugar. Both canisters were full. She smiled. It was nice living with a bachelor who liked to cook.

Finding mixing bowls and measuring cups and spoons, she set about prepping the batch of sugar cookies. Her phone rang as she took the butter sticks from the microwave after softening them.

Jake's name appeared on the screen as she reached for it.

"Hello?"

"Hey, sorry. I was in Ben's office going over the details of the bar shooting. I've been cleared and am going back on active duty tomorrow. What's up?"

"Brett's here." Her heart thumped harder as she uttered the words.

"What?" His voice deepened and grew sharp. "You're sure?"

"Pretty sure. My manager told me we have a long-term

renter in one of the units. I described Brett to him and he said that sounded like the guy. I didn't actually see him, though."

"Did anyone follow you home?"

"Not that I know of. I took a bunch of weird turns and didn't see anyone."

"Okay. I'll bring home a bug sweeper and check the car for trackers."

Mackenzie's eyes widened, and she swallowed hard. "You think he put a tracker on the car?"

"I wouldn't put it past him. You've slipped away from him twice. It's what I would do."

She blew out a breath. "Yeah. Okay." Tears formed in her eyes, and she sniffed. She hated the idea that he might have followed her home without following her home.

"Hey, don't worry about it, okay? If he checked into the motel, then he probably already knows where you live. It's not like the tracker gave away a state secret. We used my name in the social media posts. A quick background check would give him everything he needed to know about where I live and work."

Her head bobbed. "Yeah, I guess."

"Just make sure all the doors and windows are locked and stay inside until I get home. And keep your phone on you."

"I will. Don't be late, please."

"I won't. I'll see you soon."

"Okay. Bye." Her voice ended on a whisper. He echoed her goodbye, and she hung up. Blowing out a breath, she tucked her phone into her pocket and went to the back door, checking the lock. It was fine. She moved to the kitchen window, peering out into the yard after checking that it was locked too. Nothing moved outside except a few birds hopping around on the tree branches.

With a frown, she moved away from the window and checked the rest of the house. Everything was still locked up tight. Heading back to the kitchen, she rolled her neck. She'd been wrong. She wasn't more relaxed now that he was here.

For the next hour, she baked cookies and prepped toppings for their tacos. The tasks were soothing, and some of her edginess disappeared. When Jake walked in the door, she was mixing the seasonings into the browned meat.

She smiled at him. "Hey."

"Hi." He hung up his keys and shrugged out of his jacket, revealing his khaki cargo pants and department polo. "You look calmer than what you sounded on the phone."

Mackenzie shrugged. "I've had some time to think. And to process."

He walked closer. "And?" One eyebrow winged upward in question.

"And I'm okay. Still freaked out, but okay." She gave him a small smile. "I'm not ready to run."

He returned her smile. "I wasn't worried you were." He leaned in and pecked a kiss on her cheek. "I checked the SUV for trackers before I came inside. It's clean."

Her shoulders sagged as a weight she hadn't realized she still carried lifted free. "Good. Maybe the man at the motel is just a coincidence. His description could be the same for thousands of men."

"True. But still keep your eyes open." He stepped back. "I'm going to change."

She nodded. "Don't take long. This is almost done."

Jake gave her a thumbs up and trotted away. She finished stirring the seasonings into the meat, then turned off the stove and took two place settings from the cupboards and set them on the table. Finding a trivet in a drawer, she set the skillet on it in the middle of the table, then brought over the rest of the taco makings. She was getting herself a glass of water when Jake walked in, wearing jeans and a butter-soft dark-gray t-shirt. It clung to the ropey muscles of his broad shoulders.

She rolled her lips in and looked away, focusing on filling a tortilla. "Get it while it's hot."

He sat down across from her. "This smells great. Thanks for dinner."

Her eyes darted up to him. A lock of his dark hair fell down over his forehead. Her fingers twitched with the urge to brush it back. She looked down at her taco. "You're welcome. So how was your day? Good, I'm guessing, since the sheriff put you back on duty."

He nodded. "Yeah. I'll be glad to get back out in the field. Though it was nice giving Tristan a taste of what I went through while he was out on paternity leave." He chuckled.

Mackenzie smiled. "You two seem to have a good relationship."

"Yeah." Jake spooned meat into his tortillas. "We've only been partners since around the beginning of the year, but he's become a good friend. He's smart and was patient with me as I learned the ropes of being a detective."

"I can't imagine it took much for you to figure it out. You're no dummy." She lifted the taco she built to her mouth and took a bite.

"No, but Tristan has life experience I could only dream of. He was an Army Ranger—so was Ben. They were in the same unit for a while. They've got wicked instincts. Some of that's rubbed off, but not all." He grinned and took a bite of his overflowing taco.

She smiled. "You have better instincts than you think. You figured out something was wrong with me."

He tipped his head, swallowing the bite in his mouth. "I'm glad I did. It's led to a change in both our lives." The look in his eyes heated as he stared at her.

A flush crept up Mackenzie's neck.

"How about after we eat, we go for a bike ride again? There's an awesome little ice cream shop in Asheville."

A half hour crushed against him as they drove to the city? Hell, yes. "Sure. That sounds nice."

The fire in his eyes burned hotter. She knew he was thinking of the last time they took a motorcycle ride. She hoped it ended the same way.

Twenty-Three

Jake fiddled with his keys, shifting on the motorcycle seat, as he waited for Mackenzie to appear. She went to put on warmer clothes for their ride to the city.

He put the key in the ignition, then rested his hands atop his helmet, drumming his fingers on it. Recognizing the nervous behavior, he huffed and stuffed his hand in his pocket.

Why was he nervous? They'd been living together for over a week. It was just ice cream.

An ice cream date, his conscience said.

He rolled his eyes. Yes, it was a date. He wanted to date her. She'd acknowledged that she wanted a relationship. It felt like they'd gotten a good start on that this past week with all their long evening conversations. So, why did going on an actual date make him nervous?

"Sorry." Mackenzie breezed through the door. "One of my gloves was hiding." She held out her hands, adorned in black gloves. "I found it."

"Good. Hop on." He tipped his head to the seat behind him.

She walked over and picked up the helmet sitting on the

seat, putting it over her head. Jake steeled himself as she threw a leg over the bike and nestled up behind him. He covered his shifting to give himself more room in his jeans by starting the bike. He pushed the button on the garage door remote to open the door.

"Ready?"

She clutched his waist tighter. "Yep."

Jake put the bike in gear and rolled out of the garage, closing the door as they reached the street. He turned right and wove through the streets, leading them out of town. Like their last ride, after a few miles, the feel of her pressed against him left a pleasant hum through his body. It was thrilling, but also comforting. He liked knowing she was close. Safe.

The bike ate up the miles, and they soon roared into Asheville. He made several turns, taking them to a quaint little neighborhood and its amazing ice cream shop. It was as busy as he expected, and he drove toward the rear of the lot to find a parking space.

He shut off the engine and pocketed the key. Mackenzie got off and removed her helmet, shaking out her hair.

"This place is busy."

Jake took off his helmet. "It always is. And there's a reason. Come on." He took her hand and led her into the shop.

"How did you find this place?"

"My sister lives near here."

"Oh? I thought she lived in Foggy Mountain."

He shook his head, shuffling forward as the line moved. "Her husband is an insurance agent based in Asheville. She moved here when they got married." Jake missed having his sister around the corner, but he was happy for her. Her husband was a nice guy.

They reached the front of the line and Jake ordered the cinnamon churro ice cream in a cone. Mackenzie ordered the blueberry lemon cheesecake flavor in a cup. Once they had their treats, they found a table in the crowded shop and sat down.

"So, tell me about yourself," Jake said, then licked his ice cream cone to stop a drip. "Who is Mackenzie Brighton? We've spent all week talking, but you've avoided the subject of you." Every time he thought she might open up about herself, she'd steered the conversation back to him or to books or news. Or he taught her self-defense moves. He'd learned some things about her from their conversations, but not much about her personally. About her life before she met Jorgensen.

Her mouth twisted, and she took a bite of her ice cream before answering. "I'm not sure."

Jake paused mid-lick and lowered his cone, giving her his full attention.

"Honestly, I've tried not to think about that woman for the last couple of years. I needed to become Shay. To believe that's who I was. I'm struggling a bit to go back to being Mackenzie." She took another bite of her ice cream and glanced out the window at the darkened street.

"So, tell me about who she was, then."

She took a deep breath and looked at him. "She was fun. Lively, but still kind of quiet. She wanted to be a pharmacist. I'd signed up to start my degree to do just that when I met Brett. He convinced me to quit. That I didn't have time for classes." She rolled her eyes. "Yet one more thing I gave up to the bastard."

"Would you want to do it now? Once you get your life back and are free of him?"

She shrugged. "Maybe. I love the medical field. But that's a big commitment. I'm twenty-seven. Even with my associate's degree, I'm still looking at six to seven years of school before I get my bachelor's in science and my doctorate. Back then, that didn't seem so bad, but now?" She shrugged again. "I'll be well into my thirties, starting over."

Jake frowned, thoughtful. He licked a drip off his cone. "I know we haven't talked too much about where things are going between us—just that we want to explore a relationship —but I'll support you in whatever you want to do. Even if that's continuing to clean the motel."

She smiled. "Thank you. Though, I do think I'll go back to at least being a pharmacy technician if and when things with Brett get resolved. I've had my fill of the filth people leave behind." She shuddered, making Jake chuckle.

"At least the Foggy Mountain Motel isn't as seedy as some I've seen. There are a couple here in Asheville—" He lifted his eyebrows and shook his head.

"I bet. I stayed in some of those at one time. And that one I worked at here when you met me was pretty gross." She wrinkled her nose.

Jake's appetite took a nose-dive. He didn't want to think about her living and working in those places. He'd been called to places like those. He knew what went on there.

Shifting in his seat, he pushed those thoughts away and cleared his throat. "So, you're an only child, right?" He licked his cone as he changed the subject.

"Yes. My parents tried to have more kids, but after my mom had her fifth miscarriage, they stopped trying. I didn't lack for company my own age, though. My dad's brother lived nearby until I was seventeen. He had four kids. We all played together growing up."

"Why did they move?"

"He's an engineer. He got offered a job at a huge company in New York City. It tripled his salary, so he took it. They still live in a suburb of the city. He commutes. My aunt teaches high school there."

"Do you ever talk to them or your cousins?"

"I used to. Before Brett. The phone calls got fewer and further between as our relationship progressed. The last time I saw or spoke to any of them was at the funeral." She glanced down, stirring her ice cream.

"What about your mom's family?"

"Grandpa was it. She was an only child too. And Grandma died from cancer when I was just a little girl."

"I'm sorry."

Mackenzie shrugged. "I don't really remember her. Just hints of things." She looked up. "But I miss my cousins. I'd like to have relationships with them again. But I don't know how to start."

"By picking up the phone. Maybe once this is over, we'll take a trip. I've always wanted to see the Statue of Liberty and Central Park."

A pretty smile broke out on her face. "I'd like that."

Happy he'd pulled her out of her melancholy, they finished their dessert, turning to more mundane and less heavy topics. When they were done, they disposed of their trash and left the shop.

"Oh, I think it got colder." Mackenzie burrowed deeper into her coat, turning up the collar.

The chilly air ruffled Jake's hair. "I think you're right. Let's get going before it gets worse." He glanced at the sky. The leaden clouds hung low, threatening to let loose their moisture. It wasn't supposed to rain tonight, but there was snow in the forecast for later in the week in the higher elevations. He believed it. Any trace of summer was officially gone.

He pushed the speed limit all the way home, the wind cutting through his clothes. Mackenzie made herself as small as possible and tucked into his back, shielding herself from the wind. When he pulled into the garage and killed the engine, he let go of the handlebars and flexed his fingers. They were numb.

"I think that's about it for the bike until spring." He fumbled in his pocket for the garage remote to shut the door.

Mackenzie climbed off and removed her helmet, shaking out her hair. "Pity. I like the ride."

He glanced at her, the heat in her eyes warming him up. "Me too."

They stared at each other as the door rolled down. It clanked into place, surrounding them in silence. Jake got off the bike and removed his helmet. He took hers from her hands and laid both on the seat, then curled a hand around her waist, tugging her closer. "It's customary for a date to end with a kiss."

She leaned into him, her hands splaying over his leather-clad chest. "Just one?"

He growled, shoving his other hand into her hair. "No." He covered her lips with his. Pushing past her lips, he sipped at the sweet inner recesses of her mouth. She still tasted faintly of lemon. Wanting to feel her hair over his hand and the softness of her skin, he pulled back to remove his gloves. When he leaned in again, she put a hand over his lips.

"Wait."

Jake frowned in question.

She smiled and took his hand, leading him toward the door. "As much as I want you to kiss me again, I want to be warm. It's cold out here."

He chuckled and found his house key, letting them inside. Warmth blasted them both. She was right; this was much better. He shed his coat, leaving it hanging over the back of a chair. Hers landed on top of his. He took her hand and led her toward the living room.

"Where were we?" He sank on to the couch, pulling her down on top of him.

She straddled his legs, her long, dark hair creating a curtain around their faces as she leaned down. "You were going to give me another goodnight kiss."

"Mmm, yes." He feathered a soft touch over her lips, teasing them both.

She moaned, sending a pulse of need straight to his groin.

"Mack." Jake closed the distance and sealed his mouth to hers. Need built as their tongues dueled, each seeking to bring the other pleasure. He let his hands roam over her back and down over her hips, cupping the supple curves in his hands. She let out a little whimper, sinking deeper onto his lap. Jake nipped her bottom lip and held her hips steady as he thrust up, making them both gasp.

He pulled back, looking into her beautiful, rich brown eyes. "We should probably stop before we get too carried away."

"Yeah," she whispered, not moving to get up.

Jake slipped a hand back into her hair, stretching his neck to get closer. "This is a bad idea."

"Completely agree."

He nuzzled the space behind her ear. She sucked in a sharp breath and clutched his shirt. "Make me stop, Mackenzie."

"No." The single word came out on an airy sigh. Moments later, she latched onto his mouth, sealing their fate.

She ground against his hips, creating a delicious friction that made his blood pump faster. With the single shred of sanity he had left, he wrenched his mouth from hers. "Tell me you want this. I need to hear it. To know that you want this as much as I do."

Twenty-Four

Trapped in Jake's icy blue stare, need pulsed through Mackenzie's body. Moisture pooled in her core, making her ache. Any hope she had of not falling head over heels for this man evaporated as she sat on his lap, seeing—and feeling—the effect she had on him.

Scooting back, she slipped off his lap, then held out a hand. "If we're going to do this, let's do it right." Her soft smile and confident words belied the butterflies on a rampage in her stomach. Where the confidence came from, she didn't know. She didn't typically take charge in the bedroom. Brett liked certain things, and she'd learned to just let him do what he wanted. It was less uncomfortable for her.

He took her hand and stood. Tugging her into his arms, he kissed her hard, then led her down the hall to his bedroom. Pausing near the head of the bed, he clicked on the bedside lamp. Mackenzie tugged on the hem of her shirt, worrying the material between her fingers.

Jake frowned, reaching up to brush her hair back from her cheek. "You look nervous. We don't have to do this. I'm thrilled you want to. But this is all the further it needs to go."

His warm palm cupped her cheek. "This isn't a race. I'm not going anywhere."

Her smile turned tremulous. "I know all that. It's just been awhile. And my previous experiences weren't the best."

Jake's expression turned dark. "Did Brett—"

She waved a hand, cutting him off. "He never forced me, per se. But there were times I wasn't in the mood and he persuaded me. Made me feel like it was my duty. Eventually, I just accepted that as fact. And it was always about him. About what made him get off. I never got to be in control. Never got to pick the position or the place. It was always what he wanted."

His nostrils flared and something hard shot through his eyes as his mouth tightened. It was fleeting, gone almost as soon as it appeared. His expression softened. "Then we do this however you want. If you want me to just hold you, I will. If you want me to lie there and let you ride, I'll do that too. Whatever you want."

Tears pricked her eyes. She covered her face with her hands and sank onto the edge of the bed as a sob broke free. The mattress dipped beside her as he sat down. A large hand landed on her back, rubbing softly up and down her spine.

"I'm—sorry," she choked.

"Baby, you've got nothing to be sorry for. Jorgensen's a jerk. The relationship you had with him wasn't healthy." His hand curled over her shoulder, and he brushed her hair back, his fingers skimming her neck to lift her chin. "How about we hold off? I don't think you're ready."

She sniffed and shook her head. "No. It won't matter how long we wait. I'll still be nervous. Still feel like I'm inadequate. I—" His mouth covered hers, cutting off her words. Startled, she froze, but quickly loosened up. As she brought her hands up to frame his face, he pulled back.

"Once you trust me—trust us and our relationship—you

won't feel that way. You'll be ready and eager. Maybe still a tad nervous." He held up his thumb and index fingers just millimeters apart. "Hell, I will be too, because it'll be our first time, and I want it to be spectacular for both of us. *That* nervous feeling is normal. What you're feeling now isn't."

Mackenzie's brow furrowed as she weighed his words. She did feel like they were rushing a bit. But she'd just been so caught up in the moment. And wanting to please him.

More tears formed in her eyes. God! She'd wanted to have sex with him just to make *him* happy, instead of waiting until she was truly ready. What did that say about how messed up she was?

"No more tears, Mackenzie. I'm not upset that we're waiting. We'll know when the time is right."

She sniffed hard and nodded, swiping at her face. "I guess so." She had her doubts, though, that she'd recognize when that was. She'd thought that was now until he pointed out her nerves weren't normal. And he was right. When they walked in and she saw the bed, she froze. Her brain shut down. The hum of desire was still there, but her brain checked out.

Jake leaned in and pressed a tender kiss to her forehead. "Why don't you go get ready for bed? It's late, and we could both use some sleep."

Feeling stupid for pushing them to this point, she kept her head bowed and stood.

"Mackenzie, look at me."

Gritting her teeth, she flicked her gaze to his, then stared at a point on the bed beside his hand.

He stood up in front of her and took her biceps in his hands, bending at the knee so he could look into her eyes. "You do know that the only reason I stopped what was happening is because I don't want to hurt you, right? That I don't want you to regret it, or to take our relationship back several steps by moving too fast?"

She bit her lip and nodded, still mortified.

He growled, his jaw working as he straightened and glanced away.

"I'm sorry," she whispered.

"Stop saying that. You still don't have anything to be sorry for." He took her hand and pressed it to his fly. "Feel that?"

Mackenzie jumped, her gaze meeting his before darting down to her hand on his crotch, then back to his eyes.

"That's all you. Even with all this heavy conversation, he still wants a taste of your sweet body. One day, he'll get that chance. When. You're. Ready."

Emboldened by his words and actions, her fingers stroked him through his jeans, the denim rough on her skin. She couldn't help it. The man tied her up in knots, tipped her world on its axis, and left her spinning like she was in an out-of-control gyroscope. She might not be ready to do the deed, but copping a feel? She wouldn't turn that down.

A vein popped out in his neck and the muscles in his jaw worked. He leaned in and kissed her—hard. His tongue invaded her mouth, scattering her thoughts. But just as quickly, he pulled back.

"Go to bed, Mack. Before I forget I'm a gentleman."

Biting her lip, emotions and thoughts in a tilt-a-whirl, she nodded. Retreating to the door, she glanced back. "Thank you." She wanted to say more, but the words caught in her throat.

The controlled expression on his face softened. He nodded. "Goodnight, Mackenzie."

She smiled softly. "Goodnight, Jake."

TWENTY-FIVE

The bright sun bounced off the motel windows, making Mackenzie squint. She wished it was as warm as it looked. A cold, north wind swirled through the property, raising goosebumps on her arms under her long-sleeved shirt. She wasn't ready to start wearing a coat as she made her rounds, cleaning. Not yet.

She paused in front of the next room and glanced at the room number. Her stomach sank as she saw it was room 113. The "Do not disturb" sign was off the handle, so he was either up or gone. She prayed he was gone. As much as she wanted confirmation he was here, she didn't want to talk to him.

Raising a fist, she knocked. "Housekeeping." She listened, waiting for someone to answer. After about twenty seconds, she knocked again. "Hello?" She waited a few moments longer. When there was still no answer, she used her master key and let herself in.

The room was tidy. No trash lay on the floor or on the small table. In the corner, a small pile of dirty clothes sat next to a suitcase. She could see clean clothes hanging in the closet. Mackenzie resisted the urge to snoop. It would be her luck he'd walk in while she rummaged through his things. There was also the possibility the man staying here wasn't Brett. Then she'd just be invading some stranger's privacy.

Putting blinders on, she made the bed. In the bathroom, she gathered the dirty towels and deposited them in the laundry bin on her cart. She grabbed a set of clean ones and two trash bags and went back inside. Depositing the towels in the bathroom, she switched out the trash bags and went outside, tossing them into the bin on her cart.

"Your fiancé lets you clean a place like this?"

Mackenzie jumped and dread filled her stomach like lead. She knew that voice. It haunted her nightmares. She lifted her head and looked left to see Brett leaning against one of the support columns.

Heart thumping in her ears, she swallowed hard. "What are you doing here? How did you find out where I worked?"

He pushed away from the column, striding closer. Mackenzie shifted, putting the cart between them. She'd ram it into him if necessary.

"What? No, 'Hi, nice to see you, Brett.' Or how about telling me you missed me?"

"It's not, and I didn't. Go home. You don't belong here."

"And you do?"

She nodded. "This is my home now."

"Right. With what's his name? Jack?"

Mackenzie narrowed her eyes. She knew he knew Jake's name, but was playing dumb for some reason. Probably trying to put her on the defensive. "It's Jake. But you know that. Stop playing games and being an idiot. And leave me alone."

The feigned interest on his face disappeared, but the affable smile stayed even as his eyes turned cold. "I don't know what you're talking about. I'm here for work."

She frowned. "You expect me to believe a cop from a tiny

city in New York is all the way down here in North Carolina for work? What could possibly bring you down here?"

"I'm not a cop anymore. I decided I wanted more freedom and struck out on my own as a private investigator. My case brought me down here."

"What's the case?"

"Can't tell you. Client privilege."

She stopped herself from rolling her eyes. Mackenzie would eat the trash in her cart if he had an actual case here. "Okay. Well, if that's all, I have work to do." She pushed the cart forward, hoping he'd move.

He planted his feet and crossed his arms.

"Seriously, Brett. Move. I'm working."

"You're different."

"Yeah, well, it's been three years. People change."

"And get engaged."

She huffed. He wasn't going to get out of her way until he got what he wanted right now. Apparently, that was information on Jake. "Yes. Jake is a wonderful guy. I'm lucky to have him." That wasn't a lie. Every day, he proved he was a hundred times the man Brett was.

Brett hummed. "I'm sure. He's a cop, right? Seems you have a type."

"I don't like him because of his job. It's coincidence." Which was true. She wouldn't care what Jake did for a living.

"Sure it is. Or maybe you're trying to replicate what we had."

This time, she didn't stop the eye roll. "Hardly." She pushed the cart forward again, hitting his shoes. He uncrossed his arms and stepped back, the fake relaxed look on his face morphing to something much scarier. It promised retribution for defying him.

She straightened her spine and held his gaze, even as her insides quivered. Every ounce of courage she had was going into not looking away. "Go home, Brett. And get out of my way. I'm not interested in talking anymore, and I have work to do." This time, when she pushed her cart forward, he moved back.

"I'll be seeing you around, Mackenzie."

Of that, she had no doubt. But she didn't respond to him. Just kept walking to the next room on her list to clean. She'd take the little victory she just got.

Twenty-Six

Jake's cellphone vibrated, rattling the stack of papers it sat on. Absently, he picked it up and answered it, his eyes still on his computer screen as he went over notes from the cases he missed while he was on administrative leave. "Maxwell."

"Jake, it's me."

The tremor in Mackenzie's voice gained his full attention. "Mack? What's wrong?"

"Brett's here. I saw him. Talked to him. He's the guest at the motel I told you about."

He uttered a soft curse. "Are you okay?"

"I'm fine. Surprisingly, I stood up to him. But I have some information for you. He said he's no longer with the Amandale Police Department. That he's here as a private investigator on a case."

Jake snorted. "His case just happened to take him to the same city as his former girlfriend a week after she announces her engagement? Yeah, no."

"That's pretty much what I said, but he insisted it was true. He wouldn't tell me what the case was, though. Cited client privilege."

A zing of excitement shot through Jake's veins. If Brett really did quit the Amandale PD, this could give them a door into the department to get the information they needed. "Okay. Did he say anything else?"

"Not really. Just kept hinting that I missed him and was only with you as a substitute."

"You know that's not true, right? We might share a profession, but we're nothing alike."

"I know. I told him that too. He shrugged it off. We only talked for a couple of minutes. It won't be the last I see of him, though."

No, a man like Brett Jorgensen wouldn't give up so easily. "What time do you get off?"

"Three-thirty."

"Okay. I'm going to follow you home. Just to be safe."

"Good. I put on a brave front, but he's got me rattled. I'll feel better knowing someone's watching out for me when I leave here."

Jake would too. If they pushed hard enough, he could see Jorgensen changing things up and kidnapping her. He didn't think they were at that point yet—the man wasn't angry enough—but he still didn't want to take chances with Mackenzie's safety. Once she was back at his house, she'd have the security of deadbolts and his alarm, plus the firearms he kept in the house. On the road, she was vulnerable.

"Stay in sight of others when you can. And lock the room doors behind you when you go in to clean. You might want to pull your cart inside with you."

"It's too big to get through the door. But I'll be careful when I go outside and try to limit the number of trips."

His mouth pulled. He didn't like it, but it was better than nothing. And he doubted Jorgensen would try anything somewhere so public. The motel was right off the highway and saw a lot of traffic. "All right. If you feel threatened, lock yourself in a room and call for help."

"I will. I'll see you this afternoon."

They said goodbye and hung up.

Jake reran the conversation through his head. It was time to start doing some real digging on Jorgensen.

He pushed away from his desk and went to Ben's office, rapping his knuckles on the door and poking his head in. "You got a minute?"

Ben glanced up from his computer screen. "Sure. Have a seat." He motioned to the chairs in front of the desk. "What's up?"

Jake sat, balancing an ankle over his knee. "Mackenzie just called. Brett's in town. She talked to him. He said he quit his job to become a private investigator and is here on business."

Ben's eyebrows lifted. "That's the excuse he's using?"

"Right? It's plausible, but extremely flimsy. But"—he held up a finger—"it gives us a place to start. He quit his job. And he has to know that Mackenzie would tell me, so it doesn't really matter now if we call his former boss and ask some questions."

Ben sat back and studied him. "You want to tip your hand?"

"We need information. Talking to people is the only way to get that. I'm a cop, so I know other cops would understand me wanting to inquire about my fiancé's ex showing up out of the blue. Plus, we'll be able to confirm his story." He held Ben's gaze.

The older man continued to study him. Jake could see the wheels turning. After a moment, he reached for the phone.

"Who are you calling?"

"Amandale's police chief." He pulled a notebook out from under a stack of folders and punched in the number written on it.

Jake dropped his foot to the floor and leaned forward. "Put it on speaker."

"You gonna let me talk?" Ben arched a brow, pushing a button on the phone and setting the receiver in the cradle. Ringing filled the office.

"Yes." Jake folded his hands together, clutching them as a reminder to keep his mouth closed.

"Amandale Police Department. How may I direct your call?" A woman's voice echoed through the room, tinny from the small phone speaker.

"Hi. This is Sheriff Ben Davidson from Ferris County, North Carolina. Could you put me through to your chief, please? It's concerning one of his officers."

"Oh, yes, of course. One moment." A click sounded, then the phone rang again.

"Baskin." The man's gravelly voice sounded distracted.

"Chief, this is Ben Davidson. I'm the sheriff down in Ferris County, North Carolina. I'm calling regarding one of your officers, Brett Jorgensen."

"He quit. About four days ago. Walked into my office after his shift and said he wouldn't be in the next day. Said he had a family emergency. I offered him an extended leave, but he turned it down. It wasn't until later that I remembered he doesn't have any family. What do you want to know?"

"Do you remember him talking about a girlfriend a couple of years ago? Mackenzie Brighton?"

"Actually, yes. Dark-haired girl, quiet?"

"That's her."

"Yeah, they broke up a while ago. What about her?"

"She's living here and is engaged to one of my detectives. Jorgensen showed up, claiming to be a private investigator. Said he's on a case."

"What? No. I'd have seen his license. Hold on." The sound of typing came over the line, then a few seconds of silence.

"No, there's no license in our database for him. And it's an online application, so there'd be something that said pending, at least."

Ben and Jake shared a look.

"So, we have reason to believe Jorgensen's been stalking Ms. Brighton. She told my detective she moved to Pittsburgh just over three years ago to get away from him, and he followed her there."

"Three years ago, you say?"

"Yes."

"He took a leave of absence for personal issues in that timeframe. I remember, because it was right before the Fourth of July, which is always busy for us. Said he was getting burnt out and needed some time to recharge. I gave it to him because he's always been an exemplary officer and having a cop in a mental crisis on the street isn't a good idea. I wasn't happy, though. I needed all hands on deck. And he came back different. Quieter. A little edgy. Like the time off didn't help. But he said he was fine. I had no reason not to believe him."

"Probably because she took off in the middle of the night and changed her name, moving around until she was sure he wasn't following her. She's been down this way about two years."

"And you said she's engaged now?"

"Yes. She had to use her real name for the marriage application, so she came clean to her fiancé."

"How did he get access to the application? It wouldn't be public record until the marriage license is filed, right?"

"Right, but she made some other, more disturbing allegations against him. And in order to live her life free of fear, she made her engagement public in the hopes of proving some of those allegations and getting him out of her life."

"Oh, geez. Like what? Before this week, I'd have said you're crazy, but after this stunt and what you just told me about his leave back then, I'm inclined to give you the benefit of the doubt. Though, how do I know you are who you say you are? Could be she cooked this whole thing up to discredit him."

Jake shifted in his seat, opening his mouth. Ben's fierce frown sent his way, kept his words in.

"After three-and-a-half years?" Ben said.

"If she's crazy, sure. Anything could have triggered a memory and sent her down this path. I don't know that you're not some actor she hired to play a part."

Ben sighed. "Fine. Look up my department's number and call. Ask for the sheriff. I'm not lying."

A beat of silence passed. "Okay. Give me a minute." A click sounded, then the dial tone.

"Seriously?" Jake huffed and sat back, crossing his arms.

Ben shrugged. "I don't blame him. I'd do the same thing if it was one of my deputies. I'm glad he's covering his bases."

Begrudgingly, Jake agreed. But he still didn't like it.

A minute later, Ben's desk phone rang. Jake sat forward again as Ben hit a button to answer it on speaker.

"Sheriff Davidson."

"Okay, so you're not lying. Tell me more about this situation with Ms. Brighton." Defeat colored Chief Baskin's voice.

Jake pumped his fist. Jorgensen made a fatal mistake. He lied and didn't cover his tracks.

Ben's mouth quirked up, and he nodded, realizing the same thing. "Mackenzie alleges he psychologically and emotionally abused her during their relationship, which is why she ran. She also thinks he was responsible for the deaths of her parents and grandfather."

"What? They died in a car crash. I remember that. Brett was devastated."

Ben let silence speak for him.

The chief groaned. "He faked that, didn't he?" He sighed. "God."

"Were autopsies performed on her family members?"

"Let me look. I don't remember." They heard more typing. "Okay. Let's see... No. There were no autopsies."

"What would it take to get their bodies exhumed and have them done?"

Baskin blew out a breath. "You really think the M.E. will find something on bodies that were not only badly burned, but have been in the ground for nearly four years?"

"It's worth a look. He lied about why he needed time off and why he quit. What else is he lying about? I also find it highly suspicious that he'd show up under pretense after Ms. Brighton got engaged. If her allegations of abuse are true, what else would he do to keep her in his life?"

"Yeah, but murder? Jorgensen's a decorated officer. The public loves him."

"Jorgensen's a high-functioning sociopath. We've done some digging on him. His background check looks legit, but a fact-check of his claim that his parents are deceased proves false with an obituary search. There are no obituaries for either parent in any state. Not even the little blips released by funeral homes when people have no next-of-kin to write one. In fact, we couldn't find any record his parents even existed."

Baskin groaned. "I'll have a talk with our human resources department. Find out what their process is for verifying the information applicants provide. It's supposed to include getting copies of all official certificates—birth, death, marriage, etc. Someone dropped the ball or he paid them off."

Jake snagged the notepad and a pen from Ben's desk as a thought struck him. He scribbled it down, then turned the notepad for Ben to see.

Reading it, Ben nodded. "Chief, did anyone in records or

human resources die suddenly not long after Jorgensen was hired?"

The chief cursed softly. "You're thinking he paid someone off, then killed them to cover his tracks?" He groaned. "I can't believe he could pull the wool over everyone's eyes so well for so long. Are you sure Ms. Brighton is credible? The way Jorgensen painted her, she was scatter-brained and had a problem with prescription drugs. He said the reason she left and why they broke up was because she quit her job at the hospital pharmacy after her employer suspected she was stealing pills for personal use."

Jake's blood heated. He opened his mouth again, but Ben waved a hand and frowned, silencing him. Biting back a growl, Jake sat back and crossed his arms once more, fuming as he listened.

"I can assure you, Ms. Brighton does not have a drug problem. The only thing she's lied to us about is her name, and that was to protect herself from being found. But she's done hiding. And he's here. The problem is Jorgensen, not Ms. Brighton." Ben's voice was firm.

A long sigh came over the speaker. "Yeah. Dammit. Okay. I'll do some digging of my own and ask the medical examiner's office to exhume the bodies. I might need Ms. Brighton's signature on some forms. Can I fax those to your office?"

"Of course." Ben gave him the number.

"All right. I'll give you an update in a day or two." He hung up, not saying goodbye.

Ben lifted the receiver and set it back down, clearing the call. He looked at Jake. "That was easier than I thought it would be."

"The man was lied to. And made to look like a fool. I'm just glad we caught Jorgensen in a lie. We might end this much sooner than I thought."

"Yeah, well, don't get your hopes up too high. I can't arrest him for being in the area. We need proof Mackenzie's family was murdered. Then we need to prove Jorgensen did it."

"Way to burst my bubble. Thanks, Ben." Jake rolled his eyes and blew out a breath, his enthusiasm sufficiently dampened.

Ben grinned. "That's my job. Now, get out of here and go back to work. We can't do anymore about Jorgensen until we hear from Baskin."

Jake scrubbed his hands over his face and let out a soft groan. "Yeah. Okay. You'll let me know when you hear something?"

"Of course."

"Great. Thanks, Ben." Jake stood.

"You're welcome. Keep an eye on your girl. We don't know what contacts he still has in Amandale. If he gets wind of what we're doing, she could be in real danger."

"Oh, I plan to." If he couldn't be with her, she'd be somewhere public or with someone he trusted implicitly. The game just changed.

TWENTY-SEVEN

Sweat ran down Jake's face and the treadmill hummed beneath his feet. He normally ran through his neighborhood, but he didn't want to leave Mackenzie home alone if he didn't have to. It had been several days since they heard from Chief Baskin. He'd faxed a form for Mackenzie to sign to exhume her family's bodies. She'd done so eagerly, ready for answers. Now they were in wait-and-see mode. Jake knew it took time to arrange to have the bodies exhumed and then for the medical examiner to look them over in fine detail. That knowledge didn't make him any less patient. They needed evidence. Something to connect Jorgensen to their deaths. What they'd find on burned bodies that had been entombed for so long, he didn't know. He just prayed there was something.

His phone rang, the ringtone for his sister filling his basement workout room. He slowed the treadmill and hopped off, answering it.

"Yeah, Leelee? What's up?"

"Did I catch you at a bad time?"

"I was running. You're fine."

"Oh, well. Okay. Say, are you busy this afternoon? I have a photoshoot and need someone to watch Ava. My sitter canceled. She's sick. Bryce is on a business trip and mom went to the beach for the weekend with one of her girlfriends."

"Um, sure. Do you want us to come there, or do you want to bring her here?"

"Oh, I forgot about Mackenzie." Jake could hear the grin in his sister's voice. "This could be a real test for you two. Give you a taste of parenting and how you'd do it together."

Jake chuckled. "I guess."

She echoed his laugh. "In any case, you should probably come here. She'll probably still be down for her nap when I need to leave."

"That works. What time?"

"I need to be out of here by two."

"Okay." He glanced at his watch. It was lunchtime. "We'll see you then."

"Thank you so much." Relief colored her voice. "I was dreading having to wrangle her while I took pictures. I was plotting how long she'd stay content in her pack-and-play and what I could bring to extend that time."

"Well, no need now. We'll keep her entertained."

"Awesome. I'm going to go feed the beast now, then put her down for her nap. Thanks, Jake."

"Yep. Bye."

She echoed his goodbye, and he hung up. Blowing out a breath, he lifted the hem of his shirt and swiped the sweat from his face. He dashed up the steps and emerged in the kitchen. Mackenzie glanced over from where she stood in front of the sink, washing dishes.

"Have a good run?"

He nodded. "It got cut a little short. My sister called. She wants us to watch Ava this afternoon. Is that okay with you? I probably should have asked before I agreed, but she was in a bind."

"That's fine. I'd like to meet your niece." She turned on the water and rinsed the handful of silverware she held, then set it in the strainer. "When do we need to be there?"

"In a couple hours. I want to shower and eat before we go. It'll take us about a half an hour to get there."

She nodded. "Sounds good." She let the water out of the sink and rinsed her hands, then reached for a towel. "That gives me time to do a load of laundry."

"You don't have to do all the chores just because you're staying here, you know."

Mackenzie waved a hand and hung up the towel. "I know, but I don't mind. It gives me something to do and keeps my mind occupied." Her lips flattened. "Have you heard anything about my family?"

Jake shook his head. "No. It'll likely be another week before we get any answers."

Her shoulders fell. "Yeah. Okay." She pushed away from the counter. "I'm going to start that laundry. Leave your clothes outside the bathroom, and I'll throw them in." She gestured to his sweaty attire. Still frowning, she walked away.

He watched her leave, wishing he knew how to put the smile back on her face. She'd been pensive since he told her about Ben's conversation with Chief Baskin. He couldn't blame her. The waiting was driving him crazy too.

There was little any of them could do about it, though. Jorgensen was keeping a low profile. He hung around the motel, but Mackenzie avoided him as best she could. They hadn't spoken since their first encounter five days ago. Jake kept waiting for the guy to show up somewhere and try to "persuade" him he shouldn't marry her.

He snorted as he left the kitchen. He wanted the asshole to approach him just to hear what he would say.

In his bedroom, he grabbed a change of clothes, then stripped outside the bathroom door, leaving them there as Mackenzie requested. When he reemerged after his shower, his clothes were gone. Wandering down the hall, he saw her in the living room on the couch, reading a book.

"There are leftovers in the fridge," she said, not looking up.

"Thanks." He frowned, wondering if she was all right. But he didn't ask. Not yet. Maybe it was just a good book.

Meandering into the kitchen, he found last night's leftovers—enchiladas—and heated them up. Grabbing a fork, he returned to the living room and sat down across from her. When he'd eaten half his food and she hadn't looked up, he set his fork down.

"Good book?"

She glanced at him. "It's okay."

He frowned. "Are you all right? I figured you'd be darting around, cleaning. You don't sit still much, I've noticed."

Mackenzie nodded, her eyes returning to her book. "I'm fine."

Now he knew she was lying. He put his plate on the coffee table and leaned his elbows on his knees, threading his fingers together. "Okay. Tell me what's wrong."

"I'm okay, I promise." But she didn't look at him.

"Then why won't you look at me?"

Her gaze shot to his. Annoyance flashed in her eyes.

"That's better, but what's wrong?"

"Nothing."

"Bullshit."

She huffed and closed her book, tossing it onto the cushion beside her. "You're not going to let this go, are you?"

"No."

Mackenzie clasped her hands, then glanced out the window, her mouth twisting first to one side, then the other.

Finally, she looked at him. "I needed to distract myself. Reading requires my full concentration."

A small furrow formed between Jake's eyebrows. "Why do you need to distract yourself? Are you worried about Jorgensen?"

"Yes."

He laid a hand over hers. "Did you talk to him again and not tell me? Did he say something?"

She shook her head, looking down at their clasped hands. "No, I haven't talked to him. It's just more a general fear, I guess. I hate this waiting." She tipped her head toward her book. "Hence the reading. It takes my mind off things."

Jake patted her hand. "I'm sorry. I wish I could make things move faster."

"Me too."

He studied her, sensing there was more. "Is that all that's bothering you?"

She glanced away again, but nodded.

Jake wasn't sure he believed her, but it was obvious she didn't want to talk, so he wasn't going to push. "Okay. I'll leave you to your book." He started to stand, but she gripped his hand.

"Jake?"

He paused, halfway up, and sent her a questioning look.

"Thank you. For listening. And for caring."

A soft smile crossed his face. He traced a finger down her cheek. "You're welcome."

Twenty-Eight

Mackenzie held her breath, not letting it out until Jake walked away and she heard the inner garage door close as he went outside. She was glad he didn't ask more questions. And that he gave her an excuse for her attitude. She didn't really lie when she said it was Jorgensen worrying her. He was. But what had her out of sorts was her reaction to Jake. When he came into the kitchen, dripping sweat from his run, she'd wanted to strip his shirt off and watch the beads roll down the dips and valleys of his torso. Then, when she went to collect his clothes, she'd heard the shower running and couldn't stop herself from picturing him naked, water and soap sluicing over his powerful body.

Huffing as the image filled her head again, she picked up her book and opened it, flipping pages until she found the one she left off on. Words scrambled in front of her eyes as her mind wandered. Apparently, reading was only good once as a way to distract herself from thoughts of Jake naked and wet.

She set the book aside and got up. Maybe activity would help. She was tempted to get on the treadmill. But then she'd need a shower and that would just remind her of Jake in all his naked glory. Rolling her eyes, she found the broom. She'd just clean. And blast some music.

Turning on the speaker Jake had sitting on the counter, she linked her phone to it and found an upbeat playlist. A dance tune blared out, making her smile, the rhythm catching. In moments, she found herself singing along, her previous thoughts forgotten. Hips swaying and hair flying to the beat, she swept and mopped the floors in the common areas, then cleaned the kitchen counters and washed the few dishes they'd accumulated. By the time she finished, she was sweaty, but not overly so, and it was time to go.

Jake walked in as the song faded and she hung the damp dish rag over the sink divider. She glanced at him with a smile. He quirked an eyebrow.

"I heard the music from the garage. What were you doing?"

"Cleaning."

He grinned. "What happened to the book?"

She shrugged, drying her hands. "I lost interest. I needed to move."

"Well, whatever the case, it seems to have put you in a good mood, so I'm happy. Are you ready to go?"

"Yes. Let me get my purse." She hurried away to get her bag from her room, then rejoined him in the kitchen.

He took her coat from the hook and held it open. "It's chilly today, so you'll want this."

"Oh, thank you." She turned her back to him and slipped her arms into the sleeves. Heat that had nothing to do with the warmth of the jacket enveloped her as his hands lingered on her shoulders. She cleared her throat and stepped away.

Without a word, he opened the door, entering the garage. Mackenzie followed behind.

"Which car are we taking?"

"The SUV. It gets better gas mileage."

Mackenzie went outside, where the SUV was parked, and opened the passenger door, then got in. Once Jake was in and buckled, he started the vehicle.

"So, how old is your niece?" she asked once they were on the road.

"Sixteen months. She just learned to walk, babbles all day, and loves popsicles." Jake glanced at her with a smile.

She felt her mouth turn up. "Well, we won't be bored this afternoon."

He laughed. "No, definitely not."

The rest of the drive they spent chit-chatting, much like they did in the evenings. It made the journey pass quickly, and Jake soon pulled up to the curb in front of his sister's house. They got out and made their way up to the front door. Leanne threw it open before they had a chance to knock.

"Oh boy," Jake muttered. "She's got that look on her face. One that says she's glad she's leaving."

"Hi, guys! I hope you wore your running shoes." Leanne stepped back to let them in.

Mackenzie glanced around at the well-appointed home. Gleaming hardwood floors and light gray paint lent a neutral palette to the generous, two-story house. Squeals erupted from down the hall, bringing her attention back to Leanne.

The woman winced.

"She's in rare form today, isn't she?" Jake asked.

Leanne grimaced and nodded. "Yeah. Sorry. She's teething. Molars. I gave her some medicine, and she's been chewing on teethers all day. They've helped some, but she's still in a mood. It hasn't helped that her nap was shorter than normal because of it. Distract her as best you can." She started toward the noise, then rounded the corner into the living room.

In the middle of a pile of toys sat a dark-haired toddler. The girl held a block in each hand and screeched as she smacked them together.

"Ava, sweetie."

Pausing at the sound of her mother's voice, the girl looked up. A smile broke out on her face as she spotted Jake. She chucked the blocks and ran toward him.

"Unca!" Arms outstretched, Ava threw herself at him.

He caught her and tossed her in the air. Loud giggles filled the room. "Hi, sweet pea." He pulled her in close and placed a smacking kiss on her cheek. "You gonna hang out with me while Mama goes to work?"

Ava laid her little hands on his face and babbled. Leanne harrumphed, scrunching her face.

"Damn, Jake. If I'd known that's all it took to make her happy, I'd have called you early this morning." She put her hands on her hips and stared at her daughter.

Mackenzie chuckled. "Careful. You'll give him a big head."

Leanne waved a hand. "He's already got one of those."

Jake grinned, his eyes still on Ava. "Don't listen to them, sweet pea. Uncle Jake is as humble as they come."

Leanne snorted. "And on that note, I'm leaving." She patted Mackenzie's arm. "Good luck. With both of them." Turning to Ava, she kissed the toddler, promising to be back soon, then left.

Jake lifted the child higher on his hip. "So. What should we do first?" he asked the girl, then turned that bright smile on Mackenzie.

Something shifted in Mackenzie's chest. She'd been steadily falling for Jake Maxwell the moment they met, but the sight of him holding his niece, ready and excited to play whatever the girl wanted to keep her happy, pushed her over the edge. She swallowed hard and turned her attention to Ava before he could see the thoughts swimming in her eyes. "Why don't we bundle up and go outside? It's chilly, but not too cold for a little outdoor play. Fresh air always makes me happy."

"That sounds like a good plan. All right, kid. Let's find your coat. You wanna play out back?"

Ava squealed and clapped her hands. "Ow-sigh!"

"Yep, we're going outside." Jake walked into the hall and toward the rear of the house. "Leanne keeps all their coats in the mudroom."

Mackenzie's eyes went wide as they entered the kitchen. "Holy cow." The room was large, but that wasn't what made her stare. It was the six-burner gas stove and gleaming copper range hood. That and the enormous island topped with quartz and the huge apron-front farmhouse sink.

"Fancy, right?"

"A bit. I thought Leanne hated to cook."

"She does. But Bryce doesn't. They also like to entertain, and they congregate in here a lot."

He led her through the kitchen to a small room with an exterior door. Hanging on the wall, Mackenzie spotted a tiny teal coat with pink hearts. She picked it up. Jake squatted to grab a pair of pink, toddler-size rain boots.

"It's not that damp out, but she's a wiggly little thing, and these are easier to put on." He held them out to her with a grin.

Smiling and shaking her head, Mackenzie took the boots. She tucked the coat under her elbow and reached for one of Ava's legs. The girl wriggled, wanting down, but Mackenzie managed to get both shoes on her feet. Jake turned the toddler around, and she worked Ava's arms into the coat, then took her so he could zip it.

"She needs a hat." Mackenzie adjusted the girl's weight in her arms and glanced around.

Jake spotted one in a basket by the bench and picked it up, settling it over Ava's dark hair. "There we go. All set." He reached for the door and opened it, leading them out into the fenced yard.

Mackenzie took one last inhale of the girl's sweet, toddler scent and set her down. She took off for the small plastic play set in the far corner. An ache settled deep in her belly as she watched the girl play. She wanted this. A child, a family, to call her own.

Stepping closer to Jake, she wrapped a hand around his arm and hugged it, leaning into him. Her eyes still on Ava, she felt him turn his head, then he kissed her hair. A content smile tugged up the corners of her mouth. Yeah. She wanted this.

Twenty-Nine

"Jake!" The interior garage door slammed as Leanne entered the house.

Startled, Jake glanced up from building a block tower with Ava at the angry note in his sister's voice. He shared a concerned look with Mackenzie, then got up. "Leanne?" He walked into the hallway and only made it a few steps before she barreled around the corner from the kitchen, fire flashing in her eyes.

"What's wrong?"

"Where's Ava?"

"She's in the living room." He pointed behind himself, turning to see Mackenzie enter the doorway holding the girl.

"Mama!" Ava spotted her mother and wiggled in Mackenzie's arms. She set the girl down, who then sprinted to her mother.

Leanne scooped the girl up and squeezed her close. "Hi, baby."

"Leanne, what's going on? You sounded and looked mad. Now you just look relieved."

She huffed and shifted Ava onto her hip, her gaze going

between him and Mackenzie. "I had a visitor at my photoshoot."

Mackenzie groaned and Jake's stomach dropped. He knew what she was thinking, because he was thinking the same thing.

"Are you serious? I'm so sorry." Tears formed in Mackenzie's eyes. "I should just leave. Jake, can we go?"

Jake's heart flipped in his chest at the anguish on her face and in her voice. "Not yet. Let's find out what happened first." He looked at his sister.

She motioned them into the living room. "Let's sit down. Ava can play." The girl squirmed, already wanting down.

They retreated to the living room. Leanne set Ava on the floor, then sank into a chair close by. Mackenzie perched on the edge of the couch, and Jake sat down beside her, taking her hand to keep her from bolting. He had a feeling if they'd taken separate cars here, she'd have already left.

"Explain, Leanne. Please," he said.

Leanne blew out a breath and ran a hand through her hair. "We were wrapping things up. The mom from my shoot came up as they were getting ready to leave and said my husband could have joined us. That they wouldn't have minded if he watched from up close. I asked what she was talking about and she pointed to a man sitting on a bench behind me. I hadn't seen him because my back was to him the entire time, but the family noticed him. When I turned and looked, he smiled and waved. I didn't want to make a big fuss about it, so I just thanked her, and they left."

Ava toddled up to her mom and handed her a block.

"Oh, thank you, sweetie. Here, go put it in your tower." She handed it back to the girl, then continued her story when Ava went back to her blocks. "Freaked out about who was watching me, I hurriedly packed my gear, but I wasn't fast enough, and he came up to talk to me." She looked at Mackenzie. "It was your ex."

"You're sure?" Jake asked.

Leanne nodded. "Oh yeah. He identified himself. When he came up, he complimented my choice of locations for the shoot. I said thanks and asked if he was interested in booking a session for his family. That's when he told me he followed me here, hoping to get me alone so he could warn me." She rolled her eyes. "He told me his name and that he was your ex." She pointed at Mackenzie. "Said he heard about her engagement to my brother and wanted to make sure he and his family knew the kind of woman you were. A drug-addict and a con-artist."

She paused, taking a steadying breath. Jake's gut clenched as the feeling he wasn't going to like the rest of what she had to say hit him.

"He told me it would be a shame if something happened to my sweet little girl because my brother got involved with the wrong woman." Her voice ended on a whisper as emotion clogged her throat.

Mackenzie gasped and covered her mouth with her free hand. Jake cursed. He leaned forward, elbow on his knee, and ran his hand through his hair, mind whirling. What game was Jorgensen playing at? Was he just trying to isolate Mackenzie again?

"Anyway, you know me. I'm not one to be intimidated, so I looked him right in the eye and told him it would be, yes. But that I had faith in my brother and his judgement." Her gaze connected with Mackenzie's. "Honey, that man is shrewd. He knew right away I was on to him. I could see in his eyes that he understood my meaning. There was also a note of something else there. Something that said he almost viewed the whole thing as a game. That he'd accepted my challenge and it was game on." She shrugged. "I don't know. But it pissed me off.

How dare he use a child as a pawn in his sick game? And it is a game to him, I'm sure." She shook her head. "He doesn't care about you. He just wants to win. Wants the control."

Jake snorted. That was the truth. Everything about this guy screamed sociopath. He was in it for what he could get out of it. For the game, as Leanne said.

Mackenzie took a shaky breath, lowering her hand. "Well, regardless of why he's doing it, I'm sorry I've put you and Ava in danger." She tugged her hand free of Jake's and stood, then looked down at him. "I think we should go. That I should go."

"What?" Jake stood, facing her. "No. You're not running. I won't let you."

Anger flashed in her dark eyes. "It's not your decision to make, Jake. I'm putting a child in danger by being here. Do you really think he'd stop at threats? Because I don't. I've seen what he'll do to keep me. I don't want that happening again."

Jake glanced at his niece, then his sister, who watched the girl play, attempting to appear as though she wasn't listening. He was grateful she wasn't throwing her opinion into the mix. She had to be worried. He was worried. "Let's talk about this at home, so we don't upset Ava."

Mackenzie scoffed. "Yeah, that's who it'll upset." She shook her head. "Leanne, I'm sorry. But you won't have to worry anymore." Before either of them could say anything to that, she marched out of the room.

"Mack—" Jake huffed as she stormed out. A moment later, the front door banged closed.

"You better go after her." Leanne tipped her head toward the door.

He nodded. "I'm sorry."

"Don't be. Just stop the bastard. Then show her what real love is."

Mouth pressed into a firm, flat line, he nodded and walked out. Hurrying through the house, he ran outside. She stood by the car, arms crossed as she stared down the street. He pushed the button on the remote in his pocket to unlock the doors. She pulled on the door handle and got in without a word. Jake rounded the hood and climbed into the driver's seat.

"Mackenzie—"

She held up a hand. "Don't. It's not up for negotiation. I'm not putting that baby in danger. Take me back to your house so I can pack."

He growled. "Would you just listen?"

She turned to look at him. "Why? So you can convince me Ava will be safe? That you'll protect her? He murdered my family, Jake. I know he did. They're adults and couldn't protect themselves. How well do you think a toddler will fare against him?"

"My sister and her husband aren't defenseless. Leanne will fight tooth and nail—and knows how—to protect her family."

"But at what cost? I'm sorry, Jake. I can't stay."

Thirty

An ache like she'd never known filled her chest as she sat there. All the hopes and dreams she'd had for herself earlier vanished in a blink. There would be no loving husband, no children or family for her. Not until Brett was out of the picture. And she couldn't in good conscience stick around here and put little Ava in danger. Or Jake's family. Because that's who Brett would come after. It wouldn't be Jake. It would be everyone he held dear. He would seek to punish them both for getting involved. He'd want to tear Jake down as far as he could before he came for him too. It's what he did.

"Please drive," she whispered.

He sighed, hanging his head. After opening and closing his mouth a couple of times, he finally pressed the start button and put the car in gear.

She sniffed as he drove out of town and turned onto the highway that would lead them back to Foggy Mountain. Pain filled her heart as she thought of leaving Jake behind. It would crush her, especially at night in the dark when she had nothing else to distract her. But if it meant Ava stayed safe, she'd leave a thousand times.

The ride home was a silent one. Neither of them had anything to say that didn't involve her leaving, and she had zero desire to talk about it.

But still, the silence that filled the car when he shut off the engine in the garage was deafening. She yanked on the door handle, eager to escape it. At least with the hum of the car, she could pretend it was too noisy to talk.

Scrambling out, she waited for him to unlock the door and let her in, refusing to meet his gaze. Even without looking at him, she could tell he wanted to talk. It was in his posture and the way he hesitated to open the door. She said a silent prayer he would just let her inside and leave her to pack in peace.

He inserted the key in the lock and twisted the knob, walking in. Mackenzie followed, then skirted around him, heading for her room. She didn't bother to shed her coat. Her plan was to pack and then call a cab to take her to the bus station. She'd get a car wherever she ended up. She'd decided to sell her car last week after the mechanic found more problems with it, and it yielded a nice sum from the scrapyard. Plus, she had all her savings still. It was enough to set her up with a new identity and a cheap vehicle until she found a job that didn't ask questions. She should probably head south, where it was warmer. Maybe Louisiana or Texas. She'd need to stay in her car until she saved enough for the down payment on an apartment.

Crouching, she pulled her suitcase from under the bed and laid it on the covers, throwing it open. God, she hated the thought of starting over, but it was necessary.

"What are you doing?"

She glanced over at the sound of Jake's deep voice. He stood in the doorway, a fierce frown on his gorgeous face.

"What's it look like?" She walked to the dresser and

yanked open the top drawer, removing the pile of shirts stacked neatly inside.

He huffed and walked forward, taking the clothes from her hands and tossing them on the bed. "We need to talk about this."

"There's nothing to talk about, Jake. I said all I wanted to say on the subject at your sister's." She moved to step around him, but he snagged her hand.

"Well, I didn't. I don't want you to leave."

"Trust me, I don't want to go, either, but I have to."

"No, you don't. Let me do my job and catch him."

"With what evidence? Even if the autopsies conclude my family was murdered, do you really think there will be evidence linking him to their deaths? Because I don't. He's not dumb."

"I know that. But you need to give the process time to work."

"While he targets your family? No. I can't let more people die because of me. I should never have agreed to this plan in the first place. But I let my heart do the talking, and now your little niece might pay the price for that." Her voice broke as a sob wrenched itself free of her chest.

Jake tugged on her hands, attempting to draw her into his arms, but she pushed away. "No." She sniffed and wiped her face, regaining some control. "Just let me pack."

Silence stretched as he just stood there. She glanced up. Shock widened her eyes at the pain she glimpsed on his face. His gaze held hers, searching.

"I can't let you go, Mackenzie." He closed the gap between them, framing her face in his hands. "This isn't just about you anymore. It's about me too. I don't want you to leave." He closed his eyes and kissed the end of her nose.

Mackenzie inhaled a deep breath. Her eyelids fell shut and

need pulled at her. Need to be held. Need for this man. Need to have *someone* who loved her. A tear trailed down her cheek.

"Stay."

His warm breath brushed her face with the single word. Her need deepened. Oh, how she wanted to.

"I need you to stay." Voice thick, his hands left her face to cup her shoulders and trail down her arms until they wrapped around her waist, holding her close to his body.

Another tear tracked down her face. She looked at him, surprised to see a shimmer in his icy blue eyes.

"Please stay," he whispered. His breath puffed against her lips, setting off a firestorm in her veins.

Unable to form a coherent thought, let alone say something, she stood there, staring at him as his face neared. His gaze locked on hers. He paused just millimeters from her mouth as though questioning whether he should continue.

Her gaze went to his lips, then back to his pretty eyes. She swallowed, knowing the decision she was about to make would complicate everything. But she was powerless against the pull he had over her. He'd told her when the time was right, she'd know. That the fear would be gone, and the nerves would be about it being their first time together.

That's where she was at. There was no fear that she wasn't good enough. That she wouldn't please him. Desire washed it all away.

She closed the gap. Fireworks went off inside her mind at the first touch of their lips. Need exploded, wiping away every thought in her mind. She'd worry about the consequences later. Right now, all that existed was him. And her. The two of them together.

He wrapped his arms around her, pulling her tight to his larger frame. Heat traveled the length of her body. She felt a flush creep along her chest and up her neck. Sweat popped out along her hairline. It accompanied the tingles that raced along her nerve-endings. She moaned as the pleasure became too great to stay silent.

The sound galvanized Jake. His hands slid under her sweater, and he increased the intensity of their kiss. Mackenzie's hands shook as she speared them into his hair. Her body felt like she'd touched a live wire. Need zinged through her veins, leaving quivering muscles behind in its wake.

Jake walked her backward, and her legs hit the foot of the bed. She sat, pulling him with her. He hooked an arm around her waist and dragged her higher, pushing her suitcase to the floor. Mackenzie barely heard the thud. Her entire being was focused on what he was doing to her. It consumed her, from the placement of his hands on her ribcage and the thick thigh between her legs to the taste of him on her tongue and the soft feel of his mouth on hers.

Those silken lips left hers to trail along her jaw, where he found the pulse point at the base of her ear. She let out a little whimper as he nipped the skin, then soothed it with his tongue. Moisture pooled in her core, and her breasts tightened, the tips budding with a fierce tingle.

He shifted, straddling her, and moved his hands to span her ribs. They slid higher until he cupped her breasts through her bra. His fingers found the top of the cups and pulled them down. She moaned as he skimmed her hardened nipples. It turned into a ragged groan when he took the tips between his thumb and forefinger and tweaked them. Her hips rocked, just skimming the hard bulge in his jeans.

His breath caught, and his mouth crashed onto hers. A new energy gripped them as their passion flared. She found the hem of his sweater and thrust her hands beneath. Warm flesh over steel met her fingers. Muscles flexed and jerked at her touch. She counted ribs as she moved higher and spread her hands over his chest. Crisp hair tickled her palms.

Jake raised an arm and grabbed the neckline of his sweater,

yanking it over his head. Mackenzie's eyes went wide at the sight of the chest hovering over her face. The man was carved like Michelangelo's *David*. Only he was real. And she wanted to feel that hard, warm chest against hers.

She pushed him back and sat up far enough she could remove her shirt. It sailed over the edge of the bed as he tugged her back and reached for the clasp on her bra. In moments, she was naked from the waist up. But it wasn't enough for her. She wanted nothing between them.

His mouth closed around one nipple as her hands landed on his belt. Her fingers fumbled with the clasp, his ministrations short-circuiting her nerves so she couldn't perform the simplest of tasks. She tugged at his waistband, telling him silently what she wanted.

Instead of removing his pants, he reached for the button on hers. It popped free of its hole. The zipper on her jeans ticked down, and he thrust a hand inside. Mackenzie moaned loud and long as his fingers found her wet center and ran through her folds.

"Please, Jake." Her head thrashed on the pillow as he teased her soaked flesh. She couldn't take much more. His wicked fingers continued to work her, bringing her to a fevered pitch before one final stroke sent her over the edge. She let out a harsh cry and squeezed her legs together, trapping his hand.

The waves ebbed, and her muscles loosened. Her legs dropped open, and he removed his hand. She looked at him through eyelids like slits. He grinned.

"That was just the start." He curled his hands over the waistband of her jeans and underwear and tugged them down her legs.

Still numb from her epic orgasm, she could do little more than watch as he tugged the fabric free. Those pale eyes focused on the skin he exposed, and the hunger lit deep inside them.

"I'm going to taste every inch of you and make you come again. Then I'm going to bury myself so deep inside this sweet channel of yours you won't know where you end and I begin." He slowly slid one finger inside of her as he spoke.

Mackenzie moaned, and her eyes rolled back. *Holy crap.* Oh, that felt so good. Everything he described sounded so good. She wanted it all.

He withdrew his hand, and his weight lifted. She opened her eyes as he climbed off the bed and took off the rest of his clothes. When his erection sprang free of his pants, her core clenched. He was so thick. Her legs fell open a little wider, her body eager to feel him filling her. He noticed; his eyes turned a steely blue and moisture beaded on the tip of his shaft.

Feeling bold, she rolled and licked it off. When he moaned, she sucked him into her mouth and bit down gently.

"Dear God, woman." He grabbed a handful of her hair and pulled her away. "I won't last like that. Next time, you can do that." He pushed her back onto the bed, climbing over her again. "But I've got plans for you—for us—right now."

Mackenzie laid back as he caressed her skin. His hands and mouth seemed like they were everywhere at once. Touching her shoulders and along her neck. Down her chest and over her breasts. Biting her nipples and soothing the sting. At her hips, he kissed the points and skimmed the area between with his lips, then went lower, his tongue delving through the thatch of dark curls to find that sweet bud that would give her so much pleasure. An electric jolt flew through her at the speed of light when he touched it. She let out a shout and bucked.

He raised his head, grinning. "Like that, did you? Let's see what else I can find." He put a hand on both of her knees and spread them apart, holding them down.

She moaned again as he licked her. Her legs twitched, wanting to move, but he held them still. It only heightened her pleasure. "Jake." Her whispered pant did little except urge him to continue. He found that bundle of nerves again and sucked it into his mouth, teasing it with little flicks of his tongue. Heat suffused her skin, and she spiraled higher. When she was near the top, he stopped. A protest formed in her head, but died in her throat as he thrust his tongue deep inside of her. He let go of one knee to use his thumb to stroke her heated flesh and drove her over the edge.

Mackenzie broke with a scream. Light brighter than the sun burst behind her eyelids as waves of pleasure rolled over her with an intensity she didn't know was possible.

Before she could come down, he shifted, and she felt his shaft touch her entrance. Her body wept more at the touch. He slid inside, giving rise to another climb up that gilded hill.

Jake groaned as he pushed in, fully seating himself. She wrapped her legs around him, taking him just that little bit deeper.

"Mack. I need to move. Are you okay?"

"Yes. So okay."

His answer was to pull back and thrust deep. They both moaned. She'd been right about how good he'd feel inside her. He stretched her to her fullest and created a delicious friction. It wouldn't be long and she'd be toppling over the precipice again.

She neared the top, and Jake paused. Mackenzie groaned. "Why? I'm so close."

"I know." His voice was a deep growl. "I'm not." He lifted her, keeping her seated on him as he rose to his knees, changing their position. "I need a little more."

Her eyes rolled up again as he hit a different spot. She gasped. "This isn't going to slow me down."

Jake hummed and pumped into her once. Her walls

gripped him and a fine tremor went through her. She felt like a coil ready to snap.

He slid free and spun her.

"Jake?"

His hands guided her to sit on his lap, facing away. He curled around her back, wrapping one arm around her waist. She felt his other hand beneath her as he grabbed his shaft and lined himself up with her entrance. He thrust up as he pressed her hips down, joining them once again.

The new angle slowed down her ascent and gave him a chance to catch up. She felt him swell within her. The extra pressure created that little bit of heightened friction she needed to send her over the edge. Her breath caught, and she tumbled over the top with a shout.

His hands squeezed her breast, and he growled in her ear. Pumping harder, he held her tight until his muscles went slack. They toppled over onto their sides into a heap, chests heaving as they caught their breath.

As her mind came down out of the clouds and her body cooled, reality came back. Tears pricked her eyes, and she was thankful she still had her back to Jake, so he couldn't see. That was wonderful and like nothing she'd ever experienced, but it couldn't change anything. She still couldn't stay. For his sake and for his family's, she had to leave. Brett wouldn't stop. He'd hurt anyone he thought necessary to get her to toe the line. She wouldn't give him the fodder. Better he only ruined her life.

But Mackenzie would never forget this goodbye. It would have to be enough to keep her content for the rest of her life.

So, she blinked away the moisture and rolled over, pressing a tender kiss to Jake's lips. Tonight, she'd pretend that she wasn't leaving before the sun came up. And that she had a future with this man she'd fallen head over heels in love with.

THIRTY-ONE

Jake opened one eye as Mackenzie slipped out of bed. She tiptoed toward the door. Part of him hoped she just had to pee, but she dashed that hope when she came around and slowly closed her suitcase and lifted it off the floor, carrying it with her into the hallway. He stayed silent as she slipped back into the room and came over to his side of the bed, stopping beside him for a moment. He struggled to maintain his even breathing; he didn't want to clue her in yet that he was awake.

After a moment, she brushed the sheet near his hand with her fingers, then walked to the dresser, opening it again to pile the rest of her meager belongings into her arms, then tiptoed out of the room.

He couldn't believe she was leaving after all they shared the last few hours. But he also wasn't surprised. She'd been adamant that she didn't want to put his family in danger. He didn't like it, either, but running away wasn't the answer. Like it or not, they'd be in danger long after she left. Brett had to know she had feelings for him. Just because she left didn't stop how she felt. Hurting Jake or his sister or niece would still hurt her, even if she was long gone.

The door to the bathroom in the hall clicked closed, and he sat up. Determination filled him, and he got out of bed. She wasn't going anywhere without him. Hell, she wasn't going anywhere at all.

He crossed to his room and quickly dressed, then went to the living room and stood in the shadows to wait. She probably wouldn't be long. She'd want to be out of here as quickly as she could. The longer she lingered, the greater the chance he'd wake up and find her missing.

Five minutes later, she padded down the hall in her stocking feet. She set her suitcase near the door, then took her phone from her pocket.

"Need a ride?"

She shrieked and jumped. The phone flew from her hand to clatter to the floor. "Jesus criminy, Jake." She laid a hand over her heart and glared at him for a second before she bent to retrieve the device. "Why are you hiding in the shadows?"

"Why are you leaving in the middle of the night?" He pushed away from the wall to walk over to her, stopping just inches away.

She craned her neck to look up at him, fire flashing in her eyes. "You know why."

He nodded once. "Still doesn't change the fact that it's a bad idea."

She opened her mouth, but he laid a finger over her lips to stop the words she wanted to say.

"It is. And if you'd bothered to listen to me last night instead of being so stubborn, you'd know why I think so."

With a huff, she crossed her arms and lifted an eyebrow.

He removed his hand and mimicked her pose. "Leaving won't change anything. If Jorgensen can't find you, what makes you think he won't come after me or Leanne and Ava or my mom?"

The first hint of hesitation crossed her features. Jake pressed on.

"He knows there are people in this world you care about. People you'd do anything to protect. He'll exploit that weakness whether you're here or five hundred miles away. You can't run from him this time, Mackenzie. It's time to fight."

She stared at him for a moment, then looked away. A furrow erupted between her brows, and she chewed on a corner of her lip. Then her face crumpled, and she sniffed, a tear trickling out of one eye.

"I never meant for any of this to happen. I don't want you or your family to get hurt because of me." She looked at him. "What do I do, Jake? How do I keep them safe? The only thing I can think of is to give him what he wants." She took a shaky breath. "Or take away what he wants."

"What?" Fear like he'd never known sucker-punched him. He grabbed her arms and gave her a little shake. "No. I don't ever want you to even contemplate that again. That's not the answer to this. I know you feel like you're out of options, but you're not. Please let me do my job and stop him." A hot wetness splashed onto his cheeks.

More tears trailed down her face as she looked into his eyes. She reached up and swiped away the moisture on his face. "I've never had anyone outside my family care about me the way you do. I don't deserve you. Your kindness. I've brought nothing but danger to your life."

Jake framed her face and sniffed, fighting back more tears. He didn't mind her seeing him cry. But the emotion would make it nearly impossible to talk. And right now, he needed his voice. "No, you've brought so much more. You've brought laughter and purpose. And you've showed me that there's more to life than what I had. I've always wanted what my sister has, but I've never found someone I thought I could have that with until I met you. You can run to the ends of the earth, but I will never stop fighting for you. Your life doesn't have to be loveless. And even if I can't convince you to stay, my love will follow you. I love you, Mack."

Her breath hitched. "What? No. You can't. Jake, I—"

He laid a finger over her lips again. "Nothing you say can change the way I feel. Just accept it." He shrugged. "Or not. It still won't change."

She frowned and grabbed his finger, pulling it away. "Will you still feel that way if Ava dies because of me?"

"Yes. Because it's not your fault. None of this is your fault. It's Jorgensen's. You didn't do anything wrong. And we can't help who we love. If you want to blame yourself, you need to blame me too. It'll be as much my fault as yours if something happens to her, because I fell in love with you."

"God, don't say that. Now I feel worse." She thrust a hand into her hair and spun away.

He reached for her and spun her back, holding her close. "Don't. Stop beating yourself up. We're going to get through this. Jorgensen will make a mistake. And I'll be there to catch him when he does. I want a life with you. Is that what you want?" He held his breath. Yesterday, he would have been sure she'd say yes. But today?

Her watery gaze held his. Finally, she gave him a shaky nod. "Yes," she whispered. "I love you too."

Jake's heart flip-flopped, then double-timed as elation took over. "Then stay. And trust the process."

Indecision lit her eyes, and she chewed on her lip. "I hate that you're right. Not because it's you, but because of what it means." She swiped her face, dashing away the tears, and sniffed. "But you *are* right. He'll take away everything I love if he has to. And I can't let him do that again."

He wrapped a hand around the back of her head and

tipped it forward to press a kiss to her forehead. "We won't."
He pulled back and angled her face. "And in the meantime, no
more letting him dictate how you live your life. Live it."

She smiled. "I think we started that last night."

He grinned. "We did. And it was spectacular. I'm game to
do it again any time you want."

A blush stained her cheeks, but she held his gaze. Jake
stroked her cheek. "If fact, I think we should make it a perma-
nent arrangement."

She froze in his arms. "What?"

Jake found her hand and lifted it, his thumb nudging the ring
on her finger. "I intended to replace this with a better one and ask
you to marry me for real once this situation was resolved. What if
we skip a few steps and go straight to starting a life together?"

Her eyes went wide, and Jake could feel the faint tremor
go through her fingers. But what he didn't see on her face was
rejection. She was thinking about it.

"You want to get married? Now?"

He nodded. "I don't see any point in waiting. You caught
my attention the first time I talked to you at the motel back in
March. You've captivated me since. I want to spend my days—
and my nights—with you. Have little Avas of our own. Grow
old together."

Moisture shimmered in her eyes again. "That sounds
nice." She wiped her face again, a sparkle entering her eyes.
"Start living, huh?" She sniffed. "That's all I've really wanted
for a long time now. Is to live."

"Then live. Marry me, honey."

A pretty smile wreathed her face. Hope sparked in Jake's
chest. She splayed her hands over his chest, then ran them up
to his shoulders and around his neck, pressing close. "I guess
we do already have our license. It would be a shame to waste it
and then have to get another one later."

He grinned. "It would." Jake wrapped his arms around her waist and lifted her, bringing her lips to his level. "So, is that a yes?"

She nodded, leaning closer. "Yes."

Jake closed the distance and fused his mouth to hers. An inferno erupted between them, igniting the intense passion they shared only hours ago. This time, it had a new dimension, though. The love they felt for each other was on full display, no longer hiding in the shadows. It made the need, the heat, that much more intense.

He broke off, breathing hard, and rested his forehead against hers. "I'm really glad you said yes. Because I think we already started working on having little Avas earlier." That had been careless, but they'd both been so caught up in the moment. The thought hadn't occurred to him to glove up until he'd been buried deep inside her. He wasn't sure she thought of it at all.

Mackenzie's eyes went wide. "We did, didn't we?"

A little of Jake's ardor cooled at the shock in her voice. He pulled back so he could see her face. "Are you okay with that? I mean, the horse is already out of the barn, but—"

She kissed him, silencing the flow of words from his mouth. When she pulled back, a bright smile covered her face. "I'm fine with it. The timing is terrible, but seeing you with Ava, imagining what could be—I want that. If I'm going to live, I'm going to do it right."

"Full-steam ahead?" A corner of his mouth quirked.

"Yep."

"Fine by me. Wanna try again?"

In answer, she stepped back and whipped off her shirt. Jake drank in the sight. His woman was beautiful. She had small curves, her body lean—leaner than it probably should be —but her skin was flawless. It made him want to explore every inch again, this time looking for even the most minute imperfection. He was betting he wouldn't find any.

She unsnapped her bra and let it fall to the floor. He swallowed, his mouth watering as she exposed her pert, rosy nipples. He wanted—needed—to taste them again. Taking her torso in his hands, he bent his head and latched onto one. It was as sweet as he remembered. So was her little moan of pleasure.

Eager to see what other sounds he could get her to make, he dropped his hands to her jeans and quickly unfastened them, pushing them down. She kicked her feet, ridding herself of the restrictive fabric. He lifted his head to stare at her again.

"Take off your panties." His voice was a low growl.

She hooked her thumbs in the waist and shimmied her hips, pausing to look at him, a coy smile on her face. "Am I going to be the only one naked?"

Growling again, Jake stripped out of his t-shirt and removed his pants; he hadn't bothered with underwear. Once they were both naked, he grabbed her, lifting her against his body, and walked forward until her back hit the wall.

She let out a little grunt as they landed, her hands clutching his shoulders and hair. Jake nipped and licked at her neck.

"We're not going to make it back to the bedroom."

"Good." She framed his head in her hands and lifted his face to hers to latch onto his mouth.

Tongues tangling, Jake skimmed his hands down her sides to grasp her hips, kneading the firm flesh of her butt in his hands. Going lower, he wrapped his palms around her thighs and lifted, spreading her legs wide and stepping between them. She let out a little shout of surprise and pleasure as he bumped against her entrance.

Jake grasped his shaft, lining himself up, then thrust into her. He knew they were moving fast, but he couldn't wait.

Mackenzie didn't seem to want to, either. She let out a long groan and ground against him, twisting her hips to increase the friction.

It was enough to unleash the last of his restraint. He grasped her waist, pushing her against the wall, thrusting hard. The sound of skin against skin filled the room, a wonderful accompaniment to her soft sighs and his growls. In moments, they were flying high. Jake wanted the interlude to last, but was too far gone to slow down. Next time, he'd take things slow.

His climax broke like a deluge. The waterfall crashed over his shoulders, leaving a roar in his ears. It took him a moment to realize that was him expressing his pleasure. Mackenzie's own high-pitched shriek as she tumbled over the mountain joined in. As the sound faded, so did the starch in Jake's legs. He gathered her close and sank to the floor, their bodies still entwined.

"Holy crap. I think I died." Mackenzie laid her head on his chest, sucking in air.

He chuckled with what little energy he had left. "Same, baby." He stroked her hair, feeling his heart thump. "We should probably move."

Weakly, she waved a hand. "Soon."

Jake chuckled again. "Sounds good."

Thirty-Two

Humming to herself, Mackenzie rolled the vacuum out of room 227. She had one more room to clean and she was out of here. Then she was off until Monday and headed to the airport to pick up her friend, Piper. The other woman was flying in for Mackenzie's wedding this weekend. Excited didn't begin to describe how she felt. It had been three years since they'd seen each other. Mackenzie never thought she'd see her again, actually. That she'd just be on the run until Brett moved on to some other poor woman or he died.

She set the vacuum next to her cart and grabbed two trash bags.

"You've been avoiding me."

Her good mood soured at the sound of Brett's voice behind her. She glanced over her shoulder, scowling, but said nothing. Turning back to her cart, she took some fresh towels from the stack and turned toward the room. Before she could cross the threshold, he grabbed her arm. Fury gripped her. She turned a heated glare on him. "*Don't* touch me."

Surprise flickered in his eyes so quickly, Mackenzie wasn't

sure she didn't imagine it. But he released her, holding up his hands.

"I just want to talk."

She rolled her eyes. "Sure you do. Like you 'talked' to Leanne and told her I was a drug-addict? She didn't believe you, by the way. I have work to do." She stepped into the room and slammed the door in his face. He'd probably stand there and stew, but she was done being afraid of him. Jake was right. It was time to stand and fight. Brett had taken away enough of her life.

It only took her a minute to replace the trash bags and gather the dirty towels. She hoped he'd be gone when she came out, but knew she couldn't get that lucky. Reaching for the doorknob, she hesitated as an idea struck her. She took her phone from her pocket and opened the camera app. Setting it to video mode, she pressed record, then stuffed it down into her pocket with the microphone port sticking up. With a quick twist of her hand, she opened the door.

Brett stood by her cart, his expression hard and his hazel eyes flinty. Oh, yeah. He was pissed.

Good. They needed him to make a mistake, and she wasn't above goading him into it. She resisted the urge to snort. Her wedding this weekend would probably do that easily. But if she could get something on record now, maybe she could enjoy the day without a cloud hanging over her head.

"Still here?" She tossed the trash bags into her bin and the dirty towels into the laundry bag hanging on her cart. "I don't know why you're hanging around. We've got nothing to say to each other. I'm done with you, Brett. You won't persuade me to come back or trick me. I've wised up, and I found my confidence again. Not to mention a man who loves me." She grabbed onto her cart, backing up so she could steer around him.

He slammed a hand down on it, holding it in place. She met his angry gaze with one of her own.

"Make no mistake, Mackenzie. You will come back to me. Jake Maxwell is but a bump in the road to our future together. When he's out of the picture, and you've sunk so low that you see no other way to live, you'll come running. And I'll be there to welcome you back. After some groveling from you, of course."

She snorted. "I will never sink that low. You took everything from me. I've gotten my life back in spades, and I don't intend to willingly give it up again."

"I can take it all again. You think your defiance will make me stop? You're mine, Mackenzie. And when something's mine, I keep hold of it. No matter what. So, you have your little rebellion, but one day soon, you'll see that with me is the only way you'll survive."

"You're delusional, and I'm done talking. Move, or I'll call the police."

He raised an eyebrow. "You think your manager will like the police showing up here? Doesn't he try to keep the riff-raff out?"

She shrugged. "I don't really care. He can fire me if he wants. I'll get another job." She gave him a saccharine smile. "I can use my real name now."

The fire in his eyes burned brighter. She was really getting under his skin.

He leaned closer, malice written all over his face. "Careful, Mack. Don't forget what happened the last time you challenged my authority."

Her heart thumped wildly in her chest. Not from fear, but from the fact he basically acknowledged he'd killed her family. "Oh, I'll never forget. Where do you think I got the courage to leave you?" She leaned in, putting her face close to his. "Move," she growled, giving the cart a small shove.

Twin pops of red broke out on his cheeks, and the muscles in his jaw twitched. He held her gaze a moment longer, then straightened, moving to the side. "We're not done."

"Oh, not by a long shot." She pushed her cart forward, keeping her spine straight as she went to the last room on her list. She didn't look back as she grabbed what cleaning supplies she needed and went inside.

A smile broke out on her face as the door closed behind her. Damn, that felt good. Deciding she wanted to really live her life—Brett and his scare tactics be damned—was liberating. She wouldn't lie to herself, though, and say she wasn't worried about the consequences of her actions just now. She most definitely was. But she couldn't stand there and let him think he had a chance in hell of getting her to cooperate and come back quietly. He'd have to drag her kicking and screaming. And she'd never be the meek, submissive woman she used to be ever again. Not now that she recognized him for the monster he was and had the confidence to stand up to him.

After stopping the recording on her phone, she got to work. This room was a little messier than the last one, but it wasn't bad. She cleaned the bathroom and stripped the bed, then changed the sheets and ran the vacuum, replacing the trash bags and towels last. Finished, she let out a long breath, glad to be done. Stowing the cart and vacuum in the upstairs cleaning closet, she walked down the steps and headed for the office.

Pushing through the door, her manager looked up as she entered. She waved at him as she crossed to the door marked "Employees Only."

"All done?" he asked.

"Yep. Thanks again for giving me tomorrow and the weekend off."

"Well, it's not every day a girl gets married." He smiled. "You sure you don't want more time?"

"I'm sure. Jake can't really get away from work for long right now. We'll take a honeymoon later." She opened the door. "See you Monday."

He lifted a hand, and she walked through, shutting the door behind her. Opening her locker, she removed her purse and coat, then exited through the back door, making a beeline for the black SUV idling in the employee lot. She grinned as she spotted Jake behind the wheel and hurried over.

"Hi," she said, climbing inside.

"Hey, yourself." He leaned over the console to give her a quick kiss. "How was your day?"

"Interesting." She briefed him on her encounter with Brett and the threats he made as they pulled out of the lot.

He glanced at her, alarmed. "He threatened you?"

She waved a hand. "Sort of." She took out her phone. "Here. Just listen." Hitting play, she raised the volume and held the device up, hoping the audio was decent.

Jake's face hardened as the recording went on. When it finished, he looked like carved granite, but admiration shone from his eyes. "Well, you certainly poked the bear."

"It's what we want, right? I just hope he comes after me and not anyone else." That was truly her only fear. That he'd go after Leanne and Ava.

"Yeah. I'll call Leanne and Bryce later and tell them to stay vigilant. But I think he's more likely to come after me. I'm the real threat. He probably thinks if he takes me out, it'll be easy to scoop you up and run off with you." He glanced at her. "Maybe we should work on those self-defense moves a little more later."

"I wouldn't mind that." She'd been practicing the ones he'd already showed her, but would love to know more.

Jake's head bobbed. "Okay, good. I'd like to know you can put up a fight if need be."

She liked that idea too. It would be nice to have the skills to defend her newfound confidence. "Works for me."

He tangled their fingers together and settled deeper into his seat as he turned the car onto the highway to Asheville. Mackenzie put her phone away and relaxed. Her troubles with Brett could wait. They were safe for now, and she was on her way to see her best friend.

The miles ticked by quickly. They made casual conversation, talking about Jake's day at work and the rushed preparations for their weekend wedding. After his proposal in the early hours of Monday morning, they'd wasted little time putting together a ceremony for the following Saturday.

Jake had talked to the magistrates and found one who was free. Once they had an officiant, the task was on to find a venue. Leanne volunteered her backyard. That was fine with Mackenzie. It was more private than the park, which is what she'd been thinking. Tuesday, she'd gone shopping with Leanne and Belinda for dresses. She was still amazed she found a dress that not only looked like a wedding dress, but didn't need any alterations. And she loved it. It made her feel feminine and pretty.

Traffic grew heavier as they entered the interstate system around Asheville. Jake maneuvered them through the exchanges to take them out of town to the airport south of the city. Forty-five minutes after they left Foggy Mountain, they pulled into short-term parking at the airport.

Mackenzie hopped out of the car, giddy with excitement. She glanced at her watch. Piper's plane would land any minute.

Jake chuckled and took her hand, leading her toward the terminal. "You're going to vibrate out of your shoes."

"I know, and I don't care." She laughed, happier than she'd been in a long time.

They entered the terminal and waited near baggage claim,

watching travelers come and go until finally, Mackenzie spotted Piper coming down the concourse.

"There she is!" She waved. "Piper!"

The tall, curvy blonde slowed, glancing around until her gaze landed on Mackenzie. Then, a wide smile split her pretty face, and she quickened her step.

Mackenzie broke away from Jake, meeting her friend as she stepped into the baggage claim area. She wrapped the woman in a tight hug as tears filled her eyes. "Oh! It's so good to see you!" She squeezed her eyes shut, holding them at bay.

Piper hugged her back just as hard. "You too, Mack. I've missed you so much."

Pulling back, Mackenzie dashed the moisture from her face and saw her friend do the same. "How was your flight?"

"It was fine. Introduce me to this fine hunk. Damn, girl." Piper gestured to Jake, who'd followed Mackenzie over, her eyes assessing every inch of his six-foot-two-inch height. "He's even hotter than his picture."

A sexy smile broke out on Jake's face, making Mackenzie giggle. Her fiancé knew he was handsome and could flirt with the best of them.

"Thank you." He tipped an imaginary hat.

Piper tittered. "Oh, please tell me you have a brother."

"Sorry, no. Just a sister."

"Drat." Piper smiled.

Mackenzie grinned. "Piper, this is my fiancé, Jake Maxwell. Jake, Piper Riordan."

He held out a hand. "It's nice to meet you."

"You too." She shook it.

"Do you have any checked luggage?"

She nodded. "Just one. I wasn't about to ball up my new dress into my carryon."

"Which one did you get?" Mackenzie asked as they turned toward the carousel. She'd seen pictures of several. Piper had done her part to sell their engagement before it became real and went dress shopping, posting pictures of the ones she liked to her social media accounts.

"The satin one in that deep navy. With the low neckline."

"Oh, nice." She'd liked that one the best too.

As they talked, pieces of luggage filtered onto the belt. Piper stepped forward to grab a bright teal hard-sided suitcase.

"Here, let me take that." Jake reached for the case.

"Oh, thank you." Piper smiled and passed him the handle.

Jake took it, then motioned to the carryon sitting next to her. She rolled it over, and he put it on top of the larger suitcase.

"That everything?" he asked.

"Yes."

"All right, then, let's go."

The three of them headed for the doors, passing through to the bright sunshine and chilly October air.

"Oh, it's warmer here than back home." Piper lifted her face to the sun and smiled. "We're supposed to get some snow tonight. I'm glad I'm gone." She laughed.

"That's something I don't miss about Amandale." Mackenzie smiled. "It snows here—and it can snow a lot—but the season is shorter."

Piper wrinkled her nose, glancing both ways as they crossed to the parking lot. "Lucky. Maybe I should move down here."

"I would love that." She had no idea if her friend was serious, but having Piper near would be amazing. "But what about your mom? Don't you want to stay near her?"

Some of the relaxed happy look on Piper's face faded. "Mom died. Six months ago."

Mackenzie gasped. "What? Why didn't you tell me?"

"Because I knew you'd want to come back for the funeral. Or that you'd send a card. Brett knew we kept in contact—or at least suspected. I see him at the store or in the park a lot. And I know Amandale isn't that big, but I run into him much more than anyone else. He always acts like we're buddy-buddy, even though I do the bare minimum when we interact. And he came to Mom's viewing. He spent several minutes looking at the flower arrangements."

Mackenzie groaned. "I'm sorry."

Piper shook her head. "Don't be. It's not your fault he's a nut-bag."

Jake laughed. "I like you."

She sent him a saucy grin. "I like that you appreciate my blunt nature. Not everyone does."

"Then that's their loss."

Mackenzie agreed. Piper was loud and bold and not afraid to speak her mind. She'd tried to warn Mackenzie about Brett after they started dating, but he'd already begun to make her doubt herself and her friends. With her quieter nature, it hadn't been a stretch for her to doubt that someone as lively as Piper would truly want to be her friend. So, they'd gradually stopped doing things together after work as Mackenzie doubted herself more and more. It helped that in the beginning, Brett filled the time with activities for the two of them. It gave her an excuse to turn down Piper's invitations.

But the woman never gave up on their friendship, for which Mackenzie would be eternally grateful. She wouldn't have had the courage to leave without her help.

They reached the car and piled inside after stowing Piper's luggage in the back. Jake pulled out of the lot, and they were on their way home. The two women talked, catching up, as Jake maneuvered the car through the highway system and got them on the road to Foggy Mountain. As they left the city behind, the conversation turned more serious.

"So, I know you said over the phone that things have changed between you two and that your fake engagement is no longer fake, but what's the rush?" Piper waved a hand. "And don't get me wrong, I'm excited. I just want to understand."

Mackenzie glanced at Jake. A smile curved one side of his mouth, but he didn't take his eyes off the road. She smiled back, then looked at Piper.

"When it's right, what's the point of waiting? If there's one thing I've learned, life's too short and too unpredictable not to grab any happiness you can." She looked at Jake again. "I love him. And he loves me. That's all we need."

"Oh!"

Mackenzie turned to her friend to see tears in her eyes. Piper waved a hand in front of her face and sniffed.

"I'm so happy for you, Mack."

"Thanks. I just hope Saturday goes smoothly." She wrinkled her nose. "I kind of riled Brett up the other day." She relayed what happened at the motel.

Piper's eyes grew wide and her mouth dropped open as Mackenzie talked. "Holy shit, girl. Who are you and what did you do with my quiet, never rocks the boat, friend?"

Mackenzie shrugged, a smile tugging at her lips. "She found her voice."

"About damn time." Piper leaned forward to look at Jake. "I'm doubly glad she met you now. I know you had something to do with this."

He glanced at her in the rearview mirror. "I just helped her to see what it meant to live."

Mackenzie nodded. "That's true. Being with Jake showed me the difference between what I was doing and what I really aimed to do. The life I was living—it was just survival."

"Well, yeah. But for a while, that's what was necessary."

"I agree. It's not anymore, though. I'm done merely existing. I have the tools to fight back now."

"Awesome. I can't wait to see Brett's face when he finds

out you actually got married. That vein in his temple is gonna go nuts."

Mackenzie laughed, even as a pang of unease pierced her. It was more than just that vein popping that worried her about his reaction. Life could get rather harrowing soon.

THIRTY-THREE

Whistling, Jake shut off his computer, finished with the few tasks he'd needed to complete today. Ben gave him the day off to help Mackenzie with final wedding preparations, but he'd needed to stop in to check his email and update the prosecutor's office on a couple of cases. But now he was done, and he was going home.

He pushed back his chair and stood, grabbing his jacket off the back and swinging it around to put it on. Rounding his desk, he spotted Tristan coming down the hall from holding.

"I thought I saw your car in the lot," Tristan said. "What are you doing here?"

"I had a few things to take care of this morning, but I just finished." A slight frown drew down his eyebrows, and he tipped his head toward the hall. "Who'd you bring in?"

"Some idiot who thought it would be a good idea to pull out in front of me, then speed down the road at twice the legal speed. I'm glad I keep a cherry light in my truck." He shook his head. "When I pulled him over, it took me all of two seconds to realize he was tweaking out of his mind. I'm amazed he actually stopped."

"Me too. I'm glad you got him before he hurt someone." That could have been an awful scene. Tweakers were terrible drivers. Their ability to do anything at a normal speed was nonexistent, so they drove as fast as their brains whirled—light speed. "Do you need anything from me before I go?"

Tristan shook his head. "I think I can handle it. Go enjoy your last few hours of freedom."

Jake rolled his eyes. "Don't let Laurel hear you say that."

His partner chuckled. "You know I'm joking. I like being tied down. There's nothing better than walking in that door at night to her smile." He tipped his head. "Or her scowl. It depends on the kind of day she had with Wyatt. Lately, I've seen a lot of scowls. He's got some colic."

Jake grimaced. Ava had that when she was little. He remembered how much it wore on his sister and Bryce.

"Jake!"

At the sound of his name, Jake and Tristan turned to see Ben jogging toward them.

"I'm glad I caught you before you left." He crooked a finger. "You two come with me." He didn't wait for them to obey, just spun on his heel and hurried back to his office.

Jake shared a quick look with Tristan, then jogged after him. Their butts barely hit the guest chairs in Ben's office before he started talking.

"I heard from the medical examiner about Mackenzie's family."

Jake froze. "And?"

"He found evidence all three were shot before the car went off the road. Point blank through the chest."

"I knew it!" Jake pushed out of his chair to pace. "Did he find any evidence to connect anyone to the murders?"

"Actually, he found bullets in all three. They were good enough to get ballistics from."

"Was there a match?"

"Yes, but not to a gun with a name. The slugs matched to a murder of a young woman in Fort Myers, Florida just over five years ago."

Jake paused. "Just over five years, you say?" That fit their timeframe.

The twinkle in Ben's eyes said he thought the same thing. "Yep. On a hunch, I sent Jorgensen's picture to all the local police departments in the area down there. I got a hit." He flipped over a paper on the stack next to him and slid it forward.

Tristan took it. Jake came to stand behind him.

"Adam Young," Tristan read.

Frowning, Jake studied the grainy color photograph with the bio. The man was blonde and had a mustache, but the rest of the face was the same. It was Brett Jorgensen.

"I called the chief there and discovered Young was a suspect in the woman's murder. He'd been dating her sister."

Jake's gaze snapped to Ben. "Her sister? Did you talk to her?"

"No. She's dead too. Killed herself two weeks after the sister died."

Jake cursed and resumed his pacing.

"Is Young his real name?" Tristan asked.

"As far as I can tell, yes. I found his parents. They're still very much alive. I don't think they want anything to do with him, though. When I called them, I got the dad. As soon as I mentioned why I contacted them, he said they had no contact with Adam anymore and hung up on me."

"Is he still a suspect, or did they clear him?" Jake asked.

"He's still a suspect. The chief said he vanished one day. Slipped their surveillance and they never saw him again."

Jake snorted. "Yeah, because he moved fifteen hundred

miles away and reinvented himself. How did he get past the background check in Amandale? Cops are fingerprinted. And his prints would be linked to that murder case because his name is linked to it. It wouldn't matter if he changed it."

Ben picked up another paper. "Someone looked the other way." He held up the page, showing them an image of an older woman, then set it down. "I found out that the human resources director for Amandale retired suddenly around the time Jorgensen was hired. She then promptly bought a condo in Myrtle Beach, but died before she could move in. Heart attack."

"He paid her off." Jake paused, then glanced at Ben. "Where did he get the money? And how much did he give her?"

"Twenty grand. And from what I could dig up, he got an inheritance from his grandparents. They owned a fishing operation—quite a good one, from what the business filings showed—and sold it when they retired. Neither of them lived long after retirement, so the money got spread between their children and grandchildren. He got a hundred thousand dollars."

"Did he murder them too?" Tristan's voice was dry, and he lifted an eyebrow.

"I don't think so. Grandma died from cancer and Grandpa had a fatal stroke a couple of years later. He inherited the money in his early twenties. His issues in Florida didn't start until a few years later. I'm betting he murdered that human resources lady, though. But I doubt we'll ever know for sure. Her kids had her cremated and spread her ashes at the beach."

Jake scrubbed his hands over his face. "Can I go arrest his ass now?"

"Yes. Chief Baskin filed fraud charges on him this morning

and authorized extradition. There are likely others pending. The tie of the bullets used to kill Mackenzie's family to the woman in Florida—not to mention his uncanny resemblance —gave the chief probable cause to search Jorgensen's house."

"He didn't sell it?" Tristan asked.

"It's on the market, but not sold yet."

"I'm betting it's empty, then." Tristan leaned forward, planting an elbow on his knee and leaning his chin in his hand. "Which begs the question, what did he do with all his stuff?"

"Baskin was sending officers to check local storage places. If he finds a unit belonging to Jorgensen, he'll get a search warrant. My bet is he has that gun on him. So far, it's how he's eliminated threats." Ben looked at Jake. "He views you as a major threat, so I doubt he'd leave it behind. It hasn't failed him yet."

Jake nodded. "Well, it will this time. I'm not defenseless." His jaw muscles flexed as determination to bring the bastard down filled his soul. They finally had what they needed to stop the man.

"No, but you're still vulnerable. Watch your back."

Jake gave him a short nod and headed for the door. Tristan rose to follow.

"I assume you're going to the motel now?" Ben asked, making them pause. He didn't wait for an affirmation before he continued. "Take some uniforms with you." He held out a folded set of papers. "Arrest and search warrants."

Tristan took the papers.

"Be careful." Ben's green eyes held a deadly seriousness.

"We will," Tristan said. "I won't let him go off half-cocked."

Jake wanted to take offense, but couldn't. He was ready to barrel into Jorgensen's room, consequences be damned. Now he knew how Tristan felt back in March when everything went down with Laurel and that baby trafficking ring. His partner had been ready to pummel her captors into the dirt. Jake felt the same now about Jorgensen. He wanted the man to pay. "I'll behave."

"You better. We don't want him to walk because you didn't follow the rules."

His fists clenched. "Yeah, I know."

Ben nodded, then made a shooing motion. "Keep me updated."

Jake spun on his heel. He heard Tristan following close behind. They stopped long enough to get the desk sergeant to dispatch two units to meet them at the motel, then hurried outside.

"I'm driving." Tristan headed for his truck.

"Okay. I need to get my vest from my car." He loped over to his Porsche and popped the trunk, retrieving his vest and some extra ammo mags. Tristan pulled up next to him, and he got in. They squealed out of the parking lot as Jake fastened his seatbelt.

"You good?" Tristan asked.

"Yeah. I'll be fine. I know what's at stake." Knowing Jorgensen could go free if he acted rashly helped calm his emotions. He wouldn't step out of line.

"Good."

The drive to the motel was short. Tristan pulled into the lot and parked near the office. Two cruisers rolled up as they got out. Jake slipped his vest over his head as he got out of the truck. Tristan did the same. They met the uniforms in front of the vehicles and briefed them quickly. Once everyone was on the same page, Jake and Tristan went into the office to talk to the manager, who did little to hide his curiosity about what was happening right outside his window.

"Hey. You're Shay's fiancé, right?" the man said.

Jake nodded. "I'm not here about her. We need the key to room 113."

Tristan produced the warrants.

The man arched an eyebrow as he stared at the documents, not taking them. "It's not drugs, is it? I try to keep this place clean. This isn't that sort of establishment."

"No. No drugs. He's wanted on fraud." He didn't add their murder suspicions. No use riling the man unnecessarily.

"Oh. Glad it's not drugs." He reached under the desk and withdrew a set of keys. Finding the appropriate one, he took it off the ring and handed it over. "I don't know what good it'll do you, though. He checked out just a little while ago."

Jake glanced at Tristan. He could see on his partner's face that he was having similar thoughts—someone in Amandale tipped him off.

"Has anyone cleaned the room?" Jake asked. He knew Mackenzie hadn't. She was off.

"No, I don't think so. It's just Wanda today. And he checked out after the check-out time, so he wouldn't be on her list. I was going to let her know when she took her break."

"Okay, thanks."

"Yep. Make sure you bring that back." He pointed at the key in Jake's hand.

Jake nodded, and they left. Outside, Jake took out his phone. "I'm going to call Mackenzie and tell her to keep an eye out. This changes things."

Tristan nodded. "I'll call Ben."

Touching Mackenzie's name on his phone screen, he lifted the device to his ear.

"Hey, are you about ready to head home? Your mom's freaking out about the food. I don't know what to say to calm her down."

"It'll have to wait a bit. We got a lead on Jorgensen. And a reason to arrest him. I'm at the motel with Tristan serving the warrants."

She gasped.

"Someone tipped him off, though. The manager said he checked out about an hour ago. I need all of you to stay there and keep the doors and windows locked. Don't even go out in the backyard, okay?"

"Oh my. Okay. What lead did you get? Did the M.E. find evidence that he"—her voice caught, and she cleared her throat—"that he killed my family?"

"They were definitely murdered, but that's not what the warrant regards. I'll explain everything when I see you. I just wanted to give you guys a heads up that he knows were onto him. He might try something."

He heard her take a shaky breath.

"Yeah. Okay. We'll keep an eye out and stay inside. You be careful."

"I will. I'll see you soon."

"Okay. I love you."

Jake's heart squeezed. He'd never tire of hearing those words from her. "I love you too." Hanging up, he turned to Tristan. "You ready?"

He nodded. "Ben said to call him back as soon as we verify he's gone, and he'll put out a BOLO. We need to ask the manager what kind of car he was driving."

Jake nodded. "Let's check his room first. We can send one of the uniforms back to get a description of his car in a few minutes."

"Sounds good." Tristan motioned to the officers to follow him.

They walked down the row of rooms, then flanked the door. Jake put the key in the lock, then nodded to Tristan across from him.

Tristan banged on the door. "Sheriff's department! Search

warrant! Open up!" He waited several moments. When they didn't get a response, he repeated the process. Silence met them again, and Tristan nodded for Jake to open the door.

Jake turned the key, then the knob, pushing the door in.

Tristan swung into the doorway, gun drawn. "Sheriff's office!"

Weapon in hand, Jake followed Tristan inside, the uniforms right behind him. The main room was empty, which they expected. They advanced toward the bathroom. Tristan nudged open the door, which was already slightly ajar. Like the bedroom, it was vacant.

"We're clear." Tristan holstered his gun.

"Let's start searching." Jake put his weapon away. "Maybe we'll get lucky and he left something to tell us where he's going."

They spread out, turning the room inside out. Jake's frustration mounted as they found nothing of note. Jorgensen even took his trash with him. Tristan sent one of the uniforms to the office to get a description of Jorgensen's car, which he then relayed to Ben for a BOLO.

"Well, that was a waste of time." Jake stripped off his vest and tossed it into the backseat of his partner's truck.

"Can't win them all." Tristan's vest joined Jake's. "But at least we know someone's still feeding him information in New York. Maybe the police chief up there can find out who and get some useful information about Jorgensen's plan, or even where he's holed up."

Jake grimaced. "Yeah. In the meantime, though, Mackenzie and my family are in danger."

Tristan motioned for him to get in the truck, then climbed inside. "We can talk to Ben about putting a detail outside your house and your mom's. See if Asheville will put one on your sister's place. If not, I'm sure we can get some officers to volunteer."

Sighing, Jake fastened his seatbelt. "I don't like waiting. I want to act, but I can't because I don't know where he is or what he's planning. It's damn frustrating."

Tristan started the vehicle. "I get it. But we'll get him."

Jake sincerely hoped he was right. If Jorgensen slipped their net, someone he loved could pay the price.

Thirty-Four

Nerves fluttered in Mackenzie's belly. Her fingers toyed with the lace on the hem of her cream dress as she stared at herself in the mirror at Leanne's. She couldn't believe she was about to get married.

"You look so beautiful."

Mackenzie glanced at Piper in the mirror. The other woman smiled back at her as she stood just behind.

"Thanks. So do you." And she did. The navy-blue, knee-length satin dress with its wide straps and plunging v-neckline looked amazing on her friend.

Piper waved a hand. "Please. I've got nothing on you. Your dress is incredible."

Mackenzie ran her hands over her hips, staring at her reflection. She had to agree. The cream chiffon and lace concoction hugged her curves. Its neckline mimicked Piper's, but instead of a pencil-skirt style, it was tight through the hips, then flared in a modified mermaid style. She absolutely loved it.

When she'd seen it on the hanger at the store, it called to her. She'd hurried over, praying they had it in her size, elated when she hit paydirt. It only took one look in the dressing room mirror for her to know she found her dress.

There was a quick knock on the door, then Leanne poked her head in. "We're ready."

Mackenzie took a deep breath and nodded. She glanced at Piper. "Are you all set?"

"Yep. Are you?"

Taking another deep breath, she held it for a moment, letting the question filter in. Calm settled over her, and she let it out, a smile on her face. "I am, yes."

Piper grinned. "Then let's go." She picked up both bouquets from the box on the bed and handed one to Mackenzie.

Leanne pushed the door open, then led them to the stairs. "I want to get some pictures of the two of you before you go outside. Come stand on the stairs."

Mackenzie walked down several steps and paused. Leanne snapped some pictures, then motioned for Piper to come down and stand behind her. Once she had the more traditional poses, she went to the bottom of the steps, then told them to walk down, taking pictures as they came.

At the bottom of the stairs, she lowered the camera and smiled, eyes on Mackenzie. "Are you ready? Jake's practically vibrating out there."

A wide smile spread over Mackenzie's face at the thought. Her soon-to-be-husband was not a patient man, she'd discovered.

Leanne led them through the house to the back door. Through the glass, Mackenzie could see Jake standing under a tree, Tristan beside him. As she watched, he adjusted the tie at his throat and glanced around the yard, shifting his feet. She couldn't tell if he was nervous or just ready. Probably a little of both, just like her.

"I'm going to step out and get situated. When you hear the music start, Piper, you can come out."

Piper nodded.

"Where's Ava?" Mackenzie couldn't see her from her vantage point. The toddler was their flower girl.

"Bryce is right outside with her. She'll be ready once Piper heads up the aisle."

"Okay. Let's get this show on the road." She was ready to marry the man fidgeting in his sister's backyard.

Smiling, Leanne opened the door, stepping outside. All eyes swiveled her direction. Mackenzie stayed in the shadows. A few moments later, music filled the yard from the portable speaker they'd set up earlier. It played a soft, melodic guitar solo.

Piper glanced at her over her shoulder. "Here we go." A smile lit her pretty face, and she stepped through the door.

Taking a steadying breath, Mackenzie moved forward. She saw Bryce move toward the aisle, holding Ava. The little girl clutched a basket full of rose petals and watched the proceedings. When Piper reached the tree, Bryce put the girl down and pointed to Uncle Jake. They'd done a dry-run with the girl earlier so she'd know what to do. It was still fun to watch her walk and scatter the petals. She glanced around at the handful of guests as she walked, pausing to show them the rose petals, then squealing with laughter as she tossed them around. It took her several minutes, but she finally reached the tree. Belinda got up from her seat at the front and scooped up the girl, taking her back to the chairs to watch the ceremony.

The music changed to a guitar rendition of the wedding march. Mackenzie stepped through the doorway, eyes locked on Jake. A smile wreathed his face as he took her in. An answering one spread over her lips. She walked faster than they'd practiced, but she didn't care.

"Hi." She stopped beside him, drinking in the sight of him in his suit. Jake looked good in anything he wore, but his charcoal suit with its crisp white shirt and navy-blue tie set off his broad shoulders and powerful body to perfection. His icy eyes held a sparkle that was from more than the sun shining overhead.

"Hi." He took her hand, giving it a squeeze.

Their officiant stepped forward, smiling, as the music faded. "It's a lovely day for a wedding for a lovely couple. Thank you for asking me to—"

Piper stumbled half a second before a crack sounded. Mackenzie frowned and glanced at her friend. Her eyes went wide as she saw a red stain blossoming on Piper's chest.

"Oh my God."

"Shooter!" Tristan yelled. "Everyone down!"

Screams and chaos erupted. People dove for the ground. Mackenzie spun to help her friend, but Jake knocked her down and laid over her.

"No! Let me go! I need to get to her!" She pushed against his chest, but he stayed put.

"Tris, do you see the shooter?" Jake glanced back.

From under his arm, she could see Tristan sprawled on the ground. He'd produced a weapon from somewhere.

"No. Ben? How about you?"

The sheriff's voice came from the guest chairs. "Nothing." She heard the static of a radio, then him ask for an ambulance and a perimeter check. They were in Asheville, but several of his deputies volunteered for security for the wedding, knowing it could draw Jorgensen out. They'd alerted Asheville police of their concerns, she knew, and Jake told her the locals were going to increase patrols in the area today.

Mackenzie heard a radio squawk, then a tinny, garbled voice. She glanced at Jake. "What did they say?"

"They're checking the perimeter, and Asheville is responding."

"We need to get to Piper." Her friend lay on the ground, hand over her upper chest, grimacing. Blood seeped between her fingers. "She's bleeding."

He grimaced. "I know, but I don't want anyone else to get shot."

Tears spilled over her eyelids as she watched Piper bleed only feet away. "Please, Jake. Let me go to her." She pushed on his chest.

"Anyone see anything?" he called, not moving.

"Nothing yet," Ben said, his voice closer.

Mackenzie saw him move into her field of vision as he went to Piper. He took off his suit coat and balled it up, pressing it to her chest. Piper groaned.

"Hang on. An ambulance is coming."

"Good. This fucking hurts," she said through gritted teeth. "And I feel... like I can't catch... my breath."

Fear gripped Mackenzie. If the bullet pierced Piper's lung, it could have hit other structures too. She closed her eyes and prayed.

Sirens sounded, echoing through the neighborhood. Mackenzie opened her eyes, her prayers turning thankful that help arrived so quickly. Ben's radio crackled to life again. She didn't need to ask for clarification this time. The voice on the end was crystal clear when the man reported there was no sign of the shooter.

Jake got up, holding out a hand to her to help her to her feet. He glanced at Tristan. "Let's get everyone inside."

The other man nodded and turned to the crowd. "Everyone, head inside." He motioned for the handful of guests to get up and move.

"Let's go." Jake turned her toward the house.

"No." She dug in her heels and yanked her hands from his, dropping down beside Piper. "God, Piper." She took the woman's hand. "I didn't mean for any of this to happen."

Pain filled Piper's eyes as she looked at Mackenzie. "I told you... before. It's... not your fault." Her words came in short bursts as she struggled to breathe.

A tear slid down Mackenzie's face. She dashed it away with the back of her hand. "You're still hurt because he's after me."

"I still would... have come."

Commotion near the fence gate drew her attention. Paramedics came through, towing a stretcher and carrying multiple bags. She glanced down at Piper. "Help is here."

"Thank God." She closed her eyes. "This hurts."

Mackenzie backed up to give the medical team room to work. Jake came up behind her and wrapped her in his arms.

"She'll be okay," he whispered, holding her close.

She nodded, not trusting her voice. If she opened her mouth, she'd probably start sobbing. Instead, she leaned into him and watched the medics work. They cut Piper's dress, exposing her chest. One of them pressed wads of gauze to her wound to stem the bleeding. The other wrapped a blood pressure cuff around her arm. Once they had her vitals and had dressed her wound, they loaded her onto the stretcher.

"Anyone riding with us?" one of the medics asked.

"Me." Mackenzie stepped away from Jake.

"What?" Jake grabbed her hand. "No. Baby, it's not safe, and I can't get away from here yet to go with you."

"You mean like it was safe here?" She glanced at him over her shoulder, her gaze steady. He wasn't stopping her.

He scowled. "Maybe it was his plan to lure you out of the yard."

"Then I guess it worked, because I'm going."

"Mack—"

"No, Jake." She shook her head, taking a step toward the stretcher. The medics paused, listening to their exchange. "She's hurt because of me. I'm not leaving her alone. If he wants me, he can come and get me." She held up a hand when

his eyebrows slammed down and he opened his mouth. "But I don't intend to be reckless about it. I should be safe for now. The biggest danger will be getting to the ambulance. I'm sure one of Asheville's cruisers will follow us to the hospital anyway, so I'll have protection. And once we're there, I will stay in public areas at all times."

He sighed, scrubbing his hands over his face, then growled his frustration. "Fine." Spine rigid, he held her gaze. "Take your phone. Let me know when you get there. I'll keep checking in."

Mackenzie reversed course, taking his face in her hands to give him a quick, fierce kiss. "Thank you."

"Don't. You've no reason to. I may not like it, but I'm not going to stand in your way when you're right. The danger is minimal. You'll have cops all around you. But you can bet I'm going to put Kevlar on you. And maybe even a helmet."

"Deal."

A ghost of a smile emerged on his face. "Go get your phone." He glanced past her at the paramedics and tipped his chin toward the gate. "She'll meet you out front," he told them.

They hesitated, looking at each other. "Is it safe for us for her to come along?"

"Honestly? You're probably in more danger transporting your patient."

Piper groaned. "Thanks, handsome."

"Sorry."

Mackenzie patted Piper's leg, then headed for the house to get her phone, Jake right behind her.

"I'm going to run out to the car and get my vest for you. Don't leave the house."

"I won't," she said, backing toward the stairs.

He nodded and turned, walking into the throng of people watching from the living room. She ran up the stairs, snatching her purse off the bed in Leanne's bedroom, where she changed earlier, then hurried back down. Jake was nowhere to be seen, but that didn't surprise her. He probably had to give everyone an update before they'd let him outside.

"How are you holding up?" Belinda walked over, concern making furrows form on her forehead.

"I'm okay. Just anxious to get Piper to the help she needs." Moisture gathered in her eyes again. "I'm sorry, Belinda. For putting you all in danger."

"Hush." Belinda waved a hand, then pulled Mackenzie into a tight hug. "None of this is your fault."

Mackenzie sniffed, hugging her back. She so wanted to believe that. And in her mind, she did. But her heart kept telling her she was causing pain to so many people, even though logically she knew she'd done nothing to them. It was hard to reconcile one with the other.

The front door opened and closed. Mackenzie pulled back, sniffing again and wiping her face. Jake stalked toward her, a black bulletproof vest in his hand.

"They're about ready to roll." He held up the vest, pulling the sides apart and lifting it.

Mackenzie ducked so he could get it over her head, pulling her hair through so he could settle it over her shoulders. Velcro rasped as he fiddled with the straps, making sure it was secure.

He paused, staring at her, then brushed a hand over her cheek. "The perimeter is secure as far as they can tell. They still haven't found where he shot her from. If he's using a long-range rifle, he could still be out there. Though I doubt it. It was too close, and it sounded like a pistol shot, not a rifle."

Her heartbeat quickened. "Okay."

"We're going to go straight out the door to the ambulance. At a jog. No stopping. Duck your head and run."

She nodded, her heart double-timing now. Taking a deep

breath, she forced herself to relax. Freaking out wouldn't help anything.

Jake took her hand and led her to the door. "Ready?"

"Yes." She stared at the white wood, waiting for him to open it.

He twisted the knob, then walked through. Mackenzie stepped out behind him, holding his left hand. He had his right propped on the butt of his gun. Heart thudding in her ears, she tucked herself into his back and trusted him to lead her to the ambulance. Together, they ran down the front steps and across the lawn to the ambulance at the curb. He yanked open the side door, then stood back so she could step inside.

"Have a seat there." The medic closest to her pointed to a seat to her right that butted up against the driver's compartment. He eyed her vest with a wary glance, then turned back to Piper.

Mackenzie looked at Jake.

"I'll be up there as soon as I can. Pay attention to your surroundings. Note where all your exits are. Try to keep an eye on at least one security guard. If you see Jorgensen, raise a ruckus."

She nodded. "I will. I've been watching for him for three years. I'll see him coming."

Jake put one foot inside and leaned toward her, giving her a quick kiss. "I hope so. I still need to put a ring on your finger." He curled his hand over hers and squeezed.

Feeling teary-eyed again, she could only nod. With one last squeeze of her hand, he got out of the ambulance and closed the door. Mackenzie wiped her face and took a deep breath, composing herself.

Slightly more in control, she looked at Piper. Wires now snaked from her body to a monitor across the aisle and an IV was taped on the back of her hand. "How's she doing?"

"As well as can be expected." He glanced at his partner. "We're ready."

The man nodded and climbed out through the rear doors. A moment later, Mackenzie heard the driver's door open, then he got inside. She buckled up as he started the truck. The vehicle lurched as he pulled away from the curb. A moment later, the siren came on, then she heard a police siren and saw the cop car through the rear windows as it followed them away from Leanne's.

She closed her eyes and leaned back against the bulkhead, praying for a smooth ride. Something beeped, and she opened her eyes. The medic with them pressed a button on the monitor, then wrote on the clipboard in his lap. He didn't seem alarmed, so she stayed quiet.

Minutes passed as they screamed down the highway toward the hospital. Mackenzie alternated between watching the paramedic work on Piper and looking out the window at the whizzing scenery. She let out a little sigh of relief when the signs for the emergency department came into view.

The ambulance came to a halt, and the paramedic stood up. "You can exit through that door, then follow us in." He motioned to the side door.

She nodded and unfastened her seatbelt, standing. Phone clutched in her hand, she released the door latch and let herself out, meeting Piper around the back as the medical team removed her from the truck.

"You still doing okay?" she asked, squeezing her hand quick while the paramedics closed the ambulance doors.

Piper nodded, her eyelids droopy. "I'm okay."

Mackenzie offered her a watery smile, letting go of her hand as she was wheeled inside. Wiping her face, she followed.

Noise assaulted her as she walked inside the busy E.R. A nurse did a double-take at her, then hurried over.

"Um, honey, are you okay?" Her gaze wandered over Mackenzie's attire.

"I'm fine. The vest is just a precaution. It's a long story."

The woman's warm brown eyes turned sympathetic. "Okay. Why don't you come with me? I'll show you to the waiting room and make sure you get some coffee."

"That sounds great. Thank you."

She smiled and led Mackenzie down the corridor. Mackenzie pulled at the straps on the vest and slipped it over her head.

"You sure you should take that off?"

"Yes. It was just for the ride. While I was exposed outside. I don't plan on leaving this hospital anytime soon."

"Okay. Do you want a blanket to wrap up in? It's a little chilly in here."

"That would be wonderful, thank you."

"Of course." She paused at a door, then waved her hand over a sensor. The door swung out to the public area.

Mackenzie followed her down the hall and to the waiting room.

"I'll be right back with some coffee and a blanket for you."

"Thank you." She gave the woman a tired smile and went to find a chair away from others. She didn't want to talk.

THIRTY-FIVE

Mackenzie stared out the window in Piper's room at the street below. The sun was just starting to peek over the horizon, casting a golden glow on the world. She'd been watching the sky lighten for the last hour. Sleep had been elusive most of the night. Around midnight, they moved Piper to this room in the ICU after emergency surgery. The bullet tore through the top of her left lung, bounced off her scapula, then traveled down and nicked her left kidney. She'd lost part of her lung. They were hopeful she'd get to keep her kidney, though. Jake was also pretty certain the bullet they pulled out of her would match the ones that killed the woman in Florida and Mackenzie's family.

The door swished open, and she glanced over to see Piper's surgeon, Dr. Cullen Tate, enter the room. She offered him a tired smile. Jake stirred beside her, yawning as he stretched.

"Good morning." Dr. Tate walked to Piper's bedside.

"Hey, Cullen. I didn't know you were here today." Jake stifled another yawn.

Mackenzie frowned. "You know Dr. Tate?" He hadn't been here yet when the doctor came to see her. After they processed the scene at his sister's, he, Tristan, and Ben canvassed the neighborhood, along with the Asheville police, until they found the place where the shooter fired from. He'd broken into the neighbor's house, tying them up. Their attic gave him a perfect vantage point into Leanne and Bryce's backyard.

Jake glanced at her and nodded. "He's our coroner."

"Oh." A small frown furrowed her brow. "You can be a regular medical doctor and do that?"

Dr. Tate nodded. "I took some extra training to get certified. I saw a need in the county for a more experienced coroner, so I ran for office. I guess people agreed, because they elected me. I'm a trauma doctor by trade, though. I work here and at the small hospital in Foggy Mountain, rotating between them." He bent closer to Piper. "How's she doing?"

"Fine, I guess. She's been sleeping." Mackenzie leaned forward, resting her elbows on her knees as Dr. Tate gave Piper a small shake on her arm.

"Ms. Riordan? Can you open your eyes for me?"

Piper let out a soft groan. Her head rolled side to side on the pillow.

He jostled her arm again. "Piper?"

She let out another groan, but blinked, turning to look at him. "What?"

A smile lifted one corner of his mouth. "I'm Dr. Tate. Do you remember me?"

"No. Should I?"

"I introduced myself before we took you to surgery last night. I'm the one who operated on you."

"Oh. How bad is it?" She lifted her right arm and touched the heavy bandage over her chest. "I feel like I went ten rounds in a boxing ring and lost." She grimaced. "And I'm still short of breath." She touched the canula on her face, supplying oxygen into her nose.

"You lost part of your left lung and you've got a decent laceration in your kidney that I sewed up. I'm hopeful you can keep the kidney. We'll keep an eye on it and see if it recovers. You were lucky. That bullet missed your pulmonary artery by millimeters."

Piper blanched. "Good thing he missed."

"I don't think he did," Jake said, leaning forward, a thoughtful look on his face. "I think you moved. Shifted your feet or raised your arm. It was just enough to make his shot go wide. He's never left anyone alive that he's tried to kill, so why start with you?"

"You are just a ray of sunshine, aren't you?" Piper closed her eyes and leaned her head back.

Disturbed by the image Jake painted, Mackenzie got up and went to her friend's side, taking her hand. "I'm sorry."

Piper's eyes flew open. She speared Mackenzie with a green-eyed glare. "Girl, if you apologize one more time, I don't care if I can barely keep my eyes open. I will smack you."

Dr. Tate laughed. "That feistiness is going to serve you well the next few months as you recuperate."

"Months?" Piper's head swung around. "How long are we talking? I need to get home and get back to work."

"I would suggest you don't fly for at least a couple of weeks. Let your sutures come out. After that, you can go home. But you'll be off work at least another month after that to continue to heal. You'll likely need a little physical therapy as well for your shoulder. I had to cut through the muscle and spread your ribs to get to your lung. And the muscles on your back to get to your kidney."

She groaned. "It's not like I'm a factory worker or doing construction. I fill pill bottles all day."

"On your feet. You need to rest and get back to your normal activities in increments. Not all at once."

She glared at him, then looked at Jake. "When you catch Brett, if he's still alive, I want a piece of him. Bastard."

Jake grinned. "I'll keep that in mind."

Dr. Tate shook his head, an amused smile on his face. "You're going to do just fine." He lifted his stethoscope from around his neck and raised it to his ears. "I just need to check you out quick, then you can rest again."

She nodded. He pressed the bell of the scope to her chest and listened, then had her sit up so he could listen to her lungs.

"Oh, this is torture." She gritted her teeth as she leaned forward.

Mackenzie supported her arm and shoulder.

Dr. Tate straightened, putting the stethoscope around his neck. "You sound good. Let's check those incisions." He glanced at Jake. "You should probably step out."

"Right." Jake stood. "I'll go get us some coffee, Mack. You want anything to eat?"

"Not yet, thank you."

He pecked her cheek, then walked out.

"Are you all right with Ms. Brighton staying?" Dr. Tate asked.

"Of course. She's seen me naked before."

His eyebrows winged upward.

Mackenzie giggled. "Mostly naked. We went hiking one afternoon, and she slipped. Slid down a muddy hill, straight into a shallow river. Injured her wrist. I helped her out of her wet clothes when we got back to her apartment."

He shook his head again. "Your parents got all their gray hair because of you, didn't they?" He parted Piper's gown and reached for the edge of the tape holding her bandage on.

She grinned. "Probably." Her smile died as she hissed when he peeled back the tape. "Ouch. That's sensitive."

"Yeah. It's going to be for a while." He tipped his head,

looking at the wound. "It looks good, though. Let's check the other one." Pushing the gown out of the way, he peeled back the lower bandage on her side. "That looks good too. And your drain output is fine." He lifted the bulb attached to a tube coming out of her side, checking it.

"Awesome." Sweat glistened on her face.

Mackenzie frowned. "Are you okay?"

"Yeah. Getting shot wears you out." She closed her eyes, breathing harder.

"Rest now." Dr. Tate fixed her gown, then patted her good shoulder. "I'll be back tomorrow to check on you."

"Okay. How soon can I get out of here?"

"A week, at least. I don't want to push things. We need to monitor that kidney closely. You also lost quite a bit of blood. You need to rest and recover. We'll see about getting you out of bed later tonight or tomorrow, though, all right?"

Piper swallowed, then licked her lips. "Okay. Can I have some water?"

He nodded. "I'll have the nurse bring you a pitcher. You can start on some broth and gelatin too. If you handle it all right, I'll step you up to a light diet tonight."

"Good. I'm starving."

"That's a good sign." He glanced at Mackenzie. "Make her behave."

Mackenzie chuckled. "I'll do my best. No one controls Piper."

"I'm figuring that out." Smiling, he stepped back. "Get some rest. Both of you." Turning, he left the room.

"Well, that sounded promising." Mackenzie patted Piper's arm.

Piper snorted, then winced. "Ow. And you're a liar. Weeks I'm going to be laid up. I hope Jake knows I was serious. He better let me take a swing at that jerk before he puts him in jail.

This is dumb." She pointed a finger at Mackenzie. "And don't you dare say you're sorry."

Mackenzie held up her hands, then smiled. "I'm really glad you're going to be okay."

"Me too." She huffed a short breath and scratched at her face. "This thing is annoying." She nudged the canula with a finger.

"I know, but you need it right now. Once your lung has had a chance to get used to being smaller and to heal, they'll take it off."

Piper hummed and dropped her hand. "I know. It's still annoying. So is being in the hospital." She scrunched her nose and poked out her tongue before it brightened. "But Dr. Dreamy, there, makes it bearable."

Mackenzie laughed. "Leave it to you to think about men at a time like this."

"Did you see him?" She pointed at the door. "Men like him aren't supposed to exist in real life. Super smart, good job, sexier than sin—he should only exist on a movie screen." She made a face again. "I bet he's a jerk in real life. Or married already, and therefore wholly unavailable."

Mackenzie's laughter grew louder.

"Oh, stop laughing. You got your dreamboat. I'm still looking." She glared at Mackenzie, but a smile teased her lips.

The door opened again. "Boy, someone must be feeling decent. It's a regular party in here." A nurse walked in, smiling, a pitcher of water and a cup in her hands. "Dr. Tate said you were thirsty."

"God, yes. You only brought one?"

The nurse chuckled. "I'll get more if you drink all this. I'm Jeanette, by the way."

"Nice to meet you."

"You too." She set the cup on the tray at the end of the

bed, then tipped the pitcher, filling it. "I wish it were under better circumstances, but I guess that's the job."

Piper chuckled, then winced. "Oh, don't make me laugh."

"Sorry." Jeanette picked up the cup and handed it to Piper along with a paper-wrapped straw. "Do you want anything for pain? You're on a pump, and we've been giving you regular doses of pain medicine since you came out of surgery. But now that you're awake, it's all as needed, except for the aceta-minophen. We'll keep giving you that like clockwork."

"I'm all right for now."

"Okay. I'll let you know when you're close to being able to have another dose of the stronger stuff. We want to stay on top of your pain and not chase it. Don't be afraid to use that pain pump." She motioned to the IV stand next to the bed.

"I won't."

Jeanette gave a short nod. "Good. Drink that. If it doesn't cause you any problems, we'll get you some broth or Jell-O, okay?"

Piper tore the paper off her straw. "You have blue Jell-O?"

The nurse grinned. "Girl, I have them all."

"Get it ready." She slurped her water. "Oh, yeah, that's good."

Mackenzie rolled her eyes and giggled, happy that Piper was on the mend.

"So, now that I'm hydrated, can we talk about why you're still in your wedding dress?" Piper lifted a hand and motioned to Mackenzie's attire.

"I never left last night." She shrugged. "Jake didn't get here until late. By then, neither of us wanted to go anywhere, so we just sat on the couch and tried to sleep.

"Did you?"

"Not really. He dozed."

"Well, it's a shame to let the outfit go to waste. Or your hairdo. It still looks great."

Mackenzie touched her hair. How the curls were still bouncy after all this time, she didn't know. That mousse Leanne used to style her hair with must be the extra, extra-hold stuff.

Noise from the hall filled the room as the door opened again. Jake walked in carrying two cups of coffee.

"So, what's the verdict? Did Tate give you a clean bill of health?"

"He said I'm healing fine, but I'm stuck here at least a week." Piper eyed the coffee cups. "That smells amazing."

He frowned. "I doubt he cleared you for coffee."

Mackenzie took the cup he held out to her. "Don't mind her. She's starving. And high." While normally outspoken and gregarious, she doubted her friend would be this peppy without some serious painkillers propping up her mood.

Piper grinned. "I am. The world is nice and floaty. Hey. I have an amazing idea. You two should get married."

"Piper—" Mackenzie started, but her friend cut her off.

"There's a chaplain here at the hospital. Have him marry you. Don't let Brett win, Mack."

Mackenzie was all set to continue arguing until that last sentence. She closed her mouth and looked at Jake.

"It's up to you," he said. "I don't care where or when we get married, so long as we do."

"But what about your family and friends? If we invite them all up here, we run the risk of tipping him off that something's going on."

"They'd all understand if we told them after the fact. We can have a big party some other day—once we don't have to worry about Jorgensen ruining it. We can even have another ceremony if you want."

She frowned, studying him. "Do you want to get married now?"

"I don't care when we do. Whatever you want."

"That's not an answer." She wanted to know, one-hundred percent, what he wanted.

He huffed. "Yes. But only if you want to as well. We have everything here. Tristan gave me your ring back at my sister's. I think mine was in the pocket of Piper's dress, so it should be here. And the license never left the inner pocket of my suit coat."

She searched his eyes, seeing only love shining back. A smile bloomed on her face. "Well, I guess we should get married, then."

He took her hand, grinning widely. "I guess we need to find the chaplain."

THIRTY-SIX

Standing at the foot of Piper's bed, Jake stared at Mackenzie as the chaplain pronounced them husband and wife. He could hardly believe she was finally his wife. After yesterday, he hadn't a clue when they would stand in front of a magistrate—or a minister—again. Or if it would even happen. But they'd said their vows and exchanged rings. All that was left was to sign the license.

After their first kiss, of course.

He leaned in, savoring the feel of his wife's lips on his. *His wife.* Man, he liked the sound of that.

Pulling back, he noted the bright smile on her pretty face. Happiness made her dark eyes shine.

"Congratulations." The chaplain interrupted their moment.

Jake and Mackenzie turned to him. The man smiled and glanced past them at Piper and Jeanette, who they'd pulled in as their second witness.

"I present Mr. and Mrs. Jacob Maxwell."

Jeanette clapped while Piper softly cheered.

"That was great, and I'm happy for you," Piper said, then yawned. "Now go home. I want to rest, and I'm sure you two have better things to do." She waggled her eyebrows.

Jake saw Mackenzie blush as a grin broke out over his face. He could think of some things, yes. Starting with a shower. Together.

"I second my patient's advice." Jeanette's eyes widened, then she laughed. "Not the second part. Though I'm not saying you shouldn't." Her face turned scarlet. "Oh, go on. Get out of here and let her rest."

Jake laughed and tucked Mackenzie into his side. "Yes, ma'am. Thank you for being our witness."

"Of course."

"Ah, yes," the chaplain said. "We need to sign the license before you leave."

Jake took the document from his pocket, and with the pen Jeanette produced from her scrub pocket, the five of them signed the form.

"Would you like me to mail that?" The chaplain pointed to the paper. "I'd like to copy down your names and dates of birth into the little book I keep of all the people I've married."

"Oh, of course." Jake handed it to him. "Thank you."

"Certainly. It'll be in the mail by morning." He tipped his head. "Congratulations, again." Smiling, he left.

"We'll let you sleep." Mackenzie squeezed Piper's hand. The woman was already rapidly fading. Her eyelids fluttered even as she smiled.

Jake tugged on Mackenzie's hand, then waved to Piper. "We'll see you in the morning."

"Take your time. I'm not going anywhere for a while." She waved back.

"Oh!" Jeanette held up a finger. "You're going north, right?"

Jake nodded.

"A family member from one of my other patients said there was a wreck on the main road. You might want to find an alternate route."

"Okay, thanks for the heads up."

She smiled. With a final goodbye, they left the room.

In the hall, Jake grabbed Mackenzie around the waist and twirled her around, pulling her into his body. Grinning, he pressed his forehead to hers. "We did it."

She framed his face, stroking his cheeks. "We did. I love you."

Smile growing, he kissed her. "I love you too." He stepped back. "Come on. Let's go home and celebrate."

Hand-in-hand, he led her down the corridor to the elevators. They rode the car down to the first floor, then went outside.

"Oh!" Mackenzie hugged her arms around herself. "It's cold."

Jake paused, glancing at her. "Oh, crap. I didn't even think about you not having a coat. Here." He took off his suit coat and put it around her shoulders.

She grabbed the lapels, holding it closed. "Mm, much better, thank you."

Kissing her temple, he took her hand again and headed for his car. As they moved away from the hospital, it struck him, then, that in all the excitement, he failed to have her put on the Kevlar vest. Cursing to himself, he picked up the pace. Thankfully, he'd parked close since it was so late when he arrived last night.

Fumbling with his keys, he unlocked the car and helped her inside, glad he opted for the SUV. She'd have fun getting in and out of his Porsche in that dress.

"Are we ready?" he asked once they were both in and buckled up.

"Yep. Take us home, Mr. Maxwell."

He grinned. "As you wish, Mrs. Maxwell." With the push of a button, the engine roared to life. Air blasted from the vents, chilly. He dialed back the fan, so they didn't freeze before the engine warmed up, then turned on the seat warmers. Putting the car in gear, he pulled out of his parking space and headed for the exit.

Mackenzie turned on the radio, humming along as he drove. He was glad for the distraction. It helped pass the time and kept him from pulling off on some secluded back road and making love to his wife. She deserved better than the backseat of a car for their first time as husband and wife.

There was more traffic than usual on the windy mountain road that followed the river, but it was still sparse. He was glad; it meant he could go just a tiny bit faster.

Rounding a bend, movement on the side of the road drew his attention. His brain registered a man about the same time he whipped something into the road. Jake slammed on the brakes, but couldn't stop. He heard a pop. A few seconds later, his steering turned sticky, and the tires made thumping sounds.

"Shit!"

"Jake? That was Brett. What's happening?"

"I just ran over a spike strip." He tried to keep driving, but the car had virtually no traction. On these roads, it would be suicide. Glancing in the rearview mirror, he saw Jorgensen watching them. Jake turned his attention back to the road.

"What are we going to do?"

"I'm going to drive us out of sight, then we're getting out of the car." He glanced at her, grimacing. She was wearing the wrong clothes for a wilderness hike, but it couldn't be helped. "Break the heels off your shoes."

The car swerved as a tire flew off the rim. Sparks shot out as the metal struck the road. Cursing again, he ground his molars together, struggling to maintain control. The next bend was in sight. Mackenzie let out a grunt, then he heard a snap as her heel broke. A moment later, the other one snapped.

"Okay, now what?" She put the shoes back on her feet.

"Get ready to run. I didn't see another vehicle, but I bet he's got one stashed somewhere nearby. We won't have much time to disappear." Jake rounded the bend.

Mackenzie let out a frustrated grunt. "How did he even know we'd be on this route?"

"He probably orchestrated that wreck, so we'd be forced to take this road." It was a big gamble on Jorgensen's part. There was nothing to say they'd leave the hospital before the wreck was cleared. But he'd had fate on his side. Jake hoped they had it on theirs from here on out.

Steering the car onto the shoulder, he shoved it into park, then turned it off. "Let's go."

She dove out of the car. He followed her out, running around to the back to open the hatch and get what little gear he still had with him. Most of it was at his house. He'd taken it out so they could transport wedding supplies. Lifting the mat that covered the spare tire well, he took out the small pack he kept with first aid supplies, emergency rations, and a .38-caliber revolver.

Closing the hatch, he swung the backpack over his shoulders and took Mackenzie's hand. "Come on." He tugged her down the embankment and into the trees. They disappeared into the forest as the high-pitched whine of a performance motorcycle engine split the silence.

"He's on a bike?" Mackenzie glanced back. "We'll never out run him."

Jake paused. She was right. Jorgensen could ride right down into the trees and follow them. He glanced around, a plan forming. "Help me find a branch. About the length of a baseball bat, maybe a little longer." He'd clothesline the son-of-a-bitch off his bike. Shooting him would be a last resort.

"Mackenzie!" Jorgensen's voice rang over the idle of his engine. "There's nowhere you can hide where I won't find you. Just come out and let's end this now. I promise not to hurt your precious fiancé if you leave him voluntarily."

She snorted. "Yeah, right," she whispered. Anger made her eyes narrow. Lines bracketed her mouth as she pursed her lips. "Like I believe that. Come get me, asshole." She spun away, looking for a suitable branch.

Jake's mouth quirked. He liked this feistiness she'd found.

The motorcycle revved, the sound coming closer.

"There!"

Mackenzie's whispered shout drew his attention. He turned to see her hurrying toward a log on the ground. She picked it up.

"That's perfect." He reached her side and took the branch. Spinning toward the road, he hid behind a tree, watching for Jorgensen, Mackenzie huddled next to him. In seconds, he saw him slowly weaving through the trees. He glanced at his wife, setting the branch down and shrugging off his backpack. He removed the gun and slipped it into his waistband, then handed her the bag. "Go hide behind that big tree." He pointed behind her at a large oak fifteen yards away, then picked up the branch.

She looked at the tree, then frowned at him. "Why do you need the branch if you have a gun?"

"Because as much as I want to shoot the bastard, I want him to rot in jail for the rest of his life more. Death is easy for a man like him. He doesn't have to face the consequences of his actions. In jail, he'll be forced to concede that you beat him at his game."

She blinked. "Oh. Okay, fair point." Shouldering the backpack, she kissed him. "Be careful."

"I will. Stay out of sight."

With a nod, she took off. As soon as she was hidden, Jake crept forward, staying out of Jorgensen's sight as he placed himself in the man's path.

The bike crawled closer; Jake crept around the tree, ready to spring. Judging the man's location by sound, he leaped out, swinging the branch.

Jorgensen's eyes went wide as he saw the branch heading for his head. He swerved at the last second, but was too close to escape completely. Jake hit him in the shoulders, knocking him off the bike.

Dropping the branch, Jake pulled his gun. "Freeze!"

The man pushed himself up on one arm, kicking at the bike to free his other leg, but having little luck. He looked at Jake, a sardonic smile tilting one side of his mouth. "You're wilier than I gave you credit for."

"Good. Get up."

"Can't. There's a bike on my leg."

"So move it and get up."

Jorgensen pushed at the motorcycle, finally dislodging his leg. He rolled onto his knees.

"Nice and slow. Don't do anything stupid."

"Wouldn't dream of it, detective. Where's Mackenzie? I'm sure she'd love to see my demise."

"Don't worry about her. Stand up." Jake kept his eyes on Jorgensen, so he wouldn't inadvertently give away her position.

"Working on it." Jorgensen got one foot under him and rose. He put down the other foot, then let out a groan and crumpled to the forest floor.

Jake cursed. "You broke your leg, didn't you?" Dammit.

Now he was going to have to arrange a rescue. Of a dangerous individual. "Roll onto your stomach."

Jorgensen writhed on the ground, holding his leg.

"Come on, man. I want to help you, but you have to cooperate."

Gritting his teeth, Jorgensen rolled. Weapon still trained on him, Jake advanced.

In a blink, Jorgensen's expression changed. The pain disappeared, morphing into a cold, calculated look. He rolled again, bringing up a hand that now held a pistol.

Shit! Jake dove to the side, but wasn't quick enough. Searing pain tore through his left flank as Jorgensen fired his gun. He rolled, knowing if he stopped moving, he was done.

"Jake!" Mackenzie's voice carried through the trees.

He half rolled, half crawled behind a tree, then peeked out to see Jorgensen on his feet, his focus no longer on Jake but on pinpointing Mackenzie's location. Jake leaned around the tree and fired. His aim was off, thanks to the wound in his side, but he hit the other man in the arm. Brett cursed and spun in Jake's direction, firing again.

Bark splintered off the tree next to his head. Adrenaline spiked his heart rate. He blew out several breaths, then turned to fire another shot, but stopped short. Jorgensen was gone.

"Fuck," he whispered, turning around. Hand to his side, he struggled to his feet. Movement to his left drew his attention. A flash of dark-colored clothing moved between two trees. Jake raised his gun, waiting to see it again. He got a glimpse and fired.

Twigs snapped as Jorgensen ran. Holding his side, Jake pushed away from his tree. He needed to get to Mackenzie first. Dizziness made him stumble as he moved from tree to tree. He was losing blood. But he still needed to get to his wife.

Gritting his teeth, he paused at another tree. Fire spread

through his abdomen, but he ignored it. All that mattered was Mackenzie.

Jake heaved himself off the tree, doing his best not to sound like a bear crashing through the woods. Between the trees, he could see small glimpses of Jorgensen, but never long enough for him to fire off a shot. The man had wised up.

He was also close to Mackenzie. Jake paused, raising his gun, waiting for his next glimpse of Jorgensen. His hands shook, but he kept them up. Black flashed between the tree trunks. He squeezed off a shot.

Jorgensen fired back. Jake ducked behind a tree. He wanted to tell Mackenzie to run, but if she went the wrong way, she'd run right into Brett. And her white dress made her easy to spot in the sea of dark colors. He had to get to her.

Peering around the tree trunk, nothing moved. He ran. A shot bounced off another tree, then another. He wanted to fire back, but he only had three shots left and they needed to count. After a third shot whizzed past so close he felt the wind from it, he dove behind a tree, grunting in pain as the hard hit on the ground jostled his injured side.

He glanced down. His shirt was saturated, the white cotton now a bright crimson. Leaning back against the rough wood, he closed his eyes, taking several deep breaths. A rapid heart rate would only make him bleed faster.

A feminine shriek split the still air. Jake's eyes popped open, and he scrambled to his feet. "Mackenzie!"

"No! Let me go, asshole!" Her angry voice carried through the woods.

Fear gripped Jake's heart. Fear and fury. Jorgensen had found her. The fear propelled his feet forward; the fury made him forget his side was on fire and he was losing blood. Running now, he dashed toward where he left her. Her white dress shone bright amongst the dark shapes in the forest. Jorgensen had her around the waist with one arm, her feet off the ground as he struggled to carry her away. She writhed and pounded on his arm, then reached up to claw at his face. Jake could see them clearly, but didn't dare take a shot. Their movements were too unpredictable, but she was doing a great job of slowing him down and keeping him occupied until Jake could get to her.

Only feet away now, Jorgensen glanced up and saw him coming. He raised a bloody arm. Jake dove to the ground when he saw the gun come up, and the first shot flew over his head. The second hit his leg. A rough shout tore from his throat as the bullet tore through muscle and bone. Knowing he was still exposed, he rolled and avoided another bullet.

"Jake! No! Jake! Let me go, Brett! No!"

Grunting in pain, Jake stayed low behind another tree, unable to do more than listen to Mackenzie struggle with Brett. Sweat popped out on his face and neck and his stomach lurched as pain threatened to overwhelm him. His vision turned gray and his ears rang.

Squeezing his eyes shut tight, he pressed his thumb and index finger to them, then blinked several times as he sucked in a breath. *Stay awake, Jake. Don't pass out.* Gritting his teeth, he rolled onto his belly and used his arms and good leg to pull himself forward. Pain shot through his side and down his leg. He grunted again and kept going. He needed an angle—any angle. If he got a shot, he was taking it.

Mackenzie's grunts and screeches were fading as he struggled to see around the tree. Once he finally dragged himself out far enough, they were twenty yards away, and all he could see were glimpses of them between the trees. He'd never get a clear shot.

Tears pricked the back of his eyes. "No," he whispered. "No." His voice changed to a growl. He dug his elbows into the ground and pulled, tucking a knee beneath his body. It slid out from beneath him, and he crashed to the dirt with a groan.

A sob broke free and his vision blurred. He lifted his head. Blood loss and the tears in his eyes made his vision swim. The ringing in his ears got louder.

"I'm so sorry, Mackenzie." Groaning, he tried to move again, but his body gave out and refused to cooperate. A sinking realization came over him. He was going to die out here.

THIRTY-SEVEN

Mackenzie fought the entire way through the forest, knowing if she didn't, she didn't stand a chance of getting free. She wouldn't go quietly. He'd have to kill her first. So she screamed and clawed and tried to bite. But she was no match for Brett's strength. Even with only one arm, he easily held her off her feet.

Blind fear filled her mind as they left Jake behind and neared the tree line. All the self-defense moves Jake showed her this past week flew out of her head the further they traveled.

Recognizing what was happening, she forced herself to stop and think. She took a deep breath, glancing around. They were nearing Brett's bike, where Jake knocked him off of it.

He stopped beside it, but she kept struggling. Cold metal pressed against her temple.

"Stop squirming."

Breath coming in short pants, she turned her head to look at him. The barrel of the gun slid over her forehead. She swallowed hard. "You're going to have to kill me. I will never willingly do what you want. Not again." Her mind whirled as she tried to come up with a way to get free.

A muscle ticked in his jaw. "Are you sure you want to die?" He pressed the barrel harder into the skin between her eyes.

"Do it," she spat. "You've taken everything else from me. My family, my life, my husband—you might as well put me out of my misery." She couldn't be sure Jake was dead. But if she wanted to get away and help him, she needed to get a rise out of Brett. He needed to make a mistake. And letting him know she belonged to another man was the best way she could think of to do that.

Surprise flared in his eyes. "Your husband? I interrupted your wedding."

She grinned, sensing a crack in his armor. "We got married at the hospital. You didn't stop anything; just delayed it. And just so you know, we didn't wait to have sex until marriage." She raised an eyebrow. "Still want me now that I'm tainted?"

He growled and shoved her away. Mackenzie crashed to the ground, smacking her knee on a rock. Pain ricocheted down her shin, making her toes tingle. Pine needles and small twigs dug into her palms. Falling to her side, she looked up. Brett stood over her, aiming the gun at her face.

"I've put years into grooming you to be my wife. And you were the perfect woman until your mother and that damn friend of yours put ideas into your head. You were under my complete control once. I'll get you there again." He reached down and grabbed a fistful of her hair.

"Ow, ow, ow!" She grabbed his wrist with one hand, groping the ground with the other for any sort of weapon. This was her chance. She needed to take it. He wouldn't give her another.

"And you know why I'm willing to break you down and make you that perfect woman again?" He bent close, still holding her hair.

Mackenzie saw something in his eyes that sent a shiver of terror through her. She knew he was crazy—a sociopath—but what she saw now was beyond that. He'd gone full-blown psycho.

"Because I don't lose. Especially not to women." He yanked on her hair, pulling her to her feet.

She raked the ground with her hand, desperate for a weapon. Her fingers closed around a stick. As she rose, she jammed it into him, hitting him in the groin. Immediately, he released her and grabbed himself, falling to his knees. She fell back, landing on her butt, but didn't stay there. Dropping the inch thick, arm-length branch she'd picked up, she grabbed a longer stick and lunged at him, holding it horizontal. Using it like a staff, she smacked him in the head with one end. He fell back, raising his arm as he went, and fired off a wild shot. It flew past her shoulder.

Mackenzie changed her grip on the branch and used it like a bat. She smacked his wrist, sending the gun flying. It landed to her left. She dropped the branch and dove for it. Her knees hit the ground again, but she didn't feel the pain. She closed her hand around the weapon, then turned. Brett was on his feet and coming at her, rage all over his face.

The crack of the weapon sounded over the noise of their scuffle. Wetness quickly bloomed on the front of Brett's black coat, and he stumbled. Her eyes grew wide as she realized she'd shot him.

He glanced down and touched the stain. "Oh. What?" He lifted his hand, staring at the red on his fingers, a shocked bewilderment written all over his face.

Mackenzie got to her feet, keeping the gun trained on him.

Brett looked up at her, confusion on his face. "I lost?"

She held his gaze for a long moment before he stumbled forward another step, then his eyes rolled back and his muscles went slack. He collapsed to the forest floor on his stomach with a soft thud.

Breathing hard, she shuffled forward, gun still trained on him in case this was another one of his tricks. She kicked his shoulder. When he didn't flinch, she nudged his head. It turned enough she could see his eyes were open, but vacant of any life.

Letting out a long breath, a sob choked her. She lowered the gun and pressed the back of her hand to her mouth. "Oh, God." Sniffing hard, she backed away. She needed to find Jake.

Mackenzie took off through the trees, hoping she could find her way back to him. She hadn't exactly been paying attention when Brett hauled her through the woods. "Jake!" She ran, calling his name.

Head on a swivel, she moved through the forest and over fallen timbers, still calling for him. After several minutes and no answer, she paused, her emotions overwhelming her. Bending at the waist, she rested her hands on her aching knees and squeezed her eyes shut. "Please, God," she whispered, sending up a prayer that he wasn't dead, just passed out.

A soft groan reached her ears. Her eyes flew open, and she straightened, glancing around. "Jake?" She paused, listening again.

Rustling to her right sent her running in that direction. "Jake!" She scrabbled to a halt as she nearly passed him. Sliding in the dirt, she landed at his side. "Oh my God." He was so pale. She dropped the gun in her hand and smoothed them over his face. His eyelids fluttered. "Baby, wake up. Please."

He groaned again, but his eyes stayed closed.

Her face crumpled and tears streamed down her cheeks. She didn't know what to do. A sob pushed past her lips, the sound loud in the quiet forest. She hiccupped, then sucked in a breath.

Think, Mackenzie. He needs help.

Dashing the moisture off her face, she gulped in more air,

then glanced around. They really weren't that far from the road. And her phone was in the car.

"Okay." She nodded. "Okay." Glancing down, she stroked his face once more. "I'll be right back. Don't die on me." Rising, she took off toward the road as fast as she dared. Breaking a leg would not help their situation.

It took her several minutes to run through the woods. She stumbled twice, tripping on tree roots, but stayed on her feet. Sunlight hit her face as she reached the ditch.

Chest heaving, she glanced both ways, looking for the car, and spotted it to her left. She drew a quick X in the dirt with her foot to mark where she came out, then ran for the car. When she reached it, she gave the door handle a solid yank, then leaned inside. Snagging her purse from the floorboard, she upended it on the seat and grabbed her phone when it fell out. With a quick tap, the screen turned on and she touched the emergency call icon, then hit send.

Mackenzie thrust a hand into her hair as she raised the phone to her ear, making the wild curls worse. She could feel the crunch of leaves and the hard points of sticks.

"Nine-one-one dispatch, what's the nature of your emergency?" The feminine voice that came on the line was no-nonsense, but soft.

"My husband's been shot. We're on—" she paused and glanced around. "Hell, I don't know what road we're on. We were headed back to Foggy Mountain from Asheville, but we didn't take the main highway because of an accident. The road follows the river."

"Okay. I know where you are. Is your husband breathing?"

"Yes. Or at least he was." She ran back to where she marked the dirt. "We ran into the woods to get away. He's a detective with the Ferris County Sheriff's Department. Can you alert his partner, Tristan Mabley, as well as the sheriff?"

She slid in the shallow ditch, then righted herself and climbed up the other side to run into the trees.

"Yes. Can you tell me where he was shot?"

"In the side and in his right leg."

"Okay. Are the wounds still bleeding?"

"I'm not sure. I'm not back to him yet. I had to run to the car to get my phone."

"Is the person who shot him still in the area?"

"He's dead."

A beat of silence passed. "Dead?"

"Yes. I shot him with his own gun."

"Oh." The woman cleared her throat. "Okay. Where's the weapon?"

"I have it. Or I will, anyway. I left it with my husband. His is there too."

"Your husband was armed?"

"Yes."

"All right. I'll alert the police."

The only sound for the next few moments was Mackenzie's harsh breathing as she ran. She managed to avoid the tree roots this time and soon reached Jake. "Okay, I'm here." She dropped to her knees next to him and tapped his face. "Jake?" His eyelids fluttered, but he didn't make any noise.

"How is he?" the dispatcher asked.

"Unconscious, but still breathing well."

"Okay. Check his wounds. Are they still bleeding?"

Mackenzie tugged at Jake's shirt, but couldn't move it out of the way to see with just one hand. She pulled the phone away from her ear and put it on speaker, then set it on the ground. Fingers shaking, she unbuttoned his shirt and spread the plackets apart. A dribble of dark red blood ran from the wound and around his side to drip onto the ground with a steady plop.

"His side is bleeding some, but not gushing. Let me check

his thigh." Moving around to his other side, she found the hole in his pants and put her fingers in it, ripping it open wider. Blood trickled from the wound in a slow but steady stream. "His leg is bleeding more."

"All right. Find whatever you can and press it to his side wound. For his leg, if you have anything you can tie around it, do it. A belt, a shoelace, anything that will slow the blood flow."

"Okay." Mackenzie looked around, searching for the backpack they brought with them, then remembered she'd dropped it when Brett grabbed her. Muttering a soft curse, she glanced at Jake. He had a belt on she could use. She reached for it, but as she raised her hand, it brushed something silky on the jacket she wore. With a frown, she glanced down to see the end of his tie poking out of the pocket.

Something she saw on TV once hit her, and she pulled it out. She threaded it under his leg just above his wound, then looked around for a stick, finding a suitable one just a few feet away. Grabbing it, she brought the ends of the tie up and wrapped them around the wood, then started twisting until it was tight. She tucked the end of the twig under the twist and let go. It held, and she said a silent prayer of thanks.

"How are things going?" the dispatcher asked.

"I put a tourniquet on his leg. I'm putting pressure on his side now." She took off the jacket and folded it up, laying it over Jake's side. Goosebumps erupted over her skin as the chilly air hit her heated skin, but she ignored the cold. She wouldn't freeze before help found them.

On her knees, she leaned into his side with all her weight. He groaned.

"Everything okay?"

"Yes. He doesn't like the pressure I'm putting on his wound."

"Okay. Help is close. You should be able to hear the sirens soon."

Thank God.

True to her word, the faint echo of sirens reached Mackenzie a couple of minutes later. A small dose of relief washed over her, and a single tear snaked down her face.

THIRTY-EIGHT

The loud clunk-thud filled the hallway as the can of soda Mackenzie just bought fell into the receptacle at the bottom. She put her hand inside, the swinging door giving off a tiny squeak as it moved, and retrieved the can. Straightening, she turned to head back to the waiting room, but stopped at the sight of Belinda standing behind her.

"Hi, sweetie." The older woman held open her arms.

Mackenzie's face crumpled, and she dissolved into a sobbing mess. She fell into her mother-in-law, hugging her tight.

Belinda stroked her hair and back, murmuring to her while Mackenzie let out all of her pent-up emotions. It all hit her at once when she saw Jake's mom and her offer of comfort. The knowledge that it was over—that the man who murdered her mom could never hurt anyone else—removed the last barrier to the pain and sadness she'd kept bottled up all these years. So she clutched Belinda and cried. She was so thankful for this woman who accepted her so easily just because her son loved her.

Finally, a lightness entered her heart and her sobs slowed until she hiccupped. Pulling back, she wiped at her face. "I'm sorry. I blubbered all over you."

"I'm glad. You needed to let that out."

"You should be the one crying. Your son nearly died."

"But he didn't. And he won't. Not anytime soon. You watch. He'll bounce back from this better than new. He's always been that way. Never one to let an injury slow him down for long." She reached up and picked a stray bit of leaf from Mackenzie's hair. "You're a mess."

"I know. We rolled around on the ground a fair bit." She lifted a hand and found more debris.

"Come with me. I have just what you need." Belinda took her hand and led her down the hall.

"Where are we going?"

"To get you into some clean clothes. So, I talked to that lovely nurse of Piper's—Jeanette?"

Mackenzie nodded.

"She came down to the E.R. a few minutes ago. It's already all over the hospital what happened. She wanted to check on Jake for herself. I mentioned I hadn't seen you yet, but that I wanted to find you and get you cleaned up—I could imagine what a mess you were after what went on. Anyway, she led me to the nurses' lounge and gave me a set of scrubs and told me to bring you back there and make you shower and change. That she'd let the E.R. nurses know to let you in."

"Oh." Mackenzie's face crumpled again. She sniffed hard and clamped her lips together. A shower sounded wonderful. "Thank you," she whispered.

"Don't thank me. I'm just the messenger." Belinda looped her arm through Mackenzie's and steered her down another hallway.

They soon reached the emergency department. Belinda

didn't have to say anything to anyone; one of the nurses hurried around the desk at the nurses' station.

She pointed down the hall. "The lounge is down here." She led them down the corridor and around a corner, then stopped in front of a door. Waving her keycard over the reader, the light turned green, and she twisted the handle, pushing it open. "Jeanette left the scrubs on the bench in the corner, along with a towel and a patient belongings bag for your dirty clothes. There's soap and shampoo in the stalls."

"Thank you."

"You're welcome. No bride should have to go through what you have on her wedding day."

Giving the woman a watery smile, she disengaged her arm from Belinda's, squeezing her hand, then walked into the lounge.

Right where she said they would be, Mackenzie found the scrubs, towel, and bag. There was even a black plastic comb on top. She took everything with her into the shower area and went into one of the stalls. It had a little area in the front to change. She pulled the curtain closed, then leaned into the shower and turned on the water. While it warmed, she stripped out of her soiled dress and put it in the bag. Kicking off her shoes, she shimmied out of her underclothes, then stepped into the warm spray.

A sigh escaped her as the hot water cascaded over her body, soothing her sore muscles and tired mind. She soaped her hair, rinsing out as much of the dirt and debris as she could, then grabbed the comb and ran it through, getting the rest. She soaped it again, then washed her body, taking care around the scrapes on her legs. She'd have some nasty bruises soon on her knees.

Feeling more human, she turned off the water and dried herself. Her nose wrinkled as she eyed her clothes. She was fine with the scrubs, but she really didn't want to put her underwear back on.

Mackenzie picked up the scrub pants. They were thin. She was not wandering around the hospital in paper thin scrubs without undies. Nope.

She turned her panties inside out and slipped them on. Stepping into the pants, she tugged them up, then tied the drawstring. After donning her bra, she pulled the scrub top over her head. Toweling off her hair, she ran the comb through it again, then slipped on her shoes. She gathered her belongings, then dropped the towel in the dirty laundry and exited the lounge.

The same nurse who let her in spotted her when she rounded the corner to the emergency room. A bright smile covered her face. "Feel better?"

"Much, thank you."

"You're welcome. And you'll be happy to know your husband is doing well. The doctor came out just a little bit ago to give an update. The bullet in his side missed everything."

Relief rushed over her. "Oh, that's wonderful. What about his leg?"

"The femur's broken, but the artery is intact. They're placing a rod in it, so it'll be a little longer before he's out of surgery. Your mother-in-law went up to the surgical lounge."

"Great, thank you. I'll go up there now." She smiled at the woman, then turned away in search of the elevator, taking it to the third floor.

"You look much better," Belinda said when Mackenzie walked in and sat down next to her.

"I feel better. I needed that, thank you."

Belinda patted her thigh. "You're welcome. Did you hear the news about Jake?"

She nodded. "The nurse told me before I came up here. I guess now we just wait." She leaned back in the chair, slouching a little, happy to have a semi-comfortable seat. Her bed would be better. With Jake by her side.

Mackenzie sighed. It would be many days before that latter part happened. She was just thankful he would be all right. And that it was over. It was finally over.

THIRTY-NINE

Pain woke Jake. Throbbing and insistent, it speared his leg and side, creating a firestorm that made him short of breath. Opening his eyes, he let out a soft grunt.

"Jake?"

Mackenzie's soft voice pushed through his agony, dulling it some. "Mack?"

Her pretty face swam into view. She smiled. "Hi." Her brows dipped. "Are you in pain?"

"God, yes."

She lifted a hand and picked up a remote near his head, pressing a button. A tinny voice came through the speaker. Mackenzie requested some pain medicine for him, then put it down. She sat in a chair next to his bed and scooted closer.

"What happened? Are you all right? Where's Jorgensen?" He wanted to take her hand, but just tensing his muscles to raise his hand sent his pain level soaring.

She seemed to read his mind and covered his hand with hers, lacing their fingers. "I'm fine. And Brett's dead." She looked down at their clasped hands. "I shot him with his own gun."

"What? Oh, baby. I'm sorry."

She bit her lip, then let it go and looked at him. "It's okay. It was him or me, and I chose to live."

He studied her, sensing no regret or guilt for what she'd done. "What happened?"

She took a shaky breath. "After he hauled me away from you, I continued to struggle. We reached his bike, and he wanted me to be still so he could get me on it. I told him he'd have to kill me. That I wasn't going quietly."

Jake's sharp intake of breath cut off sharply as fire raced through his side. "Oh, damn." Groaning softly, he squeezed her hand, looking up at the ceiling and controlling his breathing.

"Maybe I should wait until they medicate you."

"No." He looked at her. "Listening to you helps keep my mind off the pain. Keep going, please."

She blinked twice, then continued. "I goaded him until he shoved me down. I just wanted him to let me go, so I had some sort of chance to get away. We fought, I jabbed him with a stick in the nuts, then the face, and got his gun."

"You nutted him with a stick?"

"Really hard, yes."

He winced. "I almost feel sorry for him."

Mackenzie grinned.

"How did you end up shooting him?"

"I knocked the gun from his hand, then dove for it. When I turned around, he was coming at me. I just reacted. The bullet hit him in the heart. He was dead almost immediately." Her voice trailed off as emotion choked her.

Jake growled. He wanted to get out of this bed and hold her. "I'm sorry, baby."

She sniffed. "As you keep telling me, stop apologizing. It wasn't your fault. You did everything you could to stop him. If it helps, I don't think I'd have been able to do what I did if you hadn't wounded him first. It slowed him down and made him angry. It wasn't hard to set off the powder keg after that."

"I still wish you hadn't had to shoot him." It should have been him. She shouldn't have to deal with that. With the aftermath.

"Me too, but what's done is done. Will it affect me? Sure. But I don't regret it." She squeezed his hand. "I had too much to live for."

The door opened, and the nurse breezed in. "All right. One pain cocktail, as ordered." She walked up to the computer and signed in. "Can you give me a number for your pain?"

"Nine." He couldn't imagine it could get much worse, but he wasn't screaming, so it wasn't quite a ten yet. But it was damn close.

She hummed. "That's a good one." Picking up the scanner, she scanned his wrist band, then the medicine, then her badge. Once she confirmed everything was correct, she pushed it into his IV. "That should take effect soon."

"Oh, it already is." He could feel it spreading through his limbs, leaving a heavy warmth in his bones. His pain faded away. He could feel sleep tugging at the edges of his mind.

"Mackenzie?" He looked at her through heavy eyelids. Sleep pulled harder, but he fought it. He needed to say something first.

She leaned closer. "Hm?"

"I'm glad you chose to live."

"So am I."

Her bright smile stayed on his mind as his eyes slid closed.

"I love you, Jake."

With his last bit of consciousness, he replied, his voice barely audible. "Love you too."

Thank you for reading Smoky Mountain Stalker! I hope you enjoyed it. Please consider leaving a rating or review on Amazon and/or Goodreads. It would be greatly appreciated! If you'd like a FREE romantic suspense novella just for signing up and EXCLUSIVE looks twice a month at my latest work-in-progress, you can join my mailing list at ashleyaquinn.com. You can also stay up-to-date on my newest projects by joining my Facebook readers' group, Ashley's She Shed. See you next time!

Keep reading for a sneak peek at Book 4 in the Foggy Mountain Intrigue series, Smoky Mountain Doctor.

Smoky Mountain Doctor

FOGGY MOUNTAIN INTRIGUE
BOOK 4

ONE

"Have a nice day." Piper Riordan held out the prescription bag and bared her teeth in some semblance of a smile for the woman who just berated her for the cost of her medication. It wasn't like she had control over drug prices. And she'd done everything she could to get the woman the best price. Apparently, it wasn't enough.

The woman snatched the bag; the paper crinkling and pills rattling as she took it. With a harrumph, she spun on her heel and exited the pharmacy.

Heaving a sigh, Piper closed her eyes and rubbed her forehead. She had a headache, and it wasn't even lunchtime yet.

A child's whimper drew her attention. She opened her eyes and forced a more genuine smile onto her face for the next customer. "Hello. How may I help you?"

The rest of Piper's day flew by. At the height of cold and flu season, the hospital pharmacy was hopping. She filled more prescriptions for ear infections and strep throat than she could count. It also served to remind her why she didn't have children. They were little germ factories.

"Phew! I'm beat." Piper's coworker, Melissa, followed her

into the break room. She sank into a chair at the table and popped open the spout on her water. "Is it my imagination, or did the entire population of Emery County come in today?"

Piper giggled and went to her locker. "It sure felt like it." She took out her coat and put it on. "I'm glad we're done, though. I'm ready to go home and veg on the couch the rest of the night. A glass of wine and a good book sound amazing right now." Her side ached, a holdover from being shot at her friend's wedding just months ago. Sitting down and not moving until it was time for bed sounded like her idea of a perfect evening.

"Oh, that does sound good. I'm surprised, though. You're not going out? It's Friday."

"I haven't been out dancing since I got shot." At first, she hadn't been able to because of her injuries. Then, she just didn't want to. It didn't hold the same appeal as it once did. She wasn't sure why. Now, she was more comfortable with her own company than with letting her hair down, so to speak.

"Why not?"

Piper shrugged, putting on her coat. "I'd just rather stay home. I'm pretty tired." That was no lie. She still didn't have all her strength and stamina back, even though she'd been discharged from physical therapy. Reaching into her locker, she removed her purse and slung it across her shoulders.

The door swung open and the pharmacy manager, Nikki Wells, walked in. "Oh, Piper. I'm glad I caught you. I need you to stay."

"What?" Piper frowned, her shoulders sagging. "Why?"

"Brandi called in. I need you to cover her shift."

"I just worked eight hours." Fatigue pulled at her limbs. She really wanted to go home and rest.

"I know, but it can't be helped. Maybe you can leave early. It always slows down after about ten o'clock."

Anger flared, swift and hot, in Piper's belly at Nikki's

condescending tone. Did she actually think she was doing Piper a favor by letting her leave early from her forced second shift? "Let me get this straight. You want me to work a double shift—that I may or may not get off early from—then come back tomorrow morning and work my regular shift?"

Nikki frowned. The look on her face said she didn't see the problem. "Well, yes. Sometimes, we have to work unfavorable hours. Is that a problem?"

"Yes. Yes, it is." She propped her fists on her hips. "Why can't you call someone from that shift who's off today and ask them to come in?"

"It's too late. I need someone now."

"Okay, so I'll stay until her replacement can arrive." She held up a hand. "But not past six o'clock. It's been a long day, and I need to get some rest." The ache in her side seemed to double in intensity as she acknowledged it.

"I understand it's been a long day, but—"

Piper waved a hand. "No. Look, I know the doctor cleared me to come back to work, but I still don't have all my strength back. Long days like today wear me out. I *need* the rest."

Nikki's fierce frown said she didn't like that answer, but Piper wasn't willing to compromise. Her health was more important than leaving second-shift without a full staff.

"Um, Nikki?" Melissa lifted a hand. "I can take the shift if you're that desperate."

"Thank you for the offer, but it's Piper's turn."

Piper's frown deepened. "How is it my turn? I've had all the overtime lately."

"Right. But you were out for ten weeks."

Was she for real? "Yeah, because I *was shot*."

"We all still had to pick up the slack."

Piper snorted. "Glad to know I'm such a valued employee." She looked at Melissa. "Thank you for offering to stay. I appreciate it."

Melissa cast a quick look at Nikki, then smiled at Piper. "Not a problem. The overtime will go toward Reed's birthday." She rolled her eyes at the mention of her son. "He has a list of video games eight miles long."

Piper grinned. "Glad I could help."

"Now, wait a minute." Nikki stepped closer. "I didn't agree to this."

"What's the issue?" Melissa said before Piper could open her mouth. "You need a shift covered, it's covered. Does it really matter who gets the overtime?"

Nikki crossed her arms. "That's not the point."

"Come on, Nikki. Show some compassion. She had part of a lung removed three months ago. Let her go home."

Their boss's mouth pursed for a moment, then she dropped her arms with a huff. "Fine." Whirling around, she stomped out.

Piper shook her head. Nikki had always been a bit of a hard-ass. She made sure her employees towed the line. But she'd been particularly hard on Piper since she returned. The only reason Piper could surmise was that she'd upset Nikki's orderly workplace with her prolonged absence. Giving Piper all the overtime and weekends was her way of telling everyone to expect consequences for unexpected time off.

Sighing, she closed her locker and offered Melissa a soft smile. "Thank you again for taking the overtime."

Melissa waved a hand. "Not a problem. This just paid for Reed's birthday and then some, so I should probably be thanking you."

"Well, good. We're both happy." She adjusted her purse strap and headed for the door. "I'll see you tomorrow."

"See ya."

Piper left the break room and wandered down the hall to Nikki's office. She wanted to look at her schedule for next week. Hopefully, she had Sunday off. She hadn't had a day off since she came back. Undoubtedly more punishment for being out for so long.

She paused outside her boss's closed door and looked at the schedule on the wall. Anger swelled again. She was scheduled every day this week. She'd already worked the last ten.

Furious, she didn't bother knocking on Nikki's door, just twisted the knob and thrust it open.

Nikki glanced up, frowning when she saw Piper. "Yes?"

"Okay, I get that I missed a lot of work, but is it necessary for me to work seventeen days straight? There are other people on my shift."

"Right, but I was forced to deny them all any time off while you were gone. Now that you're back, I'm working in their requests. The hospital was kind enough to allow them to roll their days over to the new year."

Piper took a deep breath and counted to ten. It didn't lessen her anger, but it gave her a chance to gather her thoughts instead of blurting out the first thought that came to mind. "I understand that, but forcing me to work more than two weeks straight is ludicrous. Even one day off would be great."

Nikki shrugged and rested her hands atop her desk. "Maybe, but that doesn't change the fact I need to make up for the time you were away. You'll get back to your normal schedule, eventually."

"Mmm." Piper rolled her lips in as she hummed, pressing them together to hold back the words wanting to break free. She couldn't get fired. Her savings took a hit when she was out. Short-term disability only covered so much.

"If there's nothing further, you should go home and rest. That's what you wanted to do, right?" Nikki arched an eyebrow.

Piper narrowed her eyes, but again, kept her thoughts to

herself. "Yep." Without a goodbye, she left the office, barely stopping herself from slamming the door.

She was so done with Nikki's crap. Life was too short to spend all her time walking on eggshells at work. It was time for a change.

A plan formed in her mind as she left the pharmacy and wandered into the main lobby. There wasn't really anything left for her in Amandale now that her mom was gone. She had no other family to speak of. That meant she could go anywhere she wanted. Even out-of-state.

The main entrance doors swished open to let her out of the hospital. She stepped through and stopped as her brain registered the sight before her. Thick snow obscured the landscape. "When the hell did this start?" She huffed and ducked her head, walking into it. At least she'd parked in the garage and wouldn't have to clean off her car before she left. Getting home would be fun, though. The streets would be a mess. Now she knew why Brandi called in. And she was doubly glad Melissa took her shift. She couldn't imagine driving home in this later after working a double.

Hurrying down the sidewalk, she made a mental note to buy the woman lunch tomorrow. And coffee. She probably deserved even more than that.

Snow trickled down Piper's collar, making her shiver. She quickened her pace. Her mind turned to her earlier thoughts. If she moved away, she should pick some place warmer. Like Florida. Or Texas. Hawaii would be amazing. But the cost to move her things there would probably be more than she could afford. She could always sell everything and buy new when she got there, she mused, then scoffed and rolled her eyes. Yeah, right. By the time she did that, she'd probably wind up paying just as much as to move it all there. She remembered the prices when she vacationed there a few years ago. Hawaii was expensive.

So, Florida, then.

She entered the parking garage and did a little shake, ridding herself of the snowflakes she'd accumulated. Walking forward, she pushed the button to call the elevator, then stepped back to wait, musing more about moving. Did she really want to go somewhere where she knew no one? She made friends easily, but it wasn't the same as being around people she'd known for years.

An image of her best friend, Mackenzie, popped into her head. She missed Mack. Her friend now lived in North Carolina with her new husband, Jake.

The elevator dinged, and the doors opened. She stepped on and pushed the button for the third floor. She rested against the wall, still lost in thought. It would be great to be close to Mack again. But could she live in the same place she nearly died?

She was getting ahead of herself, though. She needed to look up job openings and check the cost of living before she did anything.

With a jerk, the elevator stopped. The doors opened and Piper stepped out. Cold air whipped through the parking structure, bringing flurries with it. She shivered, huddling deeper into her coat as she hurried to her car. Pushing the button on her remote to unlock the doors, the car beeped. She opened the driver's door and got in, tossing her bag onto the passenger seat.

"Damn, it's cold." She started the engine, cranking up the heat. Putting the car in gear, she backed out of her space, then drove down the aisle and left the garage, heading straight into the storm. Growling, she glared at the snow. "Wherever I go, there will not be as much of this crap." White-knuckled, she turned onto the road.

About the Author

Ashley started writing in her teens and never stopped. Her first novel, Smoky Mountain Murder, came out in 2016, and she has since published two more series and has plans for more. When not writing, you can find her with her nose stuck in a book or watching some terrible disaster movie on SyFy. An avid baseball fan, she also enjoys crafting and cooking. She lives in Ohio with her husband, two kids, three cats, and one very wild shepherd mix.

Website: https://ashleyaquinn.com

goodreads.com/ashleyaquinn

amazon.com/Ashley-A-Quinn/e/B07HCT4QST

Also by Ashley A Quinn

Foggy Mountain Intrigue

Smoky Mountain Murder

Smoky Mountain Baby

Smoky Mountain Stalker

The Broken Bow

A Beautiful End

Wildfire

In Plain Sight

Close Quarters

Scorched

Light of Dawn

Pine Ridge

Sweetness

Loner

Shark

Katydid

Homespun

Also by Ashley A Quinn

Foggy Mountain Intrigue

Smoky Mountain Murder

Smoky Mountain Baby

Smoky Mountain Stalker

The Broken Bow

A Beautiful End

Wildfire

In Plain Sight

Close Quarters

Scorched

Light of Dawn

Pine Ridge

Sweetness

Loner

Shark

Katydid

Homespun